ACKNOWLEDGMENTS

Thank you to small town New England where inspiration can be found behind every curtain and door and around each corner. Additional gratitude to my family and friends who always supported my creative endeavors even when they had no idea what I was doing with my time. And to all those I've met who in some small way contributed to my knowledge of the world and unwittingly wrote this book for me.

KANE

stephen a jennings

DEDICATED TO WORKING PEOPLE IN SMALL
TOWNS EVERYWHERE

CONTENTS

1.

Carl rolled his cigarette tightly between thumb and forefinger, the dry, stale tobacco cracking into smaller pieces as he wound it tight. It was habit, custom as much as anything else. After dinner he spent every evening, regardless of season, on his front stoop rolling a cigarette. It was a short moment of calm as he unwound the day, a chance to get lost in his thoughts and perhaps the one moment in his daily life he most deeply relished. He was left to himself, the kids with the good sense to let him alone until he came back in, his wife rarely interrupting knowing this was one of his few small pleasures. He hardly smoked as it was, maybe three or four cigarettes a day, and saw no harm in taking a small amount of time to calm his nerves. Besides, the loose-leaf tobacco he bought was cheap, each bag lasting for months. It was a small price for tranquility.

Pausing to shift his feet, he put the cigarette to his lips and struck a match, taking the smoke deeply. It was just past October when the light fails early, the night coming swift and cold, the darkness punctuated only by the concentrated luminosity of the nighttime sky. Unfortunately in this particular year the autumn felt bleaker than usual with the endless rain obscuring the heavens from view, draining the clouds of their energy in great torrents, and creating a landscape as joyless below as it was above. But the leaves continued to fall as they always did multiplying his list of chores. The worst of it would be to clean the gutters, already so densely packed the musty odor of decomposition wafted through the windows of the upper floors when they were ostensibly open for fresh air. All the same it was a purposeful harvest, the family learning to make use of it by packing paper grocery bags and lining the foundation as insulation against the winter drafts coming through the basement. Even if it only meant a few pennies worth of heating oil a day it was a few more than they would have otherwise had and that counted for something, perhaps even his bag of tobacco.

Stepping from the granite stoop he made his way down the overgrown pathway, a breeze stirring up the leaves about his feet. It was a short walk from the front door to the dirt road ending at the house, their own private cul-de-sac. Reaching it he turned to inspect the property. Starting with the slate tiles along the roof edge, ever askew, a few missing, he wondered whether he could remember a time when it was otherwise. Despite having grown up in the house, his parents long passed, he was pressed when considering any of it in terms other than those of the present. The olive drab facade, its loose and occasionally splintering clapboards, the brittle windows rippling with age, the slightly crooked overhang covering the front door, all withstood the years though the decay was evident and the small neglected house was going to need a lot of work if it were to stand many more. Lost in these thoughts his eyes finally settled on Lily as she stood in the doorway. A brief feeling of melancholy flitted across his consciousness.

Giving him a weak smile, she turned and went back through the open door. He knew well enough it was an invitation to a conversation he wasn't likely to enjoy. It was funny how spoken conversation between them had dwindled over the years only to be replaced by nonverbal cues. Every subtle change of expression, of posture, even of movement, was heavy with the language the two had come to share. Some was obvious, some wasn't. Either way, the conversation seemed to leave him behind a long time ago.

Taking a final puff of his cigarette and stubbing it on the sole of his shoe he followed her into the house.

"Yeah?" he sighed entering the kitchen, Lily seated back down at the table.

She took the measure of him for a moment before responding. "We've got the first oil delivery scheduled to come on Wednesday and what was left from last year is just about gone."

"Okay?"

"Well, they want to be paid before they'll deliver."

He merely grumbled, an acknowledgment of where this was going.

"Carl, we don't even have enough money for half a tank."

Leaning against the doorway, hands in pocket, he looked away. He could feel her staring at him still in search of a new answer to what had become for them a very old problem. It was times like these she made him want to shrink away, beaten, barely half a man struggling to get even half a tank of oil to warm the house. And yet she stared.

"The kids upstairs?" he asked.

She didn't answer, looking off as he turned his gaze toward her. He noticed, not for the first time, she remained a picture of her youth. Smooth skinned, perhaps a little pale, thin of body and face, blessed with large brown eyes that could still make him jump in the right moment. But those moments seemed fleeting these days. It wasn't the lack of affection that left them stunted in their marriage, it was the lack of tender affection.

He looked away as she turned toward him once more.

"Carl, we have to get the oil."

"Can't we put it on the account?"

"We've been putting it on the account forever and can't catch up. Look, they're not asking for the money we owe they just won't deliver more unless we pay for it up front. Simple as that."

She watched him shifting on his feet as he gazed into middle nowhere. He was still wearing his work jeans and orange shirt, an ugly combination meant more for safety, and perhaps segregation, as he did his job around town for the works department. Slender despite pushing forty, she often wondered if it was his genetic metabolism or his circumstantial. Either way, his always messy dark hair couldn't hide the fact his face had become more rough and deeply etched from so much time spent working outside. Still, there was a bit of boyishness about him, some of the untamed and carefree teen. Unfortunately it manifested itself most often at times like these.

"Carl."

"Uh-huh?"

"Well?"

"I'm thinking."

A silence ensued as they took furtive glances at one another, avoiding the chance of a locked gaze. He found himself dancing around the morose idea she loathed him, and perhaps his feelings for her were not that different. It was a thought had many times and an easy place for his mind to go. Believing, wisely or not, human emotions at the base strident and

3

the motivation of an unhealthy ego more destructive to those who surround than to oneself, she was a simple read. Rarely embracing the positive, she seemed always to gravitate toward the negative when her mind met with conflict, an almost daily occurrence. While for a select few it may serve as a source of personal strength, for her it was little more than the reinforcement of a cynical nature. It was the one thing she truly embraced, a comfort in Murphy's Law, the unfortunate ability to count pessimism her friend, and the one thing he both loved and hated about her. If she could have read his thoughts she may have reluctantly agreed, at least in the more truthful moments she had with herself, another casualty of the years.

Andy came running into the bedroom he shared with Cary and jumped onto the bed beside him.

"I got it!"

"Quick, show it to me," Cary begged.

Andy hurriedly leafed through the first few pages of the notebook.

"See, it's right there."

In front of them was the name Chris Larson with a little red heart where the dot of the 'i' should have been. It was simply too extraordinary for the boys, too out of character for Beth, a little red heart suspended so carefully above the black handwriting. They broke out in a fit of squealed laughter, proof positive she was out of her tree and off her nut.

"Oh, Beth, you look so divine," Andy cooed and they again went into hysterics. Grabbing a pillow he continued his soliloquy, "Oh Chris, hold my hand, give me a kiss my sweet..."

Beth wandered down the hall at the sound of their laughter with an inkling it was at her expense. It usually was with these two who seemed to never miss an opportunity to torment her and she knew full well it was always Andy leading the charge with Cary simply following his lead. It was lamentable really because she felt where he was brash Cary was quite pliant and pleasant and so it wasn't that he was necessarily a natural born leader in her eyes, far from it, it was that Cary was a natural born follower.

"Give that back you jerk!" she screamed realizing the object of all the commotion.

Reaching out she simultaneously pushed Cary away and grabbed for the notebook just snagging a corner as Andy tried to bury it beneath he and the pillow. With a little leverage, and an instant rage, she pounded his back with her free hand trying to loosen his grip. The beating did its job and he lost possession. Spinning around in response he kicked at her with both feet landing a blow to her thigh.

"Oh, you friggin' jerk," she hissed through gritted teeth, smacking him with such force the sound echoed through the sparsely furnished bedroom.

"Ow, stop it you freak!" he shouted just missing with another kick.

"You're the freak," she shot back, turning on her heel.

"Get your skinny butt out of here," he added, a last insult as she was exiting the room.

After taking a few seconds to sulk he looked over at Cary and grinned while rubbing his reddening cheek. "Damn, that hurt."

"You should see your face," he snickered, "she left her hand print on it."

"No way."

He made his way to the mirror and sure enough there it was, a red splotch with the faint trace of fingers radiating toward his earlobe. "Dang, would you look at that."

"Told ya."

He cocked his head hoping to get a better view of the damage. Noticing his hair a mess he tried playing with a few strands before giving up, the whole thing a pointless endeavor. It was nothing new for him really, his hair usually was a disaster since he hated the idea of a haircut and did his best to avoid them. The reason was simple, his mother did all the cutting and had no skill with a pair of scissors. She was forever creating an even larger disaster than letting it do what it wanted on its own could ever be. Cary, barely eleven, had yet to realize just how awful these haircuts were and to be sure, his patchwork of varying lengths was simply tragic. But at twelve Andy had awakened to the fact with some help from the kids at school. These days it was shoulder length, much easier to hide her mistakes on the rare occasion he let her trim the ends. Being slight of build he had no desire to raise his profile at school beyond where it already was, which was pretty low.

"Dang, that really hurts."

"What was that about?" Audrey asked as Beth came storming into their bedroom.

"Those jerks took my notebook."

"Why?"

She paused, "Never mind."

"Okay," Audrey said sarcastically as she turned back to the mirror and continued combing her hair. Long and brown with flecks of red when the light hit it just right, it was the envy of Beth. Hers just seemed to be more thin, a dull, plain and completely uninteresting brown. She neither could seem to grow it to any length that satisfied her or could rival her sister. Scarcely fourteen, she often wondered if she would ever be the measure of her seventeen year old sister. In her eyes Audrey was to beauty what she was to invisibility, a definition. Although she was cognizant that at her age she wouldn't be as naturally developed as Audrey, it was something her impatience refused to recognize. In truth, Audrey was too thin and she even more so.

"What?" Audrey asked glaring at the reflection of Beth in the mirror.

She realized she had been intently watching her sister run the brush through her hair. Suddenly self-conscious, she turned without saying a word and slouched on the edge of the bed thumbing the pages of her notebook. She looked from her thin, bare legs to her long slender fingers. Try as she might she couldn't get her fingernails to grow without breaking. True, they were brittle, as often breaking while doing her chores as simply running her fingers along a wall, yet more than that was her unconscious habit of biting them. Before she realized it she could chew a fingernail to the nub. Undignified her mother would scold even though she would catch her doing the very same when she thought no one was watching. It was a nervous habit they shared, she wished the only.

"So, Chris huh?" Audrey asked with a sneer as she tied her hair in a bun.

Beth looked around, "Did you give this to them?"

"No, we share a room don't we? I'm bound to see things I shouldn't."

She walked to the closet, Beth watching as she went.

"You do realize he's in my grade, might even be eighteen?" she pointed out while rummaging around for a sweatshirt to ward off the increasing coolness of the evening.

"Yeah, I know."

"Well, I don't have a problem with it but what do you think mom and dad would say?"

"I don't care. Besides, we're not doing anything," she trailed off.

"No?" Somehow she wasn't surprised.

She continued poring over the pile of clothes strewn on the floor of the closet while Beth sat in silence, her attention still fixating on her fingernails. Finding the gray sweatshirt she was seeking she turned to face her.

"How come?"

"I don't know. He barely notices me in school."

"Have you tried talking to him?"

"No."

Audrey continued watching her while she in turn remained staring at her nails. Although they shared the same room, and had for all their lives, they'd never been all that close, not as you'd expect anyway. Sure, they shared life's standard moments; joy, anguish and all that resides in between. But it was more as acquaintances than close family relation, and certainly not as friends. Odd really, she thought, because Beth was a rather harmless soul with her nervous habits and self-imposed vow of silence. And maybe that was at the heart of it – she spoke so little, especially of herself, and rarely betrayed an emotion of any kind, present circumstances excepted. She sought no help with problems, and at fourteen they were there in abundance as she recollected, and asked no advice on clothes, makeup, or even homework. Sadly, she was in many ways a nonentity, a part of the scenery, a pitiable creature. In fact, she realized, it may not be a matter of like or dislike, respect or scorn, just plain indifference toward her sister.

"So?" Audrey continued with the inquiry.

Beth glanced up at her. "I don't know," she quietly replied but then more stridently, "why do you even care?"

"Look, I'm just trying to help. Why don't you talk to me for once instead of getting yourself stuck in your own little world? You know, if you don't ever talk about anything how do you expect anyone to talk to you? That's probably why he doesn't." She paused. "Honestly Beth, even when I listen to you I'm left wondering if you're actually saying anything."

She simply sat staring at her fingers. With no reaction, the short reprimand saw Audrey getting more agitated and it gained momentum. Stomping back to her place in front of the mirror she turned on her again.

"What's wrong with you? Can you put together more than a few words for me, a full sentence maybe? Christ, you just sit there staring at the floor, a freak in her own little freak world."

"Go to Hell," Beth mumbled.

"Excuse me?"

"Go to Hell!" she repeated rather more loudly than she intended. Still, it felt good.

Audrey was a little taken aback with her vehemence, and a little pleased too. Though she knew there was something masochistic about going after her sister the way she so often did, she couldn't help but play out the status quo. It was an expectation as much as anything else and getting her to raise her voice, well, that was just a satisfying rarity.

"At least that's something I can understand."

Carl ignored the first outburst he heard between Andy and Beth knowing the use of it to escape the conversation with Lily would seem as transparent as it really was. But the second provided a convenience further aided by she arching her eyebrows in matched concern. She knew it was unlike Beth to be so expressive even once, let alone twice. Despite the closed shell she presented to the world, especially toward her, she thought she was still more in tune with her young daughter's emotions than anyone else. A mother's misguided intuition perhaps, kindred spirit more likely.

"I better go see what's going on," he offered, lingering a moment for approval. More accurately he was waiting for a sign of disapproval and sensing none he turned and went upstairs. She watched him go, running her fingers the length of her hair.

Reaching the landing he poked his head in the boy's room. They were carousing and pretending nothing was out of the ordinary, taking no notice of his presence. The ruse was for naught, he knew full well his movement on the creaky stairs told his arrival. It was one of the great advantages to an old house, you could always tell who was moving about and where based on their weight and stride. In this way he'd always been able to keep track of the kids without ever having to actually watch them directly. Of course, from their perspective it was a distinct disadvantage. They'd spent many frustrating hours trying to find the perfect path to take that would minimize the noise and grant at least a little success in their quest for some entertainment free of a parent's watchful eye. It seemed the worn floorboards of the old house would forever keep them imprisoned.

"Hey, cool it," he advised fixing a stern glare on Andy.

"What?"

"You heard me."

Cary giggled, clear in the belief he was the innocent bystander to all these goings on.

"You too."

"Yes, dad."

He moved across the hall to the girl's room as Audrey came out brushing past without a word.

"What's going on?"

"That strange daughter of yours is just having a meltdown," she gleefully reported over her shoulder.

"Hey, I don't need the attitude, I asked what's going on?"

"Go ask her."

His eldest daughter was always the most mysterious to him. Although the image of her mother during her youth with the long hair, tall slender build, graceful movement and soft, pale skin, she couldn't have been more different. Outspoken, extroverted, flirtatious, emotional, agile; they were traits running in neither the Kane family nor the Morse, his wife's side of the tree. The boys he knew and understood, Beth he knew and misunderstood, this creature he could barely comprehend.

Watching after her he took a deep breath and turned to the girls' room. Standing in the doorway he found Beth sitting on the edge of her bed, attention focused on her fingernails.

"Okay, what's wrong?"

"Nothing," she replied barely above a whisper. The rehearsed conversation began exactly as she imagined it would. He would first ask some generic questions, lose interest when she wouldn't part with any information, and then offer a couple of inane words of encouragement before taking his leave. He'd feel better for having tried, she'd feel better for having won.

"Look Beth, something's wrong. So what did the boys do this time?"

"It's nothing dad, really."

He watched her rubbing her fingers together, gaze fixed downward, body hunched as if she were trying to crawl inside herself. Although she rarely invested herself with the family making inclusion of any kind an excruciating chore, he often felt more love for her in these moments than he did in any other. He also found her more beautiful in these moments than any of his children could ever be.

"Look honey," he said, sitting on the edge of the bed and putting his arm around her shoulder, "don't let them bother you, they're just a couple of punks."

She shrugged his arm away, "I'm fine dad."

"If you're sure?"

"I am."

He took the rejection of his affection in stride having grown far too accustomed for it to have any effect on him now. Where Audrey would greedily soak up any affection he gave, or anyone it seemed for that matter, Beth remained a desert. In this she was her mother's child, alone and unto herself.

"Do you want to come downstairs with me?"

"No, just leave me alone, dad, I told you I'm fine."

He stood, hesitating a moment longer, "Okay, but if you need anything..."

"Yes, dad."

After he left she sat in front of the mirror carefully tracing her features. Nothing in the reflection thrilled her.

Before he made his way downstairs he stuck his head back into the boys room, "Leave her alone."

"Well if she wasn't such a baby..." Andy protested before he cut him off.

"I mean it."

Wandering into the kitchen again he found Lily sitting where he left her and Audrey rummaging through the cupboards looking for a snack. Neither paid him any mind as he entered, a small relief. He didn't really want to resume the conversation with his wife, necessary though it was, nor was he in a mood to have a meaningless conversation with his daughter.

"Isn't there anything in this friggin' house to eat?" Audrey asked in a manner that came off as accusatory as it was bitter.

"Hey, I don't want to hear that language," he scolded.

"Just eat some Saltines," Lily calmly responded.

"That's all there ever is," she complained taking the box with her into the living room.

"Well?" Lily asked the moment she left.

"It was nothing, the boys teasing her again I guess. She seems fine."

She nodded, otherwise making no sound or movement. He waited to continue the conversation but she seemed content to leave it where it was. He knew the circumstances and with that she was fine. Nothing had changed, ever did for the Kanes. She just hoped they'd find a way to get by and that he understood this time the oil company didn't seem inclined to negotiate anything. The terms were clear, pay and get the oil, don't pay and don't get the oil. She was doubtful he would get them to change though reckoned it wouldn't hurt to let him try. At least he could feel he was doing something and when it failed finally realize the seriousness of their situation and work toward finding a better alternative. One thing she knew for sure was their combined income, his for the town and her part-time clerical work at the clinic, couldn't be stretched any farther. She couldn't get any more hours, there were none to give, and with what little work they had it was a strain for them not to cut the existing hours she had. Knowing what they did of her family's trials, and being a small town they knew more than they should though not as accurately as you'd expect, they found things to keep her busy. Besides, she knew they liked her, she was a pretty face around the office and pleasant, if a little distant, and it always amazed them how a pretty face with a nice smile put the patients at ease even when with them she had no direct contact. It was, quite frankly, a truth known to her in virtually every facet of life. It was also the reason she kept cloistered, letting go of her dignity too high a price in her eyes.

Somehow she felt that idea had been lost on Audrey and it troubled her. Of all her children she seemed the most destined to escape. To where or to what she was unsure but she often wondered if her eldest daughter realized there was a price to be paid for that choice. And when the time came, would she disappoint her and pay it or would she disappoint herself and refuse? Equally troubling was Beth, so sullen, so frail. She hated to admit it but there were times when she felt almost dispassionate toward the girl. Where there was a certain fascination and admiration for Audrey, for Beth there was little but pity. Of course she loved her and wanted her to succeed like all of her children. Yet at the same time it was almost satisfying to know she would struggle for her happiness as she herself had always done. That said, if she found it, it would be on her own terms and through her own accomplishment, no compromises. There was little price to be paid for that and the value was inestimable. And perhaps that's really all she wanted for her children, the temerity to stand up and be counted, to matter. No doubt the boys would, she thought, ignoring concerns she had for Cary as well, because boys just do. They scorn the helping hand, compromise anathema to being a man. Life is what you make and if you fail then its your own undoing and either you find the strength to remake yourself or simply get pushed aside.

While lost in these thoughts she never noticed Carl reach for his tobacco and return to the stoop in the crisp night air. Rarely having a second cigarette following so closely on the after dinner smoke, he felt he needed it to settle his nerves and get away for awhile where he could think about the oil and their troubling cash flow, about the kids, about Beth. He also took the time to think about Lily and her unnerving acceptance of their lives, and of him when you come to it, as if there was no fight left. It's not like their lives were somehow awful, or more worrying than half the people he knew, it was just he felt one should always fight for something a little better than you already have and if you've given that up then what do you have left? In his mind an emptiness, an unending void, a daily existence, but not a life.

2.

Beth was now two months into her high school existence and still felt like she was struggling to get used to the place. Though the academics were fine, she found the work less than challenging. It disappointed her as she was expecting a more dynamic environment than the one she left behind. In middle school everything was rote learning – names and dates in history, standard equations in algebra, rules of grammar in English. Finding the same methods taught in high school was an immense letdown yet in the end, she reasoned, it was the grades that mattered, not the knowledge gained. So what if the teachers were dull, and so what if she felt some of them were little more than creatures of invention, making things up on the spot, the game was an easy one for her and so excellence was just a matter of course. Really it was everything else that was proving a struggle. Some was mundane; the halls too wide and painted lime green, the classrooms seeming to reek of formaldehyde, the bathrooms dimly lit, the lockers too narrow, the floors too shiny. She even felt the exterior bricks were too red. And these things counted for something in her mind. They obstructed learning, a sense of place, a sense of comfort. It was all so cold and sterile. In middle school they put up vibrant posters made in art class, the desks had colorful chairs and seemed always new, the classrooms bright and airy, but here every bit of the building was as dull as the education she was receiving.

That wasn't all that was troubling her though, there were new cliques, groups, teams and friendships forming every day. As the younger kids maneuvered through the first few weeks they were being taken in and fitted by the older kids. Sometimes it wouldn't last very long, a misjudgment on the part of one or the other, and the kid would fall backward or into another group. Other times it stuck by virtue of a sibling. So and so is the brother of so and so therefore he must be cool. And that worked conversely as well where you could be pigeonholed simply by the elevation an older sibling failed to achieve before you. In those cases she bore witness to the tragic internal struggle of the kid as he or she came to grips with the fact that although they were all of it in middle school they were none of it now. In the worst cases those kids would be scooped up by the dopeheads who provided an instant safe haven, a belonging they couldn't find elsewhere. Of course, she also felt that was just plain business savvy as it provided a steady stream of customers for the narcotic of choice. But the end result in all cases was the same, each person found their group, settled in, jostled for position and then ranked the other groups in relation to their own. Satisfied the choice was made, or made for them, they then tried to navigate high school with as little investment as possible.

In her case the path was somewhat carved out by Audrey before who, now a senior, was a very popular girl and, oddly, with all groups. Everyone, from students to teachers and staff, seemed to react positively to her and her gregarious nature. She even transcended the economic stratum which was a much uglier side of high school. The kids from wealthier families welcomed her into their circle and, incredibly still, with no protest from their parents who often seemed to regard the less fortunate as somehow dull or indolent. So when Beth entered the school a hand was extended in the natural assumption she was equally impressive, but it didn't last. They found her silence unsettling, her face and body too expressionless. She was, in fact, perceived to be more their parent's assumption; dull, indolent, uninterested, somehow shabby. Audrey didn't help either as she appeared to slap the hands away the moment they were extended. It was as if she would take the shine from her sister's star, that she somehow would cause her to fall from her perch in the wide cosmos, the one she so long worked to reach. It hurt, and as much as any other experience in her small corner of life, was most formative.

So it was this Monday as she walked to school tracing the usual route by herself through the small downtown. It was a fifteen minute journey she shared alone with groups of kids walking, laughing and pushing. The week ahead seemed endless, the in between tiresome. Approaching the entrance she would have given anything to be anywhere but here.

Audrey saw her arrive while she was socializing with some of her friends before first bell. She watched her slide up the stairs and enter the building with scarcely a glance sideways and nobody looking in her direction either. With all the kids milling about and moving up and down the stairway not one welcomed, spoke or even gave her a friendly wave. Indeed she was invisible in every way and about that Audrey felt a little uneasy. Part of it was the messy scene the two played out last night. She wasn't sure she would call it remorse, perhaps just a little unfortunate, but she knew in a way she was guilty of making Beth's introduction to high school a bit harder than it need be. When some of her friends tried approaching her sister only to be brushed off she feebly explained she was a little shy, a quiet girl. When still more friends inquired about her she told them not to bother and by the time the first few weeks in school had passed she actively, though inadvertently, created a perception of Beth as a loner and someone upon whom any attempt at friendship would be lost. Sadly, she herself believed it to be true. After all, hadn't she known the strange girl all of her life and spent every evening in her company, or lack thereof, and still failed to break through the hardness of her shell? What was queer was she often believed she knew no more about Beth than any of they.

Straying from her thoughts she tried to reengage the conversation before noticing Chris Larson standing a few yards away chatting with some of his friends. Though she didn't know him well, as with most she was friendly enough that making an approach wouldn't seem strange. She was unsure exactly what he was but on the surface appeared to be a nice kid, a little sloppy in his faded jeans and canvas sneakers, most probably musical, his type always were, and like Beth a rather quiet kid seeming to socialize little and to be often alone. Yet unlike Beth he had an easy manner and an affable smile. Regarding him this way she began to see the attraction her sister had for him, it was a natural fit.

"Hey Chris," she called out bouncing toward him.

"Hey Audrey."

"You got a minute?" she asked walking him away to a more discrete location without waiting for an answer. "I'm wondering if you can do me a favor?"

"What's that?"

"You know my sister?"

"The skinny one?"

"Yeah, Elizabeth."

She was unsure why she used her sister's full name just then, she hadn't done it in years. Nor could she remember hearing anyone else do the same, except perhaps her mother in a fit of anger. It was nice, almost regal, the way it rolled off the tongue. Perhaps all Beth needed to change her fortunes was to start using her full name, she mused.

"The quiet one?" he continued.

"Yeah. Could you talk to her?"

"About what?"

"Anything."

"Why?"

She rocked back and forth, scrunching her hands in her back pockets and looking up at him.

"Well, she just kind of needs a friend and I think you two would get along."

"Audrey, I don't know about that."

"Please?"

He hesitated, "Isn't she a freshman?"

"Yeah, but she's already fourteen," she responded quickly in an attempt to close the deal.

The last statement confirmed his fear about what this conversation was about. He didn't know the first thing about her sister and fourteen was a little on the young side. Besides, he was well aware she wasn't highly regarded. He couldn't actually tell you why, he just knew.

"No Audrey, I don't think that's a good idea."

"Why? I'm just asking you to talk to her. That way you can get to know her a little. It's no big deal, just ask her about herself, what she does, what she likes."

"What does she like?"

She hadn't the faintest idea. "You know, a lot of the same things as you, music and stuff."

She was completely out on the limb. Not only was the list rather on the weak side, consisting of one, but she was making assumptions based on his attire that he was into music. And stuff, whatever the Hell that was.

"Yeah, I don't know Aud."

His use of her familiar moniker was encouraging so she pressed on, "Please?"

"Look, if I get a chance I'll see if I can talk to her." He followed with the standard caveat, "but I'm not promising anything."

"You're the best Chris."

She rubbed his arm as they parted, never missing the chance to add some innocent flirtation as an inducement. Bouncing back to her friends she took a last glance over her shoulder and smiled fully confident he would be watching her go. He was, they all did, and life was easy.

Reflecting on the conversation she realized an added benefit of he talking to her sister was she may learn more about her as well. How strange, to be caught almost speechless when asked what someone you've known for her entire fourteen years, with whom you share a house and a room, likes. Not one thing came to mind. She was never one for dolls, toys, or games of any kind. She did like to swing a lot but was probably too old for that now. She recalled her climbing trees and reading, a lot of reading. She couldn't remember her ever listening to music yet she must, everyone listens to music. She was an excellent student, though rarely trumpeted the fact, and appeared to have little interest in clothes, or anything of a material nature, and certainly not friends. It was all quite baffling, the damn girl very nearly a blank slate. So it was tree climbing, swinging and reading. In fourteen shared years that's all she knew of Elizabeth.

Carl took an extended mid-morning break and drove through a pounding rain to Whyte's Heating Oil hoping he could do something, anything, to loosen up the conditions they gave to Lily. He wasn't terribly optimistic. For years his father was close friends with Danny Senior and able to get some leeway with the bill when times were tough, a frequent occurrence for a Kane. But with his passing the friendship did too and so any clout he thought he may have appeared lost. To make matters worse, the elder Danny had these days turned most of the operations over to Danny Junior who wasn't as inclined to friendly relations. Unhappy about the Kane's account he took every opportunity, public or otherwise, to let them know and though the chances were infrequent, the embarrassment stuck. His only solace this morning was the meeting wouldn't be occurring on the street.

Approaching the door it was held open by Junior's wife giving him the opportunity to dodge a few raindrops. They exchanged brief and common pleasantries; both doing well, kids okay, weather atrocious.

"Yeah Lois, that's why I'm here. Danny spoke with Lily about the delivery for Wednesday. I guess you won't make it until we can pay for the tank up front."

"Yes Carl, I think that's right. The account's gotten pretty high and you know with prices and all. Danny says we just can't afford to keep delivering until you pay it down some."

"I know, but we've been making the payments haven't we?"

"Mostly, though you have been late quite a few times."

"I know, I know, but times are tough and with the weather being so cool and damp..."

Lois gently cut him off ushering him to the far end of the counter as another customer came in, "I know Carl and that's what I'm saying. Look, Danny's in his office. Why don't you talk with him. I don't think it will change anything but really he's the one you should be talking to about these things."

He followed her around the counter and into the office where Danny was perched behind the desk with his morning coffee and a newspaper open to the sports page. He scarcely noticed them come in giving Carl a moment to survey the scene in a vain attempt to find some common ground. With his striped button-down shirt, purple tie and gray slacks he could scarcely have presented a more altogether different portrait from he in his damp jeans and orange t-shirt. Mumbling under his breath, he hoped Junior was just reacting to the story he was reading.

"Danny?"

"Yeah, hon, in a minute."

"Danny, Carl's here to see you."

"Carl who?" he asked without looking up from his paper.

"Danny."

"What?" Snapping his head up he noticed Carl standing at the end of his desk. "Oh, hey Carl. Have a seat. Lois, clear off those newspapers for him."

Lois cleared the papers away from a fraying parson's chair on the opposite side of the desk before retreating to assist the waiting customer.

"Look," Junior started without missing a beat, "I know why you're here and you just have to find a way to pay for the oil before I can deliver. This isn't dad's business anymore and I try to be fair but in this economy we just can't run things like he did."

"I know Danny, but..."

"Look Carl, do you know how deep into this you are?"

"Well, I know we owe quite a bit."

"Quite a bit?" He became animated, "Carl, you owe us over three thousand dollars. Paying a hundred bucks a month won't cut it anymore when we're delivering nearly two thousand worth of oil every winter. C'mon, you must see that?"

"Yeah, I know, but things are a bit tough."

"A bit tough? Carl, when haven't things been tough for you?"

Danny raised the volume on the discussion sufficiently that Lois returned and closed the door while shooting him a look of marked disapproval. Without a potential audience he modulated his tone a bit.

"Look Carl, you know when your dad died he left us holding thousands in unpaid oil bills. We had every right to try to collect that from you since you inherited his house. Now I know he had no money but that place is worth more than enough. We didn't do that because we knew you didn't have the money and we weren't going to force you out of your home. But damn, this is serious business. We carry a lot of accounts here and do our best for folks that are struggling but of all of them you're always in the most serious trouble. And I gotta tell you Carl, I just don't see it changing at this point."

They sat in silence, Carl staring at the newspaper spread on Danny's desk, Danny staring at him. He noticed the assumption was made he was here to beg rather than pay his bill. It consumed him when he should have been more clearly concentrating on finding a resolution, some common ground on which to build. In fact, it bothered him more than the attempt to shame him in front of the waiting customer.

"Look," Danny said quietly to break the impasse, "isn't there some kind of assistance or something that can help get you through? You know, the state runs a home heating program, have you tried contacting them? I don't know about any other charity but..."

Carl responded forcefully, "I'm not getting help from a charity."

"Well, suit yourself. I guess there's nothing more to say."

With that he arose from his chair and opened the office door inviting Carl to leave. After a slight hesitation he made his way out refusing to make eye contact with or otherwise acknowledge and engage Danny further. Indeed there was nothing more. Then on his way through the lobby he found the exit held open by an incoming Danny Senior.

"Well, well, little Carl Kane. How the Hell are ya my boy?"

Danny Senior was always convivial, ready with a joke, a kind word and a quick smile whenever Carl chanced to run into him. He remembered as a young boy he used to see him quite often until his growing family focused his attention elsewhere. Despite that he and his dad had still managed to get together once in awhile for a few beers. What he recalled most were summer bonfires in the backyard where they would all gather to regale each other with wild and fantastic tales. At least that's what they were to a boy's fanciful ears. As the night wore on and members of the gathering slowly peeled away he vividly remembered peaceably falling asleep with the murmuring voices of his father and Danny floating through the open window. It was one of his fondest memories of youth, when the idea of an inclusive adulthood waiting around the corner was his fortune.

"Hey Danny, doing okay I guess," he replied weakly, "How about you?"

"Can't complain, would you listen if I could? How's the kids?"

"Doing okay, Audrey's a senior, still trying for a scholarship I guess. Beth just started high school, the boys are in middle school."

"That's fine, that's fine. How about that pretty wife of yours? You know, I knew her dad Stanley real well, God rest his soul. Knew her too. Well Hell, you remember, Stan used to stop by your dad's for a few beers with us down back."

"Yeah, that's how I met her."

"That's right too, I remember that. I even remember the look on your face when...ah Hell, been awhile since I've seen you. Poor Jim, I still miss him you know?"

"Yeah, we all do."

"You know, I don't think I ever mentioned it but I nearly dropped my end of the casket at his funeral. Yeah, there I was you know, caught up in the emotion, not paying attention and boy, it sure was hot that day. Well, anyway, me and this fat boy," he squeezed a roll of his ample girth, "were really struggling and then on the way up the stairs of the church I caught my foot on the last step. It's a bit higher than the others you know? Well, I started to stumble and felt it pass down through the other fellas and for a moment we staggered backwards. I don't know if you noticed but sure gave me a fright." He paused a moment, "Anyways, looks like the rain's on again so come back inside for a minute."

"I really ought to be getting back to work Danny."

"Yeah I know, just give me a couple minutes."

Carl followed him inside. Passing by the counter Lois gave him a quick smile and a wink as they continued through to the office where Junior was back to reading the newspaper.

"What's the news son?"

"Those dang hockey players are talking about another walkout and..." he looked up, stopping in mid-sentence.

"Fine, well I met Carl here just as I was coming in. So, what are we gonna do about this?"

"About what?" He leaned back in his chair wrapping his arms behind his head, "I already told him I need to be paid for the Wednesday delivery before I can make it."

"Hmm. Do you have the money Carl?"

"Not really sir."

"Well, what are we gonna do then?" he asked turning to Junior.

"Look, I told him we need the money for another delivery up front. He doesn't have it, I suggested seeking assistance, and that's where we left it."

"I see. Can you get assistance?" he looked back to Carl.

"I'm gonna try home heating but I don't know from there."

"That's fine, that's fine. See what you can do, maybe get some help for the winter. But don't worry none, the delivery will be there on Wednesday as scheduled."

Junior reddened at his father's dismissing of the issue so easily. Not more than five minutes before he had the terms with Carl set in stone. He felt sure he would find a way to pay. Somehow the poor always managed to find a way to get by, to skate, to do enough to keep a low profile and stay just out of reach of their debtors. This was his chance to get him to pay the bill down once and for all, to realize life wasn't forever free.

Jumping from his chair he shut the door. "No dad, not this time, not anymore. He owes us over three thousand dollars."

Danny stared him down. "Don't presume what I don't know, who do you think does the books around here? This is still my business you know, I'm not pushing the daisies yet. And this business," he added motioning to Carl, "is my business."

"But he keeps getting deeper, he'll never pay."

"Don't you worry about that, Carl will take care of this when he can."

He was getting more agitated, "No, dad, not this time."

"Son, sit down for a minute."

Junior wavered, shooting a look of disgust at Carl before sitting back down. Instead of being treated like the businessman he was he was being contradicted, scolded by his father in front of a man who moments before humbly left in search of charity elsewhere as he should.

Carl was embarrassed, the caustic remarks from Junior biting as they intended, the contempt like lead in the heated air.

"Let me tell you both a little story. Years ago, before you were even born Danny, your mother and I went through a rough patch. We waited awhile to have kids because in the early years the business wasn't good. You know, we weren't always the only business in town. Anyway, your mother and I were doing everything, the orders, the deliveries, the books. We only had the one truck and there were times when we barely kept the lights on."

"Yeah, I know the story," Junior said impatiently.

"No, you listen!" he furiously snapped before sitting on the edge of the desk to face Carl, his back to his son. "When we were struggling we had to lean on friends. I used to go over to Jim's and we'd sit up until the early hours of the morning just talking and staring at the fire. Jim was one of the kindest and gentlest people I ever knew. Anyway, I'd talk about the business, your mother, the troubles we were having with the marriage. All of it, things were just snowballing out of control. I really thought I'd made some terrible choices, mistakes I couldn't get my head around. Your mother nearly left me you know?" He glanced at Junior before continuing, "So anyway, Jim would just sit and listen as I talked my way through the problems, never troubling me with his own in all the years I knew him. And I know he had troubles. God, no one ever worked so hard for so little. Anyway, we were at our lowest, the holidays the year before you were born. The electric had been cut and the business was going to be lost any day. Your mother couldn't stick it out any longer and I sure couldn't blame her because I'd have left by then if I were in her shoes. Well, Jim invites us over for Thanksgiving dinner which we gladly accepted. Oh, it was a beautiful dinner they put on for us and we didn't have a thing to bring. But it didn't matter, he wouldn't have had it any other way. Well, as we settle in for a few beers after dinner he lets me know the lights will be back on tomorrow at the business. Matter of fact, just like that. Turns out he had a couple bucks laying around so he went and paid the bill. It wasn't much, not much to you these days, but it was probably all he had. All that time with me jabbering in his ear over a few beers through the summer and him not saying a word, he was listening the whole time even long after I thought he'd fallen asleep. But that's just a little thing. For the next few months he helped me in his free time with deliveries, maintenance, anything he could while we saw our way through the winter and kept the doors open and our own heat on. You see what I'm telling you? Jim didn't have much, but what he did have was a sense of loyalty to his friends. He gave me everything he could, his ear, his hard work. That's what kept us going, that's what gave you this business. That's what made Jim who he was and it went a long way to making us who we are. I know we didn't see each other as much once the business really got going and the family grew but he was always there if I needed him."

Junior squirmed in his chair, feeling properly disciplined.

"So you see son," he turned to face him, "you take care of folks. After all, they're the ones who are taking care of you. Carl here, he's fine and he'll do you right. But don't put him or his family through this again, not while I'm around."

Getting off the desk Senior extended his hand to Carl, "Good to see you my boy. Give my best to Lily and the kids. God, I have to get up there real soon to see you folks. Maybe we can get a little fire going in the backyard and have a beer. We'll raise a toast to your dad."

"Thanks Danny, I'll see you soon."

Carl shook his hand on the way to the door, then turned to address Junior, "We'll clear this up just as soon as we can."

"No worries Carl," he replied watching the rain beat heavily against the windowpane.

As he was making his way through the lobby Lois caught his arm, "All set Carl?"

"I think so."

"I knew the old man would see ya right."

"Thanks Lois," and with a nod he left.

The end of third period saw Beth weaving through the halls careful to avoid the clusters of kids milling about their lockers and loitering in classroom doorways. Her locker was at the other end of the building forever making getting from where she was to where she was supposed to be a rather trying endeavor. All freshman lockers started at the far end of the building and worked forward segregated by class. Despite that small issue, she found the whole locker thing fascinating. Until now her personal space during the school day had been an unsecured cubby. As one who closely guards her privacy it's understandable she would have had a trepidation bordering on paranoia about making use of it. While other kids packed their space with books, clothing, toys and any other manner of childhood detritus, her cubby remained empty. It wasn't really a fear of theft, her possessions would have attracted little interest in the material sense, it was more an unwitting rejection of the communality of it all and an unwillingness to display the remains of her own childhood for all to see. But now she had her own space, secure and unreachable.

She was further fascinated by the way other kids decorated those spaces. So many rock stars, sports heroes, family pets, stolen mementos from summer vacation spots, friends and lovers. The more creative treated their locker as an art project, the Jesus freaks a shrine, the athletes their own personal hall of fame. The girl to her left paid homage to a lost sibling replete with rosary and funeral announcement while the boy to her right seemed to regard his space as a rubbish can. Squeezed in the space between, her locker looked little different from the day she moved in, just some books on the shelf, neatly stacked, and a sweatshirt on the door in case of a chill. It was unused, no mementos, no photographs, no shrines. She held her sentimentality close.

When she reached her locker Audrey was already there waiting.

"Hey Elizabeth."

"Elizabeth?" she answered, perplexed, while pushing her way in to undo the lock.

"Beth," she repeated in a low, mocking tone.

"What?"

Opening the door she added and took books from the small pile to look busy. These were the types of interruptions that really upset the pace of her day.

"Just thought I'd say hi, see how your day was going."

"Fine. Why?"

"No particular reason. And sorry about last night, I really didn't mean to make you feel worse."

She'd heard these apologies before and they rang hollow. Nothing would have stopped Audrey in the next moment from tearing her down again if the opportunity presented. Ignoring her, she let her continue babbling while she shuffled through the books until the bell rang, a welcome relief. Fourth period was a free period for her, just time enough to get away somewhere quiet and read. Unlike most students, who undoubtedly procrastinated, she chose not to do homework during the break preferring instead to leave it as an escape at home.

"Well, I have to get to class so I'll see you later," Audrey finished with whatever nonsense she was spouting before skipping away as she herself went in search of a warm, dry place away from it all.

Andy and Cary made their way home after the final bell through the same route traced by the girls. As they built new schools in town the residents had the foresight to build them in a cluster. This made the logistics of running a small, ever strapped system much more simple. Busing could be consolidated, custodians shared, facilities and athletic fields serve students of all ages. It also made easier the task of keeping up with the kids when everything was centrally located. Certainly most families felt that way as older siblings could be pressed as sitters and minders while their parents finished up work for the day. Peace of mind, a few dollars saved, it amounted to something. But the older kids didn't quite see it that way and this was true of Audrey who for years had the job of keeping watch over her sister and the boys during the trek home. Now the responsibility fell to Beth as she was deemed old enough and as Audrey demanded more of the freedom associated with someone her age and in the last year of school.

"Do you have to follow us so close?" Andy protested impatiently, still not used to Beth tailing them after the laxity of Audrey in prior years.

She ignored him and the boys went back to their snickering, inside jokes and foolishness. She hadn't wanted the job and, if truth be told, she didn't actually do the job. She was just walking home via the most direct route and Andy and Cary had yet to catch on that it was all she was doing. If she kept track of them, all the better. If they got away from her, well, all the better too.

Nearing home the boys took off at a sprint bounding across the stoop and into the house. It was Monday, grocery shopping day, and they knew what that meant; tasty treats. Every week was the same, their mother would get the staples and then whatever she had left over in the budget would be used to get little cakes, sugary cereals, chips and pop. Like jackals at the kill they would hover around waiting for her to finish putting them away and turn her back at which time it was every man for himself as they tried tearing into everything at once. But she was wise to the game hiding a portion of the treasure to be doled out as the week went on using it as inducement, bribe, payoff for good behavior, an extra chore done or, if the moment demanded, consolation.

Today there wasn't much of a budget left.

3.

Having seen Carl off to work and the kids off to school Lily finished her morning coffee. She would ordinarily do some minor housework, choose a task that could be easily taken care of before being to work by ten, but after she and Carl discussed the outcome of the oil problem it was decided she would make some inquiries into the state's offer of home heating assistance. It was a difficult chore for her, the first time they'd been put into a position where they sought help, very public help, and it bored itself into her mind. Such a departure from her sense of a normal life it felt like a new and dark beginning with no pleasant end. She wondered would they soon need food assistance, help with the utilities, clothing donations? Would they end up crawling on all fours just to feed and clothe their children? Or would they end up penniless, more so, and be forced into low income housing while their few possessions were sold off? It was mental hyperbole, and she knew it, yet these questions were indicative of the Apocalyptic thoughts ruling her world and overriding her reason this morning.

But in truth this cut her deep, to the very core of her being, something she was sure Carl didn't fully appreciate. It was undignified, for herself, for the kids in whom she had been working ever so hard to instill a sense of decency, of character and grace. She feared it could be a transformative moment for them when they wrongly learned some things in this life are for free. Or conversely, it may be a moment of sudden despair, a sense of purposelessness, the realization that hard work may not be enough. Though in reality it would likely never have registered with them, especially the boys, it was altogether too much for her to contemplate rationally after a sleepless night and a watery cup of coffee. Besides, it didn't help she was making the call because it was decided a woman asking for help was more likely to illicit a positive response and hence gain a positive outcome than a man. Somehow a man, and in particular Carl, would be abrupt and defensive and, after all, a man asking for help wasn't much of a man. On the last point a part of her had to agree. Nonetheless, she resented the fact she was being necessitated to use her limited charms not as a human being, but as a woman.

Nervously running her hand through her hair she leafed the phone book looking for the appropriate agency to call. Finding nothing specifically pertaining to heating assistance she decided the state welfare office would be a likely starting point. The very word, welfare, stuck in her throat more than her last gulp of cold coffee. With a glance at the clock, she hesitantly dialed.

"Welfare."

The woman who answered was gruff and abrupt. She had a fleeting picture of her as rather obese, ear and nose hair, bad ankles, drove a Buick.

"I'm calling to find out about heating assistance." Her voice cracked ever so slightly as she spoke, a betrayal of the steely tone she was intending. She hoped it was audible only to herself believing it would be seen as a sign of weakness and knowing all too well how events can change the moment someone feels they have something over you.

"Yes?"

"I'm trying to find out if there is a program or who I should call?"

"We administer the heating assistance."

"Can you tell me how it works and how we might qualify?"

The woman responded as though she were reciting from a well-worn script, quickly dispensing the rules of the program, how you apply, how you qualify and what to expect. It was done with a monotone only an overly rehearsed scene could deliver. Try as she might, Lily couldn't keep up and found herself interrupting several times after which the woman would sigh impatiently and repeat her last sentence treating her the fool, incapable of grasping simple concepts. Then the more the woman spoke the more her attention strayed from what was being said to who was saying it. She grew ever fatter in her mind and had hair growing from a mole on her face. She even put her in a pair of horn-rimmed glasses, a hair net, rollers and polyester stretch pants, dirt brown with a crease running the front. No, in fact her thighs were too fat for the pants to have a crease and she was so large she had a custom built Buick with some sort of enhanced suspension to prevent the vehicle from collapsing beneath her.

Her thoughts were drifting like this for mere seconds when the woman said something that snapped her back into the conversation. She asked her to repeat it and there it was, an oddly gratifying statement, a statement of truth, a statement that wiped everything clean; they earned too much money to qualify, and just.

She was elated, ignoring the tinge of guilt telling her she shouldn't be, and thanked the woman before putting the phone down. How fortunate, despite the feeling they were finding barely enough to keep her busy at work and, in all reality, should have cut her hours further or let her go altogether, it was those precious few dollars putting them out of reach for assistance. Though she may have ever so briefly tarnished her sense of decency by talking to the welfare office, she no longer had the same irrational worries about herself or the kids. The stain on the family simply wouldn't be and the backward step wouldn't have to be taken and after all, thanks to the elder Danny, they wouldn't be going cold. She knew much of the gratitude belonged to Carl as well but was reluctant to give it for it was he who put her in line to make the call in the first place. He had no right to do that to her, or to his family, so he had no right to gratitude of any kind. What he did have was a duty to find an answer that involved no one but themselves and to put it on his shoulders alone.

There was a definite jump in her step as she left the house that morning, something exceedingly rare for her.

"Nice shoes dingus," one of the kids called out.

Cary's worn out sneaker tore as he kicked the soccer ball trying to get a pass off to a teammate on the side of the net during mid-morning recess. He caught a piece of turf bringing his foot down and it was enough to open the seam a couple of inches near the sole. Now his big toe was unceremoniously poking through generating a round of laughter from the other kids. Plagued by the shame of both misfiring on the pass and ruining his sneakers so publicly he moved away, stopping to dawdle near the swing set. As one of the kids ran off to find adventure elsewhere he sat on the vacant swing and began fingering the hole. His sock had already accumulated quite a lot of debris over the short walk so he started picking out bits of grass and pebbles and brush the dirt away as best he could. Looking closely he could see each end of the tear was straining at the threads and was sure to widen further if he tried to walk but he couldn't move around in his stockings, or bare feet for that matter, so he was at a loss as to what he should do. Getting up from the swing he tested out a few different ways of hobbling around that would afford him to keep his dignity intact, such as it was, and prevent the sneaker from all but disintegrating. He could find no middle ground and as the bell rang was left with no choice other than limp off and join his classmates in line.

Entering the building he still heard a few of the kids reveling in his misfortune. Taking a peek over his shoulder he was just in time to see Jeremy Watson in the middle of a parody, exaggerating his limp to the delight of the other boys who were in turn inspiring him to even greater lunacy with their hooting and hollering. Eventually Miss McCall stepped in to quiet the boys yet, oblivious to the object of their derision, she was unaware their now muffled voices were still keeping up the fun at his expense when they reached class.

As the day wore on things didn't get much better. She continued teaching English after recess, for him an easy gambit, but then it was on to math where fractions were as bedeviling as ever. He just couldn't seem to get beyond the basics of numerators and denominators. Proper fractions, improper, equivalent, reciprocal; what did it all mean and what did it represent? Simple equations with their divided fruits, times and groups were hopelessly lost on him. Already his young mind was framing the question he would ask a thousand times during his school years, why do I have to know this? All the while he failed to realize he used them everyday, most often when he would eye an after school snack given to he and his brother to share where an argument would ensue as to whose half was bigger. It wasn't really surprising the lesson was lost though, might always triumphed over reason.

"Cary, are you with us?" Miss McCall noticed he was lost in his own thoughts and not paying proper attention.

"Yes, ma'am."

"Well good, then maybe you can come up here and show us how to convert this number to an improper fraction?"

He stared unblinking at the blackboard. Looking at the numbers, and they could have been any numbers, there was no way he could solve the problem.

"Well?"

"No ma'am."

"No? Could you at least try?"

Hesitating, he replied the same.

"Mister Kane, get your little bottom up here and try," she demanded.

"No ma'am, I can't."

He was never very good at defying authority, it just wasn't his way, and so he was as disappointed hearing his own refusal as she may have been angered. But the pain of walking up there, torn sneaker opening him to more barbs from his classmates, and failing to solve the problem overruled his nature.

"Yeah, c'mon Cary, go ahead and walk up there for us," Jeremy taunted.

Realizing something more was going on, and having witnessed his recent tendency to belittle other classmates to the delight of his little gathering of chums, she turned her attention to him. "Okay, Mister Watson, you come up here and convert this number to an improper fraction."

He was surprised by how quickly the tables had turned.

"Well?"

"Yes, ma'am."

He made his way toward the front waiting for her to turn her back. She did so at just the right moment. Making the best of his opportunity he whacked Cary in the back of the head with a pencil causing him to let loose a sharp cry that caught her attention. She eyed the pair of them.

"Right, what did you do?"

"Nothing, I didn't do anything," his denial emphatic. It was a feeble defense.

"That's it, down to the office."

"Why?"

"You know why." Grabbing him roughly by the arm she pulled him from the classroom and pointed the way, as though he needed any direction. "Now march."

She returned to a wide-eyed and silent class. Looking Cary over she decided the best course of action was to try and move on, salvage what she could of the lesson, but it didn't feel so easy for him. With few options, and feeling the overwhelming need to flee, he asked for the bathroom pass and went to one of the stalls where he closed the door and sat, and cried.

The shock of the pencil to the back of his head was far more than the pain, it added to his humiliation, a feeling that had been scratching at the corner of his life for some time now. And while he wept he just kept wishing over and over to begin the day again. There would be no soccer this time, he would go to the swings as he usually did and play there alone. He castigated himself for ever daring to join the other kids. A low profile was best, pass unnoticed. Andy did it well, never straying too far, never the first to speak or act, always siting in the back of the class. When he became too assertive for his own comfort he pulled back. He needed to emulate his brother this way. He needed to conduct himself in a manner that he got by with as little attention given his way as possible. He needed to be a ghost, pass unseen.

After a time Miss McCall noticed he wasn't returning. She hoped it wasn't a case of the two boys meeting in the hall and hashing out their differences. Worse still was the thought he might have left school grounds because that would fall on her. Deciding either outcome wasn't good she went in search. Passing the boys room she heard his quiet sobs and pushed the door open a crack.

"Cary?"

He quieted himself.

"Cary, is that you?"

"Yes, ma'am."

"Do you want to come out here?"

"No ma'am."

She wasn't going to play this game with him again. Finding his stall she pushed the door wide, then softened when she saw the state of him. "What's wrong Cary?"

As hard as he tried not to, he burst into tears. She watched them stream down his thin cheeks and gather on his chin before falling to the floor. He tried wiping them away as though his balled up fists could stem the flow but it was no use, they kept coming. Her heart dropped, the significance of Jeremy's games becoming more clear in her mind.

"Cary, tell me what's wrong," she appealed kneeling in front of him.

He just shook his head. Reaching up she gently pulled his hands away from his face and led him from the stall where she bent and hugged him close. As she did so he grasped her tightly and tried stifling the tears by burying his head in her shoulder. They only came stronger. She nearly broke down along with him, the rims of her eyes filling with moisture. And there the two of them were, holding one another, Cary weeping, and neither with the need to say a word.

Finally cried out, she lifted his head and looked at him for a moment, his eyes reddened and swollen. "So, are we better?"

"Yes, ma'am."

"I'm glad." She brushed the moist hair from his forehead, "So are you ready to tell me what happened?"

"I ripped my shoe."

"Is that all?"

He lowered his eyes, "But they made fun of me."

"Oh, don't listen to them. And don't pay any attention to that Jeremy."

Pulling him close again she gave him a firm hug while quietly scolding herself for not taking more immediate notice of Jeremy and his antics. She knew better, and she knew he and his ilk better. In her few years of teaching she'd seen the type, all types, come and go. They largely left the same way they came in, the abusers continuing to abuse and the abused continuing to allow its happening. As she saw some of them even now reaching high school it surprised her how little they changed. Yet at the same time, and with few exceptions, she was sure she could have mapped their future from day one in her class.

"Well Cary, what shall we do now?"

He shrugged.

"Are you ready to come back in?"

"Not really."

"Well, you can't stay in here all day." She thought for a moment, "I tell you what, do you want me to call your mom or dad, have them come pick you up? Maybe they can bring you out for a new pair of sneakers," she suggested giving him a playful poke. The humor was lost.

"No, but can you get Andy for me?"

She nodded and with her arm around his shoulder led him to the office. She saw the pleading in his eyes, the embarrassment, perhaps of his parents knowing, maybe even of her knowing. She was sure he very well would have stayed in the bathroom the rest of the day if it were left up to him. Making the proper arrangements with Lily she sent them home together.

Leaving the building, Andy tousled his hair, "Thanks for getting me out of school early."

Cary quietly limped along on his ruined shoe, the humor still lost on him.

Beth was waiting outside the boy's middle school when it emptied with no sign of them. After about ten minutes, and annoyed the little bastards left her standing, she stormed off just hoping she would run into them somewhere along the way. For a time she imagined them playing one of their games on her by hiding and watching her go all the while flitting from corner to corner and having a hearty laugh at her expense. Looking around periodically she never caught sight of them so abandoned the idea. Then she thought they may be setting up an ambush for her where she'd come around some corner and they'd pelt her with clods of dirt, or worse. When that didn't happen either she finally settled on the idea it was their way of causing her trouble at home, that she wasn't up to the job of keeping track of them so why bother have her try. This could be a win-win for them, she'd get scolded and they'd be credited with being big boys, big enough to walk without someone by their side. At first she was determined they wouldn't get the satisfaction but as quickly as her anger had come it faded and she resigned herself to whatever fate was waiting at home. She simply didn't feel she had the energy to fight with them anymore, hadn't for some time, and quite frankly didn't care one way or the other if her esteem was diminished in her parents eyes because after all, she never wanted the job of walking with them in the first place.

Entering the house she made her way upstairs and sat on her bed. She could hear Andy and Cary playing in their room, home after all. Her mother, having ignored her as she came in, was downstairs making dinner, Audrey probably off with some friends, her dad still at work. Thinking she'd get some reading done she pulled out a book. It was no use, visions of escape were crowding her thoughts.

4.

Audrey waited the rest of the week for news from Chris on how any potential conversation he'd had with her sister may have gone. It was a long wait. The whole idea of somehow getting Beth involved with someone, especially he, had become a crusade. It was the focus of all she did during the day, from planning to be near classrooms she would be exiting to walking home with her after school. Daily she quizzed her on the course of her day, her classes, what she learned, to whom did she talk? She'd even come to convince herself Beth was the same as she only timid, a bit reserved, just in need of that someone to pull her out of her shell and then she'd be a little social butterfly and sister in whom she could be proud. Chris would be that someone, behind her machinations of course.

Beth found Audrey's interest in her life peculiar and discomforting. No matter how hard she tried pushing her away, in ways subtle and unsubtle, she was persistent. For a time she dropped her guard and though unintentional at first, she did so afterward thinking if she shared some minor details perhaps her sister would be satisfied. So they talked about school, mostly superficial gossip, and a bit about clothes. They were topics on which her sister was well-versed and in which she herself could care less. Yet she unfortunately at one point found herself inexplicably divulging the regret she wasn't a bit more outgoing. This just delighted Audrey, feeding her increasing hunger for information like nothing before and driving she herself to again clam up. Finally reaching the return point where they barely exchanged a word as they walked side by side on the way home, she saw the strain it had on her sister, dying to talk, dying to pry, and she was satisfied, a moment's peace at last.

It was short-lived. She hadn't given Audrey's perseverance enough credit. Walking the hall Friday morning she felt a tap on her shoulder.

"Hey Elizabeth."

She didn't turn, confused someone would call her by her full name, but kept walking sure she must have heard it in error.

"Hey Elizabeth, wait up."

She turned, on that there was no mistaking.

"What's going on?" Chris asked.

She stared at him, speechless and still.

He stared back, then tried again, "So what's up?"

It took her what felt like several baffling minutes to respond, it felt that way to them both. "Uh, I'm fine." Just as the words escaped her she realized she'd given the wrong answer to the question, or the right answer to the wrong question. Either way she was flustered.

"Okay, I'm good too then."

Reddening, she nervously fidgeted with the spiral binding of her notebook. Interminable seconds passed before she finally stammered, "Well, I gotta be going, so uh, nice talking to you Chris."

He watched her walk away wondering if that could possibly be the most awkward conversation he'd ever had with the strangest girl he'd ever met. Audrey owed him, big time. He tried, he did just as she asked, and the whole thing went by in the blink of an eye.

Beth was mortified. Reaching her locker she wanted nothing more than to crawl deep inside and lock the door. It was the first conversation she'd ever had with him, one of the few with another student of any kind all year, and she fled like a little girl seeking the folds of her mother's skirt. She rehearsed the scene many times in her head, sometimes effervescent, charming, flirtatious, she would come off as a queen. But most often it played out in her head about the way it just played out in the hall where she would be artless, stultified, and he would turn and walk away.

Audrey saw Chris approaching, shaking his head. "So?"

"That was just weird. She's an odd girl."

"Why? What happened?"

"Well, at first she wouldn't turn around when I tapped her on the shoulder and then when I asked her what's up she just stared at me. I asked her again and she kept staring and then said I'm fine which wasn't really what I was asking. It was just weird."

"She's shy."

"Yeah, you think? She got all embarrassed and walked away."

"That was it?"

"Yeah. What was I gonna do, chase after her?"

"Well, you could have."

"Look Audrey," he cut off any more dialogue as he walked away, "I did what you asked."

She watched him disappear down the hall getting lost amongst the crowd of students. She immediately made for the other end of the building hoping to find Beth still at her locker. She was as angry with her as with Chris whom she felt she had set up just right for the girl. She led the horse to water and all her sister had to do was give him a swallow but instead she left him parched. All week she'd waited on this and from the sound of things it was worth but a few seconds, long enough for the damn girl to unravel all she tried doing. She really deserved this loneliness, she worked at it, she earned it. And in a sense she felt beaten, the girl spurning even her own attempts at connection and now doing away with the one person she seemed to have an interest in and for what? Was it spite, hatred? Did the girl despise her so much she would forsake a chance at her own redemption for the chance to thrust a spear in her older sister's side?

Indeed she was at her locker but as Audrey approached she slowed, finally stopping unnoticed a few feet away. Sitting cross-legged in front of the open door, a few books at her side, she wasn't doing much of anything, just staring down at her hands, rubbing them together, fingering each nail. Her long brown hair fell forward, gathering on her thighs, obscuring her face, and for a long while she stood watching her sister quietly melt down lamenting the day she was unwillingly thrust into the world, or it into her.

"I want you to take Cary to buy some sneakers in the morning."

Lily looked at Carl, her expression enough.

"I don't care. Find the money."

He left the conversation there and went outside with his tobacco, the cool mist of the night tingling on his flush skin, dancing through every exposed pore. He took a deep breath, enjoying the sensation of a moist rush of air flooding his lungs. Despite all it signified, the cold drafts, increased monetary pressure, the onset of winter, he enjoyed autumn's crisp and clean air as it blended with the musty, sweet, earthy, essence of the soil. He loved the way the morning frost twinkled as it lay its blanket across the landscape, the wonderful deep reds and oranges magical in the afternoon sun. Or how on a clear, moonless night the cosmos came alive as millions of stars competed with one another for his attention. He liked nothing more than to just sit and contemplate, really try to encapsulate, the sheer size of the universe on these nights and after all the years his head would still swim, confused, almost dizzy, as it failed to comprehend the magnitude of it all. Those moments were solitary yet he felt like all that existed throughout the universe, from time's beginning and on in perpetuity, accompanied him in a shared moment of awe. He wished it was a clear night.

Breaking the reverie, he sat and rolled a cigarette. Lily came out and joined, sitting just beside him. They silently watched over the night as a breeze rustled in the trees trying to shake free the few leaves stubbornly refusing to let go. The mist gathered in tiny droplets in the troughs of her wavy hair, sparkling in the light pouring from the house. He handed her the cigarette he'd rolled. She took it, and he rolled another for himself. Striking a match he first lit hers, then his own.

"Winter's just about here so I don't see the rush to get him new sneakers," she stated simply.

"The kids are picking on him because he's wearing his boots."

She contemplated his words, "But he hasn't said anything to me."

"I'm not surprised." Realizing too late what he'd said, and the way he said it, he added, "Andy told me."

But she understood. Snuffing the cigarette on a slate paver she went back inside without another word.

He finished his cigarette and rolled another putting it behind his ear. It had been a short, unnecessary and unpleasant exchange with his wife and for that he cursed himself. By now he should know enough to say as little as needed and to choose those remaining words wisely. Much of it was the propensity for her to impregnate everything he said with more meaning than what was actually there to begin. Though at times he had to admit he was flattered she thought him clever enough to speak a double language, something he would never have credited himself capable, over the years he tried to combat her assumptions by shrinking his vocabulary considerably. His words were now more often direct and sentences short. In the end, one result of the issue was he had lost subtlety and was guilty, as now, of saying exactly what he meant when the wiser course would have been to say nothing. The other and more hazardous consequence was the two most often said precisely that, nothing.

As he rose to go back inside Andy stepped out onto the stoop. He invited the boy to sit.

"Have they been real rough on him at school?"

"Yeah, pretty rough. I don't think he's going to play soccer anymore."

"He likes soccer, huh?"

"Yeah, and he's pretty good."

"No kidding, who would have thought?"

The two sat quietly for a moment, Andy tracing a line in the dirt with his shoe, Carl closing his eyes and enjoying the cool air.

"You getting him new sneakers?" he asked looking up at his dad.

"Uh-huh, your mother's taking him in the morning."

"Good," he smiled.

Looking down he returned the smile, noticing not for the first time his twelve year old nothing of a boy was on the verge of becoming a man. It was another uncomfortable marker of his own age.

"So you know son, the rink will be opening next week."

"Yeah? We going?"

"I think we should. Maybe do something nice for Cary, huh?"

"Yeah."

He stood and brushed the back of his pants, Andy doing likewise.

"Right, off to bed with you."

"Dad, it's like eight o'clock or something."

"Is that all?" He winked at the boy, "Well go read or something then."

He pulled the cigarette from behind his ear lighting it as Andy ran back inside. Things must be different these days, he mused, it seemed not too long ago what you wore didn't carry all that much importance, with others or yourself, as long as your clothes were clean and fit right. At least that's what he thought he remembered.

Finishing what was left of the dishes Lily went upstairs to her bedroom. She kept it immaculate, an echo of her mother. Every morning the bed was made, every night the shoes put away. She did her best with the rest of the house yet four kids would allow only so much cleanliness to spoil a good time. Spacing the chores out as she did, it was impossible to have things as she wished but with that she was okay, years of conditioning by the children and Carl rubbed off on her to a degree her mother would never have tolerated. When she was a girl not a toy could be left on the floor at night, a shoe or jacket out of its place, dish undone or even a spot on the bathroom mirror when you were done brushing your teeth. Everything had to be just right. It was odd to think how cluttered the home in which she grew up really felt with photographs, knickknacks and books everywhere and if you ran a finger on a binding or frame not a speck of dust could be found. The myriad reminders of a life unlived had their place in her mother's home and she could sense if even one item had been shifted, no matter how small, when she entered a room. It was uncanny, and it was Lily.

For her it was all very rational. She'd set the closet up so her clothes were sequential from left to right according to bolt weight, lighter articles to the left and the heaviest to the right. Her shoes lined the floor using the same reasoning. Her dressing table was organized so the evening's first use items were to her left and so forth through to her hair brush on the far right. It was a quirk that Carl was quite used to and found rather amusing. He didn't much care because this was her haven, her one place that was sacrosanct. While he was comfortable spreading himself anywhere in the house to read, converse or simply to think, she was most in tune with herself here. This is where she most often worked out the family's problems, absolved herself, castigated others and reminisced.

There were times though when she felt he really didn't understand much at all. He thought it was great fun to mix-up her dressing table, leave a stray shoe about or turn up the corner of a sheet. To him it was being playful, a gentle tease, harmless, but for she it wasn't nearly as much fun. It broke her concentration, hindered her ability to work through problems. A cluttered space necessarily translated into a cluttered mind. She couldn't differentiate between the chaos around her and the chaos in her head. Inevitably it would lead to a downward spiral of sorts where she would proceed to redo and remake everything in the room to reassure herself that all was in its place and all was right in her world. Only then could she feel free, liberated, clear of mind. And all the while Carl would be off playing with the kids, putting them to bed, reading to them, waking them up, and they would stop and wonder to where she'd gone.

Tonight she didn't have the luxury, she was exhausted. Sitting in front of her mirror she replayed the week, a jumbled mess of events. She knew it would turn out that way after the issue of the heating oil seared itself into her brain and into the pit of her stomach. After all the years of struggle she still couldn't get used to the feeling she was standing on the verge of an abyss and as she was forced to look over the edge would nearly collapse, her innards twisted and knotted. Off the rails already, the call from the school pushed her ever closer. Stroking her hair she felt it a wonder she wasn't going gray. Still youthful, few lines, somehow the toil had no effect on her visage, it just tore her apart on the inside. Eventually the two would have to catch up to one another she thought.

She heard Carl creeping up the stairs, stopping at each bedroom for a few moments. It was still early, the boys could be heard occasionally, Beth likely alone in her room, quiet as ever, Audrey out for the night. He eventually made his way into their room approaching her from behind. Caressing her hair as he gazed into the reflection she gave him a weak smile before he kissed her bare, slender neck, her ear, and rested his chin on the crown of her head. She gazed back into his eyes, expressionless, then shut her own. Lingering for a moment he quietly sat on the edge of the bed watching her. Then taking his shoes off he crept to the closet and placed them neatly on the floor closing the door afterward. Taking a last peek, he left as silently as he entered. That was his apology.

Carl felt something wasn't quite right when he looked in on Beth. Although she was laying on her bed, reading as usual, he noticed almost right away it was an illusion. Her countenance was only a part of the betrayal. Downcast and disheartened, it was too unlike her usual mask of stoicism, somehow darker, more distracted. Yet more than that, in the few seconds he was watching she never moved her eyes across the page. Deep in thought, distant, unaware he was even there, she lay unmoving and in a way he found it enthralling. She was statuesque, alluring in her musings, so dark and brooding. Her obvious ache, her pain, was attractive and always had been to him. It was the same with Lily, the two were so like one another. It stirred in him an overwhelming need to protect, to sooth the hurt, to embrace, to do whatever may be necessary, to shine a light though he couldn't for one moment comprehend what thoughts were swirling in their minds. It was edifying. He broke the silence anyway.

"Beth?"

She vacantly looked his way, "Yes, dad?

"What's going on?"

Indeed what? She'd been replaying the scene with Chris over and over in her head unable to shake its indelible mark. It was such a little thing, such a small moment in her life. Yet it was a meaningful moment, it was her moment, and she failed to make it precious. She felt inept and graceless.

"Is everything okay?" he asked inching into the room, hands in pocket.

"Yeah, dad, I'm fine."

He wasn't going to be so easily moved off this time and she sensed it. At the same time she didn't know how to have this conversation with him, or with anyone. While for most the act of talking through one's emotions was cathartic, for her it felt like a walk through a minefield with every footfall perilous, a backward step safer than a forward, and if you froze, unmoving even for an instant, you were exposed.

"Come sit, dad." She thought she might mollify him as she'd done Audrey by parting with something inconsequential, with nothing.

He was grateful for the invitation, sitting on the bed with her as she sat up. Not a word was spoken, he received what he wanted, a closeness, a feeling he was helping in some small way by virtue of being there and she gave what she intended, nothing. Brushing the hair from her face he rubbed her shoulder trying to massage away the obscurity of her thoughts. She didn't recoil this time, instead feeling soothed by the touch. Pulling her close he embraced her more tightly and she felt warm, and for a moment, needed. In that brief time she told her father all she could never saying a word, and he understood.

Audrey spotted Chris on the other side of the fire trying to hide himself from her view. She'd gone out cruising for the night with some friends in hopes of finding a suitable gathering and wedging themselves in for some Friday night fun. It was a custom in town among the teenagers when nothing of consequence was happening, no planned house party, bonfire or hunting cabin where they could content themselves with a few beers and a few laughs. Instead it was a night of spontaneity, a favorite with her, where a sizable enough group would find themselves together and decide on one of a myriad remote locations they traditionally used with the virtue of being out of view of parents and the police. Driving by the usual spots they found what they were looking for, a gathering of some twenty odd kids, mostly boys, standing about or jumping from car to car, plotting the night's mayhem. Some whoops went up when they pulled in, always did when a car full of girls arrived, especially when Audrey Kane could be counted amongst them. It was decided before their arrival that the old pasture would be the spot of choice. Tucked between a grove of trees near the road and a river on the far side it was hidden from view until you drove down in and had the added advantage of a small sandy beach ideal for a campfire and comfortable seating. The water in this part of the river was fairly still and barely two or three feet deep so was deemed safe enough for the midnight drunken swimmer. And if the party came off right there was always at least one, even at this time of year.

Surprised he was there she moved around the fire and planted herself in front of him blocking everyone else out. After witnessing Beth glumly squatting in front of her locker she resolved he was going to try again. She would not be so easily beaten by her sister and neither would he. They exchanged greetings, some minor chit-chat, but both knew the topic at hand.

"Look Audrey, what do you want from me?"

"I want you to try again."

"I know, but why?"

"It's important to me."

An inner dialogue had been playing out in Audrey's mind over the last few days over how much information she should share with him. From the beginning she anticipated there may be, likely would be, problems getting these two talking. At some point she may have to share what little she knew of her sister's feelings but that in itself was a multifaceted problem. It could easily scare him away and seemed probable given his expressed desire not to get involved with her in any romantic way, or in any way at all. At the same time, it may be her last and best hope of piquing his interest enough to keep going forward, especially when there were no more cards in the deck to play. Another aspect, and a bit more troubling, was Beth herself. It was a serious breach of the girl's privacy to even be talking to him about this and if she discovered the betrayal their relationship would likely be forever destroyed. Considering all that had come before, there was little doubt on this point, even if there wasn't much of a relationship there to destroy.

"I get that Audrey, but why?"

"It just is."

"Not good enough."

She was surprised by how adamant he was about not getting involved with her sister. Taking him by the hand she led him away from the fire to a location more discreet. If she was about to play her last card it wasn't going to be under the watchful eye and listening ear of others.

"Look Chris, she likes you."

"So," he responded flatly.

"Well, I don't know if she's ever really liked anyone before. She's just so private it's hard to know what the girl is thinking. But now I know and I want her to be happy and I think you can do that for me."

"Do it for you?"

"Well, for her."

"What about me, who the Hell do you think I am?"

She was getting a bit testy. Obstacles for her were ordinarily not this difficult to overcome, particularly when the male animal was involved.

"What's your problem Chris?"

"My problem is that you keep pushing this girl on me."

He made to move off toward the fire but she caught him by the arm angrily pulling him back.

"Why won't you talk to her?" she demanded.

"Audrey," he complained, "I'm just not that interested in her. Can't you just let this go?"

"No, I can't."

They exchanged point for point in a conversation at times bewildering to both. Neither would back down, after a time appearing they were holding their ground for nothing more than the sake of argument. He was trying to work his logic, she her charms, because in the end his position was rational, hers emotional. It was fun, engaging, and they continued for quite some time. Finally Audrey had an inkling on how to break the impasse. She found she was holding another card, a well used one. Drawing him close, she wrapped her hand around his head while running her slender fingers through his hair and kissed him with all the passion she could muster. Pulling herself away, she ran her hand down his arm and squeezed his own.

"Is that good enough reason?"

Later in her room, still deliberating the day, a thought struck Beth. It was very nearly the same time Audrey was winning the argument with Chris. It had to be her, she had to be at the root of this disaster. His approaching her was curious, even more so when he called her Elizabeth. She remembered her sister doing the same earlier in the week and how odd it was then. The damn girl must have told him what she'd written in her notebook, what they had so briefly and savagely discussed. She had to have put him up to it and now she looked even more the fool, in her own play no less. Standing in the blinding light she couldn't remember what she was supposed to say or do so she fumbled about, reaching for anything, and when all was lost fled the stage in retreat. Now here she was, replaying the defeat, her chance to find a place to shine, even a little, now lost. It was the worst betrayal. Why couldn't the damn girl, everyone for that matter, do as she wished and just let her be? Couldn't they see she was happiest when she was alone and was really only ever miserable with their intervention, their misguided, fabricated, noble charity? After all, if the universe wanted her involvement then surely she would have been made in another image, not the sordid reflection on which her twilight thoughts now played.

5.

Lily left early with Cary hoping to get in and out of the department store before the weekend rush. Though Andy was disappointed to be left behind she knew the boys would spend too much of the time heckling one another and she needed to be quick. Crowds were a source of discomfort for her. She found the jostling and closeness of a busy shop far more worrisome than perhaps any other venue in her world. Rudeness seemed to abound, ungracious acts by ungracious people. And really it was the way they moved helter skelter pushing past one another for a choice item on the shelf or a better position on line. They were their own unconcerned center of focus. It even extended itself to the parking lot, another source of tedium. Everyone packed their cars as closely together as possible to mitigate an additional six foot walk to the entrance. It was no wonder people were so enormous these days, she often thought, because walking anywhere for anything had somehow become passe.

It was a phenomenon she'd noticed with her walk to work as well where she rarely met anyone else on the sidewalk. People were instead crammed in their cars, stopping and going, listening to music, belting out the tunes as though no one outside their tin cans could hear. Even if she and Carl could afford a second car she would have preferred the walk because she enjoyed her thoughts for those ten minutes. Free of he and the kids, away from the house, her mind had time to stretch. Gratefully it wasn't important thoughts, those ruled her psyche all other times of the day. It was instead a moment to make light observations, gaze at the world around, simply be an unassuming part of it all. To be sure, it was a conscious effort as she would often find her mind polluted by fragments of home life and those stray thoughts were enough to put a black spot on her day. Squeezing real hard she usually managed to push them far to the back and let the aimless wanderings invade the fore of her mind. It was a small step toward bliss.

Pulling into the parking lot she painfully felt how fleeting those moments were as it was far busier than she'd expected for such an early hour. Already there were lines forming, cars blocking those behind as they waited for a parking spot closer to the door taking far more time than if they'd just parked in the first open space they found and walked. Oh well, she mused, another dollar for the newest diet guru as the world continues to wobble in its orbit. She found her space, well away from the doors, and said a little prayer she didn't run into anyone she knew. Of that there was little chance. Warning Cary not to stray they made their way to the shoe department.

"Mom, I want these ones."

He excitedly pulled the first pair he came to off the shelf, much to her displeasure. The more expensive were always in front to have just this effect on children who so often ruled their parent's purchases. But he rarely had anything new with he and Andy being so close in age. The allure was immense and reason, as much as could be done with an eleven year old, was an added challenge to her day.

"No, those are too expensive."

"No they're not. Look, they're not as much as those ones," he pleaded while pointing out another pair nearby.

"No Cary, we have to keep looking."

"But mom?"

"No, I can't afford to get you branded shoes like that."

She took him by the hand pulling him farther down the aisle. Somewhere toward the middle she suspected the prices would become more manageable. Scanning the tags she realized it was a relative thing, very relative. Despite repeated ventures in shoe shopping she never ceased to be amazed at how dear they'd become.

"Look at these ones Cary."

Eagerly taking them from her he analyzed them close. Though his spirits were buoyed by the sheer variety of colors and styles, his eyes were keen. He felt the material, checked the seam and passed judgment; they wouldn't do. Rolling her eyes she returned them to the shelf.

"And these?"

He put the sneaker through the same inspection, this time also testing the cushion of the sole, the ruggedness of the tread. It failed, and again she returned them to the shelf.

"Alright then." Scanning the aisle for the basic price breaks, "you choose something. But only from this area here."

She circumscribed a fairly confined area in which he had to work. Disheartened his choice was so narrowly curtailed the excitement waned and for a moment he sulked, refusing to pick a pair of sneakers off the shelf. He looked from one end of the aisle to the other questioning her logic. Clearly those on either side of him were of higher quality while those in front would soon tear as the others had done.

She was losing her patience as he looked everywhere but straight ahead. "If you don't choose a pair then I'll choose them for you."

"But mom, these ones are just cheap."

"No they're not, they're fine."

"But they'll rip."

"Look, Cary, these are your choices so pick a pair. Now," she warned him.

What to do with the boy. She felt Carl should be here doing this with him since he was the one with so much concern. But then he would probably have given in to the boy's desire for an expensive pair and she would have been left worrying from what budget the choice would come.

With he still in a huff she bent close, arched her eyebrows and icily breathed, "Pick a pair now or you are not getting anything."

Looking up at her uneasily he strode over and pointed to the pair she originally picked out for him. He'd been holding out hope for sneakers he could boast about, maybe lord over his brother since hand-me-downs never moved upward, but from those which he had to choose the pair his mother suggested probably were the most attractive. He preferred a dark color rather than what he was getting since white always screamed new shoes inviting further inspection and efforts to scuff them. Indeed it was no way to begin an inconspicuous life. Checking his size, she took a matching box from the shelf and pulled him along to the register.

On the way Cary spotted Jeremy passing through one of the aisles. He was alone, wandering through a row of jackets, fingering some but otherwise paying little attention. Feeling too exposed he moved to the other side of his mother using her body to block the line of sight. As he did so Jeremy changed direction and started coming toward them. Again he moved around her to hide himself and as the boy came closer and closer he continued to nervously move around, clinging tightly to her as he spun.

"What the devil is wrong with you?" she growled.

Looking down at him as he snapped his head up she saw the anxiety, for an instant thinking she struck fear in the boy then quickly realizing his attention was elsewhere. Seeking the source of his alarm she easily settled on Jeremy as he passed behind and Cary moved directly in front of her, all but burying his head in the folds of her thin sweater. Brushing her hands over his head she pulled him closer and watched the boy go. Looking back down she regarded the way he shrunk away, eyes wide, barely taking a breath even as the kid moved down another aisle and out of sight. Glancing back up at her he lightly pushed himself away.

Making their way outside she followed his eyes as they scanned the parking lot for any signs of the boy. He kept his distance from her while she contemplated the matter. After loading themselves in the car she looked down to regard him. He was staring at his feet.

"Shall we get some breakfast?"

He nodded, giving her a faint smile. Easing away from the lot she was pleased for the moment she would have with the boy. It was time away, from Carl, from the house, the other children, and her own anxiety.

Carl had the other kids out doing yard work all morning. They began the process of bagging leaves to place around the foundation of the house. Saving paper grocery bags for months gave them all they needed to get the job done and with what had fallen thus far in the cold and damp weather they were lucky they'd saved what they did. The lawn was positively blanketed from end to end with the foliage gathering several inches deep in corners of the house or hollows of the land, places the wind helped gather them in deep, moist heaps. He had Audrey and Beth raking while Andy, reveling in the chance to get down in the muck and mire with the insects and all manner of beast, handled most of the bagging. By mid-morning they'd harvested enough for one complete layer around the house yet there was still work to be done if they were to achieve the bounty's full reward. His hope was they could get the pile two high, a chore for sure, but this year they needed to realize as much savings as possible. Though in a real sense it failed to register with him as any more significant than other years.

Following Beth most of the morning he was a bit morose his bonding with the girl didn't seem to improve her outlook a great deal. Feeling the two had silently come to an understanding with one another, at the least an attrition, he was now left to wonder just what he achieved knowing whatever it was it passed in that moment and no other. She kept to herself, most of the time raking on the opposite side of the lawn. While Audrey and Andy were having a grand time frolicking about, covering one another in the leafy debris, she concentrated on making perfect each sequential square yard of turf. He found the compulsiveness of her work amusing, wondering if her mind was as organized. If only he'd been able to get a glimpse of the chafing thoughts infesting her morning he may have understood it wasn't.

"Well, I think it's time for a coffee break," he proclaimed dropping the pruning shears he'd been using on the trees.

"Sounds good to me," Andy chimed in.

"Oh, you having coffee then?" he laughingly asked of the boy.

"Sure."

"Well, okay then young man. Audrey, Beth, you coming?"

Dropping her rake Audrey skipped toward them pausing long enough to deposit some leaves down the back of Andy's shirt. Chasing after her with his own handful he found he was no match for her long legs.

"Beth, you coming?"

She deliberated, not possessing much of a taste for coffee yet feeling as though she needed to give her dad something in reward for reaching out to her last night. It wasn't much but at least he'd made the attempt, a certain improvement over the first fourteen years of family life.

"Yeah, I guess," she said dropping her rake and walking toward him as Audrey and Andy continued the chase inside.

He slung his arm around her as she neared, "You okay honey?"

She was sorely tempted to shrug his arm away, partly out of habit, partly to redraw the lines in her wavering mind. She was sure every other sentence he uttered to her consisted of some variation of that same question. It was tiresome, yet she let his arm stay as they walked in the front door.

She deposited herself on the couch while he ambled into the kitchen, whistling as he went. Starting the kettle he prepared the four mugs including his favorite, deeply stained yet still proudly emblazoned with the Chicago skyline. He'd been there once, his lone venture out of state, to attend a public works convention. It was something the town took part in every other year, a bone they threw out to everyone at work. Each getting their turn in pairs, all expenses paid, it was a wonderful time had mostly on his own. He'd never seen living on such a grand scale. It wasn't only the sheer size of the buildings, so densely packed together, but the metropolitan spread. Coming into Midway he couldn't help be in awe of a place so large, so colossal, that from airplane height his eye still couldn't find a horizon empty of some structure or other piled closely on top of another. It stuck with him, his now favorite place, his favorite mug.

The kettle whistling, he called to the kids, Audrey and Andy still chasing one another through the cramped confines of the house. They bounded down the stairs reaching the kitchen just ahead of Beth who made her way in but remained standing in the doorway. He handed them all their coffee with a wink and a smile and sat at the table where they quietly sipped taking in the sharp, bitter flavor of the instant brew. It was a sensory joy after a chilly morning of good, hard work.

"So, that's quite a bit done for one morning?" Carl eventually broke the silence.

"Sure is," Andy agreed.

"So how's that coffee, boy?"

"Hits the spot, dad."

"The spot, huh?" he chuckled. Andy was rarely allowed coffee and it was only over the last few months so he wondered how the boy could already have developed a spot?

"Dad, how much longer are we going to be at this?" Audrey asked, finishing her cup.

"Why, somewhere better to be?"

"Maybe."

He measured her for a moment, always on the run, never taking time enough to stop for a breath. In a way she was no different from Beth in that neither had time to invest in the family, one by virtue of being physically absent, the other by being emotionally vacant. How queer, family life, he thought.

"Well, I suspect we'll get most of what we can by lunch. If you still feel the need to split after that then fine." He looked over at Beth and then back to her, "Why don't you take your sister with you?"

"I don't know dad?" she replied looking alarmed at the prospect.

"I'm fine dad." Beth set her mug on the counter and resigned to the living room.

He knew as soon as he'd asked it was a mistake. Worrying he may have just spent what precious little capital he'd gained with her over the last twelve hours on a foolhardy suggestion he was again left marveling at his inability to stay quiet when silence was the best language he could employ. Perhaps if he carved out his tongue he'd be a torment to no one, especially himself.

"C'mon Andy, let's get this cleaned up."

Beth, sitting cross-legged on the couch in the darkened living room, caught Audrey as she was leaving the kitchen. "Why'd you do that to me?"

Unclear what the question was, and thus equally unclear how to answer, Audrey prevaricated. She couldn't recall doing anything, the two hardly saying a word all morning. Then the thought struck, perhaps her sister was somehow aware of the previous night's festivities and her concluding arrangement with Chris. As unlikely as it seemed, it was really the only idea that came to mind. Still, it was a dubious question, the only course to remain unequivocal, an attempt at vacuousness to betray nothing her sister may believe she knows.

They stared at each other, one in practiced deception, the other wearing her tortured and bruised innocence, until Carl broke the spell rounding them up to finish the work. Audrey gratuitously took the interruption, hugging him as they made their way back outside and confounding him as usual in the process. Beth lingered a moment seething at the scene her sister played in front of her before joining them to neaten another square yard of turf.

Lily and Cary found a nice corner table at Brett's Cafe back in town. A little breakfast nook with a flair for the arts, they specialized in french toast. She found the place an oddity, he thinking it brilliant with the red and white checkered tablecloths, the vases with a single daisy, the watercolors lining the brick walls. And there was Brett himself cooking up the french toast with fresh berries, nuts, powdered sugar or nutmeg and maple syrup in full view of his guests with a pristine white apron complete with ruffled chef's hat. For Cary it was a bit magical, a feast for the eyes and for the belly. It was rare to eat out, rarer still to be in a place such as this which was especially nice in his eyes. Lily was simply relieved the prices were reasonable because buying a child's confidence had become more and more expensive over the years and their budget barely scored a hug.

"So what are you going to have Cary?"

"French toast," he answered excitedly.

"Of course you are," she snickered, "but what do you want to drink?"

"Can I have orange juice?"

The waitress approached the table already writing OJ on her pad having overheard his response. He followed by ordering his french toast enthusiastically demanding heaps of strawberries and whipped cream. Lily ordered coffee and nothing else figuring at worst she'd be finishing his.

"So let me see those shoes on you?"

Cary, beaming, got up from the table and modeled them for her. He'd taken the sneakers out of the box on the ride back to town and laced them up. Glad to be rid of his winter boots, he marveled at the sheer blinding whiteness of his new footwear. It was going to take a lot of work to get them scuffed up in time for Monday but he was sure Andy would be more than pleased to lend a hand. Being home for the yard work would have done the trick though perhaps, he thought, for the rest of the day it would be best to leave them clean. She would be none too impressed to see what he had in store so he might as well give her the day.

"They look really nice."

"Thanks mom."

"You're welcome."

He turned his attention back to Brett, sure the batch he was now preparing was his own. Lily watched his fascination, fearing to interrupt. He was entranced and Brett was clearly enjoying the audience as he seemed part cook and part circus clown. Tossing the eggs high in the air he caught and juggled them before cracking them on the edge of the bowl.

Looking over his shoulder with a wink he took the french toast off the grill balancing it on the edge of the spatula behind his back and flipped it high over his head onto the plate waiting in hand. He swerved, dancing and whistling as he gathered the toppings, piling them with a flourish of exaggerated gestures. All this was to the delight of Cary, his glee complete when Brett himself delivered the breakfast with a mountain of whipped cream teeming with strawberries and a little French flag on top. He was such a young eleven year old.

"So can I have a strawberry?"

"Sure mom."

She took it, first disposing of the whipped cream, then biting it to the stem. A trickle of red juice flowed from the corner of her lip where she quickly dabbed it away with her napkin. Indeed they were fresh.

She'd been trying to consider the best way to ease into a conversation about school and his boots but found it quite difficult. Fearful it would dampen the fine time he was having, she was also afraid it may do nothing more than supplant the good memory she was hoping to create with the darker reality she thought his life sometimes had to offer. Ultimately she decided to just out with it since there was no natural or delicate way to bring the conversation around and desperate as she was to know something of the boy's troubles.

"So what's been going on at school with the other kids?"

He paused before continuing to stuff himself. Mouth full, he responded, "What do you mean?"

"You know, with your winter boots."

He considered the question carefully. She didn't often ask such things, or any things for that matter, so he was unrehearsed on the appropriate response.

"Mom, why did you name me Cary?" he asked in reply.

"Why, don't you like it?"

"I guess, I just never seen another kid with that name?"

"Nobody picks on your name do they?"

"No, not really."

"Well, is it no or not really?"

"I guess not."

She hated how indirect were kids. Tending to answer questions with other questions their responses seemed always deliberately vague when you managed to drag anything out of them at all. It was as though they were already suspicious of your motives, paranoid and jaded at a young age. She resented it, their spirits had a lot more bruising to go before they were entitled to feel those things.

"So is it no?"

He nodded.

"Well, what about your boots?"

He stalled by pushing a strawberry around his plate picking up maple syrup and melted whipped cream. Feeling her eyes on him he knew he couldn't delay much longer. Besides, his food play was less than convincing, his hunger long sated.

"Some of the kids thought it was funny."

"What was funny?"

"When I ripped my sneaker and when I went to school wearing my boots."

"Why?"

"I don't know."

"Well what did they say?"

"I don't know. They just picked on me about wearing boots when there's no snow."

"Was that boy in the store one of them?"

He replied with a nod, still pushing the same strawberry around the plate which had by now become pulpy, swamped with an amber glaze. He sorely wanted the interrogation to end preferring instead to think about his new shoes and the fine breakfast he'd just eaten. The day had thus far been a bit turbulent, much more than he would have anticipated when it started out, and while seeing Jeremy in the store where he was buying the very sneakers he hoped would bury his torment was nerve-wracking enough, the line of questions from his mother was simply adding to the hurt. He wished the matter dropped, he wished to be left alone.

She eased up realizing she was achieving little save the ruination of his day which was hard enough already. Though she didn't recognize the boy in the store, no real surprise, she did feel he looked the type, miserable and apathetic, who could cause a great deal of trouble for Cary, for any boy really.

"Alright then, let's pay the bill and go home." When he didn't look up from his plate she put her finger under his chin and led his gaze to meet her own. "So, are we better?"

An odd choice of words, he thought. He was appreciative of the sneakers, really loved the breakfast and the time away, but was unclear on how things were suddenly much better.

By the time they arrived back home it was after lunch. Carl and the kids had nearly finished an entire second row of bags around the house, exhausting the leaf supply in the process. Being into November he was skeptical they would have enough as planned. He put it down to the dampness of the season and the resulting compaction this year as opposed to others. Audrey had left, gone off with some friends and then on for destinations unknown, while Beth had taken a walk. Andy was waiting outside, following his dad around and picking at the dirt. Sporting his new sneakers Cary jumped from the car just as it rolled to a stop.

"Wow, pretty cool, and pretty white," Andy exclaimed when he saw them.

"Yeah, nice ones there Cary," Carl echoed.

Moving past on her way to the front door Lily gave Carl's arm a squeeze. He watched her go the length of the yard. Andy, deciding he was going to remove some of the shine from his brother's sneakers, chased Cary until he caught him and the two started wrestling around the front yard. It was doing its job, so much for a proud mother's day, and in a matter of seconds the virginal sneakers were tainted, proudly advertising their soiled essence. Cary cared not, Andy rejoiced, Carl lamented and Lily was oblivious.

"So it went pretty well then?" Carl asked following her into the house.

"Yeah, it really did," she smiled.

He was impressed with her spirit, and quite relieved. He knew he'd left the matter with her on very tenuous footing. Yet he also knew there were times when you need to push the more worldly concerns to the side and a child's happiness, or unhappiness as it were, was one of those times. It's a small thing really, should be both an afterthought and at the fore of your mind at all times. It was parenting, it was family life, it was one of the few aphorisms he knew to be true and he hoped it was the end of his questions as to whether she shared that vision.

Beth's walk saw her aimlessly wandering the neighborhood enjoying the chance to pore over the variety of approaches her neighbors took with their landscaping, yards both large and small. While most had no inspiration or purpose, their shared vision a flawlessness in the way they wore their plush cushion, others resembled the best cared for golf courses with consistent greens, manicured shrubs, proportional trees, and boring ascetic. But what really intrigued her were those with the impertinence to redefine a lawn and landscaping in the process. There was the old man on the corner a couple of blocks away who decorated his lawn with all manner of household refuse in an ever-changing riot that was surely an affront to the traditional country homeowner. Hanging laundry detergent bottles from trees as wind chimes, shaping a variety of indescribable ornaments from bits of metal and plastic, using an abandoned and rusting car as a planter with a mix of flowers and vegetables, he nonetheless carefully clipped his lawn and trimmed the trees around them. Another was Mrs. Jensen a little farther on who simply did nothing at all. Whether from infirmity, apathy or a carefree existence it didn't matter, her lawn was perfectly wedded to the natural environment with all its native species, plant and animal. During the warmer months she was compelled to stop for a time and watch the dragonflies, the myriad birds and squirrels, cicadas, butterflies and moths, ants, beetles, ladybugs and a horde of other creatures dancing around and among the brush. She wished it was warmer now.

Though she'd never met any of these homeowners in a meaningful way, only occasionally chancing a wave, she imagined they reflected the lawns they kept. Those with the most fastidiously trimmed and ornamented lawns were likely by and large to be uptight, conventional, concerned how the one avenue others had into their lives communicated how they lived and what they thought. Their presentation was an exhibit of their unease with the world. On the other hand was the old man who found solace in creating his ideal of beauty out of the junk around him, the remains of our lives, of his life, a semblance of order from chaos. He'd probably lived a long time in the same town and the same house and cared not what the world thought because he'd paid his dues already. The same could be true of Mrs. Jensen who had no time for pretense and enjoyed watching the native species from her window as much as she did. In the end she reasoned the more interesting displays a sort of truth, a presentation of comfort with oneself.

Returning home she stopped to muse on how her own lawn reflected the lives within. It was orderly, a few large trees, grass a little long. There were no flowers and no shrubs other than what others would consider an oversized weed, a nuisance for the compulsive. Nor were there any ornaments, no wind chimes, no cleverly planted wheelbarrow, no flowers in the mailbox in front of the house. The land heaved a bit here and there, fell away toward the far edge of the house. It certainly wasn't neatly maintained yet neither was it rough or neglected. In a way, the whole scene composed a portrait, the somewhat dilapidated little house, bags of leaves lining the foundation, broken and missing clapboards and roofing tiles, frame a bit askew, crooked granite stoop with slate pavers forming an overgrown walkway, that was, in her estimation, a fairly accurate reflection of her family.

Breaking off her study, she ignored the sprinkles that were starting to fall and pushed past the house, through the backyard and up the small hill in back enjoying the soft crunch of leaves and twigs underfoot as she climbed higher. Up here was an area of her own. She carved it out over the summer completing it with a small wooden bench she chanced upon as it was being discarded. She'd spent considerable time trimming back the brush, leveling the land and keeping it free of debris. Shaded by the oaks and the maples with a healthy screen of evergreens it was her own place for quiet reading, watching the forest, or contemplation and meditation. Today she had a lot of thinking to do.

6.

Audrey returned home in the wee hours of Sunday morning, the night largely a repeat of Friday's affair, sans Chris, where she and her friends sought the comfort of a warm fire and a few beers. Not much of a drinker, she usually contented herself with just having a couple throughout the night more as something to have in her hand along with the others than for any real enjoyment. She was pleased with the reality her life presented outside of the home and saw no reason to muddy it up. She'd also borne witness, all too often, to the repercussions for some who were out of control whether it was the physical danger, the loss of esteem, a reputation or worse. She had a focus, a center point in life, an arrival on which she desperately needed to keep her eye. Such things were an impediment to all she had thus far cultivated and there was no time to delay by putting obstacles in her own way. Yet not all obstacles were under her control and one such was Beth.

Like many of life's crusades, they border on unhealthy obsession as they gain momentum and this was the case with Audrey and her desire to turn Beth into herself. The girl was pretty enough, perhaps a little makeup or more style to her hair. She was awfully thin but not much could be done with that other than her natural development. It was really the depth of her gloom and her petulance that so bedeviled Audrey. She felt she was making an effort in good faith to bring her sister around, to make her happy, but was ever spurned by the confounding nature of the girl. She even used her considerable charms on Chris to keep his interest alive, weak though it was, and tonight she began to realize the enormity of that mistake.

Tongues were atwitter at the bonfire before she ever arrived. It seemed her final point in the previous night's argument with him hadn't gone unnoticed. Audrey Kane, the girl who rebuffed most boy's advances, had somehow become romantically entangled with Chris Larson, a boy who, though with no substantial marks against him, was by no means supposed to be the object of desire by someone of her distinction. It was gossip, good gossip, and it was making the rounds. Some had it pegged as surely an alcohol fueled transgression, others that she was somehow playing the poor boy, like all beautiful girls, and he would only be hurt in the end. Oddly still, some were giving her credit for looking past the normal adolescent dating game by seeking someone who made her happy based on qualities other than popularity or looks. In this she was more mature, less superficial, even more understanding a person than they'd previously given credit.

Any way they played it she was in a corner. She couldn't tell the truth because it would be a further break from her sister's confidence. Based on her reaction earlier in the day, and already doubts were again clouding her mind as to how much her sister really knew, it would be a mammoth betrayal that made even she squeamish. And though she'd made the best decision she could at the time by doing what she did, it was a mistake to be indiscreet when so many others were around. Yet, if she allowed the rumors to persist there was no doubt even in her sheltered world Beth would eventually hear. If no one told her directly it didn't matter, the girl was smart and would intuit something was amiss when suddenly all eyes were on her, a girl who went unconsidered through life.

Weighing all excuses in the brief time she had, she settled finally on allowing alcohol to be the root of it all. Although it wouldn't stop the tongues wagging, it would at least give the episode a less harmful, wanton taint. Moreover, it did have the potential to more easily and quickly close the story. The ideal was to put the explanation out there, spend as little time as possible on it, and just let it die on the vine. By Monday, with some fortune, there would be little left to discuss hence few people left who needed to hear the latest in high school farce. As added credence, she had a few more beers than usual. Not enough to lose her faculties or become in any way incoherent, but enough to give the story weight.

Now she found herself in a heap, fully clothed, lying in bed, staring at the ceiling in the dark. She hoped it had all worked, desperate to have it all work. Unfortunately, Beth wouldn't let the subject go, nor was she asleep.

"Why'd you do that to me?"

Her voice, abrupt and close, echoed through the dark. Ruminating most of the afternoon Beth found a certain resignation in the matter. Still, her mind as far as her sister was concerned was clear.

Waiting a moment with no response she repeated the question. "Why'd you do that to me?"

"I heard you the first time."

By the very way Audrey lived her life she was indelicate hence the level of nuance this was going to take was for her taxing, and especially so when she was vague on where her sister's knowledge began and where it ended. Though her silence was intentionally obfuscating, she needed the room to tie the whole thing up as neatly as possible, if indeed it were possible.

"Well?"

"I didn't do anything to you Beth so I don't know what you're on about."

"Why'd you tell Chris?"

It at least gave Audrey a clue as to what her sister knew.

"What makes you think I said anything to him?"

"I asked you why?"

The damn girl wasn't going to let even a shade of nuance be used here, she thought. Perhaps it was better to come a little clean on this matter rather than let the girl continue to fume over the affair and potentially uncover the entire thing on her own.

"I didn't mean to, it just happened."

"How does it 'just happen'?"

"It just did."

"How?" she repeated forcefully.

"Why are you so worked up about this, he talked to you didn't he? Isn't that what you wanted?"

"How?"

"Just go to sleep Beth."

Fed up with the line of questions, Audrey tried to end the conversation there by rolling over to stare at the wall in the dark. Beth remained silent for a long time, recounting some of her darker thoughts from the previous evening. She hated her sister. Measuring the words carefully, she broke the silence.

"I didn't want him to talk to me, I wanted to talk to him."

"What's the difference? It's done anyhow."

"There's a world of difference."

"Yeah, whatever, in your world maybe."

"I asked you to stay out of my life. I've always asked you to stay out of my life, but you never listen. Now you do this to me."

"What? What have I done? So a boy talked to you, big deal. Be thankful, at least now he knows you exist - it's a far cry from everyone else in school."

"But I wanted to talk to him."

Agitated, Audrey rolled back over and sat up, "What the Hell are you on about girl?"

"I wanted to talk to him, in my own time, on my own terms," she responded evenly.

"Listen you little freak, I did you a favor. Would you have ever talked to him anyway?"

Beth refused to rise to the bait, weary from the same trap being used over and again on her.

"Maybe."

"More like no," she corrected her, "you'd never talk to him."

"You're missing the point."

"Yeah, apparently so."

"It was my decision," Beth continued, "and now you've taken that away from me. It doesn't matter whether or not I talk to him, it matters that the choice was mine, not yours. Taking that from me wasn't fair. You already have everything your own way as it is so why you did this is just..."

Beth was on the verge of uncharted ground. She was clear of mind as the evening closed in having had time to put everything in perspective but now her thoughts felt incomplete as they were vocalized and left hanging out there. And that's just how she felt, like she was hanging out there, incomplete, dangling in front of the one person in her world she felt was as callous as anyone could possibly be. She wanted to leave it there, Audrey's ire wouldn't have it.

"Just?"

"Cruel," she breathed finally.

Whether it was how she said it or the fact she did it didn't matter, for Audrey it surprised and hurt not because she'd done her best for the girl, but because she'd done her worst, and it was true. It was a more honest thing than any her sister had said, perhaps ever if she'd been listening. The silly girl, forever closed, in a most rare of open moments and with one solitary word gave a glimpse of her person showing in turn all she had done to damage her. It seemed such a frivolous thing to get the boy involved yet it was so clear, so simple, and so cruel. Indeed she had unwittingly played the girl, set her up to appear foolish. More than that, she realized she forced the girl to peer more starkly in the mirror and catalog her inadequacies, learn who she wasn't, who she would never be and lose the comfort of knowing who she was at that very moment. Rather than accept her sister, at worst just leave her alone as she so often wished, she'd been spiteful, scornful of the frail, tired girl. It was a lot to absorb, much more than she could in this sliver of time in consideration of a lifetime that had come before.

"I'm sorry," she whispered laying back down.

Sunday's breakfast was more scintillating than usual. In typical Kane fashion it was most weekends taken at leisure and exclusively consisted of cold cereal and toast. They wandered in and out of the kitchen as they awoke, Carl and Lily first, followed by the kids, Audrey ordinarily being the last. It had always been this way and it functioned well. It was the one day everyone was allowed to sleep in, chores be damned. If there was any work to be done it could be done later, or not at all.

However, inspired by her fine mood and the previous day's shared breakfast with Cary, Lily was this morning hard at work making french toast. She wasn't particularly good at it, uncomplicated though it was, because breakfast had never been a staple in this house or her own when she was a child. It was then much as it was now, cold cereal and toast. If you wanted something hot you had to make it yourself and be prepared to share, even when she was the littlest of girls. She therefore never learned to make a proper breakfast and frankly never at all thought much about it since it was nothing more than utility, something to have if you felt the need to plug a hole in your belly.

This day, unaccustomed to such niceties, the magnificent aroma drifting upstairs awakened each in turn. Carl and Cary came bounding down the stairs together, Andy in pursuit. She greeted them at the entryway to the kitchen.

"It's about time."

Carl, thinking the scene a little odd, took his seat at the table eying her bemusedly while doing so. The boys rolled with it not caring to consider how rare an event this was just thankful the event was occurring at all. That was especially true of Cary who was now going to have a specialty such as this two days running. He was having a wonderful weekend.

"Where are the girls?" Lily asked turning her attention back to the stove.

Beth wandered in before anyone could answer. Lily, hearing another chair being pulled from the table, glanced over her shoulder, "Where's Audrey?"

"Still in bed."

"Still sleeping?"

"No, she's awake."

Beth had moved noiselessly around the room when she first awoke looking for some clothes to throw on before going downstairs. Audrey appeared to be still asleep, laying on her side, back to the room and scrunched up making a tight ball of herself. As she moved past her sister's bed she noted at some time during the night she'd taken the time to remove her street clothes and replace them with proper bedclothes. She also chanced to see her eyes wide open. Hesitating, thinking she might speak to her, she as quickly realized there was nothing to say.

"Carl, can you see what's keeping her?"

Walking to the foot of the stairs he called up a couple of times. With no response he returned to the kitchen. "Beth, are you sure she's awake?"

She nodded.

The boys were deeply tucked into their food. Unlike yesterday there were no strawberries and whipped cream, no nutmeg, no flags, nothing to fancify the food, but there was plenty of syrup and they dumped gobs of it on their plates to where it was oozing over the sides every time they would slice another hunk. Lily caught sight of what was happening and seeing her take notice both Carl and Beth steeled themselves for the inevitable reprimand. It never came. Looking at one another, astonished with her silence, Carl wasn't about to question, and neither was Beth. The sheer novelty of it all was enough to keep everyone quiet.

"Carl, can you go up and see what's keeping her?"

Making his way upstairs he knocked on the door. There was still no response so he pushed it open enough to glance inside. She was laying in the same position, back to the room. Creeping over he looked down, her eyes closed and unmoving. He whispered her name a couple of times with no reaction. Yet he saw no tranquility, no peace to the way she lay there so he was sure she was indeed awake. He whispered her name once more.

"What dad?" she responded without stirring.

"Aren't you coming downstairs for breakfast?"

"No."

"How come?"

"I'm not hungry."

He knew something was troubling her and his instinct was to find out what. But she was forever an enigma and he was unsure how to approach her especially since she rarely, if ever, showed signs of anything weighing on her. This lack of history, and her vexing nature, made the situation difficult, yet his instinct overruled his reason.

"Is something bothering you?"

"Yeah, you are."

Her response was pithy and immediate. It stung him a bit. Feeling a need to excuse himself, to explain he was only trying to help, reason overruled his instinct this time and he instead left her to her own devices returning to the kitchen.

"Well?" Lily asked.

"She's not hungry."

She felt a bit dejected having made breakfast for them to share together, all of them. It shouldn't have bothered her, she knew that, yet somehow it did, the effort being put in for the family unrewarded by the absence of one. Sitting down with her plate she looked over at the boys.

"Mind what you're doing, I have to clean that up you know."

Audrey had slept fitfully. It was guilt, something to which she was unused. Her callousness toward Beth over the last few days, years when you come to it, was disturbing her. She turned over in her head past transgressions, moments when she could have acted or reacted better, times when she could have been a better sister, a true big sister. She knew these things couldn't be changed nor, perhaps, would her relationship ever have been any better even if they could. At the core of it her sister's personality was what it was and so too was her own. Nothing would ever alter that basic fact and regretful as the affair was, their relationship was probably as good as it would ever get.

That said, what was distressing her most was it could get a whole lot worse. If Beth found out what she'd really done, altruistic though it was, what little was left to build on would surely fall away. There was no explaining it, her sister was a literalist and would take it for what it was on the surface, a kiss was a kiss. She could never hope the girl would grasp what was behind it, what it represented, how it was meant to help, and it couldn't have been any other way because as Beth was so keen to point out, she wished to be left alone. Instead of understanding it would be defined as further meddling. Even the excuse she was promulgating, a mindless drunken transgression, would carry little here. To her sister it would be nothing more than a most disgraceful type of treason, a Judas kiss.

In the end she was left sitting up half the night with her new-found conscience and its attendant fears. Getting to Chris before anyone else would be paramount. She needed to be sure he paid adequate attention to Beth and somehow with the appearance he was acting of his own accord. The one variable over which she had no control was what anyone else might say. That was just going to have to play itself out. If through the whole mess some good could come of it then maybe the situation, and she, would be redeemed, but only just. She had the feeling it was going to be a long and delicate path she would have to tread.

With this she was finally thought out. Every angle had been as examined, every outcome as analyzed, as she was able. If the scenario lacked a basic logic it didn't matter, she was often better at action than thought anyway, leastwise the entanglements of emotion. And she was hungry. Putting on the same clothes she'd worn the night before she joined her mother in the kitchen who seemed to be struggling with finding respite of her own. Standing at the counter, staring blankly through the window, she hardly took notice of Audrey moving behind.

"Mom, is there any food left?"

"No, the boys finished it off," she replied waking from her stupor.

"What did you make?"

"Just some french toast."

Audrey frowned, "And there's nothing left?"

"You should have come down when your father called."

Lily watched her rooting through the cupboards for something else to eat. She couldn't help think the girl was alluring, even in last night's clothes. Though she bore a stunning resemblance to herself in her own youth, she doubted she was ever as lovely to look on or as graceful in movement as this creature. She could remember the boys being interested but it never seemed to last, she somehow in their eyes becoming coarse, her quirks less easy to overlook the more they knew her. Audrey was altogether different in this regard and always had been. She possessed an odd ability to make people feel both loved and ill at ease in her company. Off balance, they were quick to cave to her whims. It was powerful and fascinating, and she was as uncomfortably entranced by the girl, and nearly as easily led, as anyone.

"Great, generic rice puffs again," she complained.

"Or you can have nothing," Lily snapped back before turning her attention to the window once more.

Audrey left in a huff.

The day's weather was an echo of the season, periods of showers interrupted by periods of drizzle. It was as monotonous as the gray white sky. It seemed they were barely able to get two days of the week in which sunshine was the main feature, never in sequence. With the rapidly diminishing light, trees mostly shorn of their leaves, the days had a pallid, almost sickly glow. Even when the sun struggled an appearance it was low on the horizon creating stark, ugly shadows. They'd reached the in between, that stretch of time from the normally enchanting colors of autumn to the blinding luster of the first snows. It was a period of stasis, when all of creation perceptibly held its collective breath in anticipation of the hard season to come, before the cold winds blew from the north and the drifts draped the loathsome landscape in sparkling brilliance. It all felt very ominous.

Turning her attention from the window she focused on the bills spread over the table. She had to find a way to account for the shoes and the guilty pleasure of sharing a private meal with Cary. Already the electric bill was late, nothing new since it was the easiest to ignore by virtue of the difficulty involved for the municipality in shutting it off. That was especially true at this time of year with the early nights and increasing chill. The food budget was already stripped to the essentials. She could move some money set aside for the property taxes, which weren't due for some time, but that was a game she was reluctant to play. A matter of public record, delinquent payers were published in the agenda delivered to all citizens in preparation for town meeting day. Once it arrived, the first pages to which everyone turned, including herself, were those with the overdue tax listings. It was yet another chance for misinformation to be passed from one citizen to another and having the Kane name mixed amongst them would be to her nothing short of calamitous.

Giving up, foul over such a trivial expense, she angrily determined Carl would have to fix this one. Returning to her watch at the window she was grieved, equally as much by her emotions as the situation. They always had a predictable rhythm to them, something like a wave with its troughs and crests. She knew when she was rising, when she was falling, when she barely registered a ripple. These days she felt less in tune with herself. She didn't seem to know when or whether she was rising, or if she was falling, the steadiness had vanished. She'd always known she spent more time in the troughs than the crests but now they seemed deeper, more difficult to escape, and the day's weather was not aiding her liberation from herself in any way.

7.

Audrey left earlier than usual on Monday morning dodging the rain as she hurried to school so she could find Chris and rectify the weekend's mistakes. Avoiding Beth as much as she could since their disagreement she just managed to make it out of the house without any significant interaction. Knowing her sister there wouldn't have been much anyway, she said all she needed and likely all she was going to on the matter. Now it was up to Audrey to salvage what she could, to make amends with her actions rather than try talking her way around the problem. Right now, however, the biggest problem was finding Chris.

Not expecting to see him at the front of the school so early she went to the common haunts; the quad, the picnic tables, the smokers lounge, so-called though it was only a small clearing in the woods just off school grounds. He wasn't a smoker, at least from what little of him she knew, but she figured he at least had some friends who were, everyone did. Several of her own friends were known to carry a packet of cigarettes for social smoking on the weekends. She herself had tried, and still now and again had one, but the burning in her chest afterward and even into the next day was enough to swear them off as a potential vice. If she were to find her way to a sin or two it would definitely have to be something a bit more benign.

Having no luck she returned to the front of the school where the congregation of kids anxiously waiting for the first bell had grown considerably. Scanning the crowd looking for any signs of he or his closest friends and finding none she did chance to see Beth approach, eyes as ever glued to the ground. With ample time to wade into the mob and avoid an accidental meeting she kept her focus on the girl just in case she became suddenly less predictable and took an unexpected detour. Not wavering from the path even a bit, her certainty a close companion, someone else did, Chris. As she was making her way up the stairs and into the building he was following close behind trying to catch up with her hasty, nervous step. The situation was already showing signs of spinning from her grasp.

Breaking free from the other kids she followed them into the building at a distance keeping careful watch as the door opened and closed to be sure they hadn't stopped just inside. Though it might have given her a chance to take control it was too ungraceful to be worth the effort. Standing outside the main office she spied them talking together halfway down the hall near one of the science rooms. She wasn't sure what it meant but Beth wasn't running away in fear, no doubt a positive step for the girl, and after a few minutes they parted with a smile. As Beth made her way farther down the hall Chris turned and was heading her way. She stepped in front of him just as the bell rang.

"So what was that about?"

"What, Elizabeth?"

"Yes, Elizabeth."

"You wanted me to talk to her, yeah?"

"Yeah."

"So I did."

"About what?"

"Nothing much."

"Why?"

"Uh, because you asked. Well, you kind of asked I guess."

It was his turn to be confused. Wasn't this what she'd been pestering him about these last few days? Wasn't this, much to his dismay, what their Friday night interlude was about? The thought couldn't escape him that the Kane girls were a most peculiar lot.

"Look Audrey, I have to get to class," he said pressing past.

"But I want to talk to you about Friday night."

"I know, you were drunk. I already heard."

He continued on his way without looking back. She watched him go, now feeling guilty about this end as well. She cursed her conscience, she cursed Beth, she cursed Chris. Up until last week she hadn't a worry about such trivial things yet now the dualities were damning, afraid if he showed an interest in her and equally afraid if he did not. She should have heeded her sister's own and best advice and just continued along her own path, oblivious. Once this little story played itself out she vowed she would never again spend effort or emotional capital on anyone, especially Beth. It was just too hard. And this whole idea of introspection, she determined, was meant to be a dirty activity of the bored and regrettably, she was anything but these last few days.

On the positive side, the fallout from Friday night wasn't as bad as she feared. The idea she had been drinking too much seemed enough to quiet things down, it also appearing most students were unaware of anything having happened at all. She was much relieved, perhaps that part of the problem already resolving itself without much effort. Reputation could be a wonderful thing.

Andy spent nearly the entire walk to school trying to help Cary dirty up his new sneakers. It wasn't as easy as it first might seem. Hoping for a more natural tarnish, he no matter how hard they tried just ended looking like a boy in dirty new shoes. Even enlisting help from a couple of other kids didn't help as together they scuffed and scrubbed only adding more dirt to their own shoes while the remarkable brightness remained showing through his. It was hopeless yet endless fun and it carried them laughing all the way to the schoolyard where Miss McCall stood to greet them. She'd been watching over Cary since the initial incident and he noted the kindness even if the attention was something to which he was unused. He was at the same time feeling a bit sheepish about her acting as both teacher and protector because down the line he may have to pay a price for that and he wasn't sure she fully appreciated what that might be or how such things can stay with a boy.

Still unready to play soccer with the other kids, the wounds too fresh, they instead made for the swings. Despite feeling he was personally too old, Andy sensed Cary's apprehension thinking it better to forsake his own small group of friends to stay with him for awhile. His brother's sensitivity was something never lost on him. It wasn't just he knew him so intimately, it was he too had been the object of derision from time to time. He never really understood why, couldn't remember doing anything that would cause someone to see him as an enemy, felt he was always kind enough, friendly enough and quiet enough to escape attention. It nonetheless taught him how to keep his head down and stay well clear of the domineering type.

They were hard lessons but he'd learned them well and now sought to teach Cary. Full of advice on how to avoid the other boys, stop their pursuit, show them the respect they coveted and ultimately how to move them along until they found a fresh victim he was unknowingly and simply reciting a litany of cowardice, deceit, supplication and deflection. It was nothing more than survival for the weakest only serving to strengthen the schoolyard caste system. A strictly hierarchical community, it's where the kids in the middle, the preponderance of children, are left to observe, to catalog, to remember and, though unaware, as sure as any to participate for it is they who unwittingly keep the order in place. Neither making a move to stop the oppressor nor console the oppressed, they learn to fear the ruffian and loathe the victim while doing their level best to steer clear of the whole affair lest they become the quarry. Rare is the child martyr, the one who refuses to stand by and watch while the warriors and their servants destroy one another, and though Andy loved his little brother, he didn't have the strength to be anyone's schoolyard sacrifice recognizing his lot had been cast with the lowest an unfortunate long time before.

Engrossed in their conversation his initial lessons were already falling away as an entourage of boys approached unnoticed. Led by Jeremy they formed a circle and immediately started in on his new sneakers. When that wasn't enough they began teasing him about his intelligence, his lack of friends and his sexual preference, a subject as confusing as it was unknown to a still too young Cary. While they continued with the usual playground insults Andy tried getting him to move along and form up with the other kids waiting to go inside. He simply stood, immovable, feet stuck fast to the turf with no idea how to answer.

"In a hurry there, Candy Kane?"

It had been awhile since Andy heard the taunt thinking he'd put it well behind. Low profile or not, some things just seem naturally to roll off the tongue and that disparaging nickname was one.

"Just leave us alone."

"Aw c'mon guys, we just want to help you break in the new sneakers," one of the boys pleaded.

"Yeah, they're too nice for the rest of your crappy clothes. Look at this poor loser," Jeremy said motioning to his pals, "not enough money to get new pants to go with those sneakers, dumbass?"

"C'mon Cary, let's go," Andy whispered sternly.

"You ain't going nowhere yet, not until we see those nice new shoes. Why don't you take them off for us Cary?"

He shook his head.

"Aw, c'mon, I promise I'll give them back."

Andy finally managed to pull him free from where he'd taken root feeling they were just a short distance from a physical confrontation they couldn't win. As they were moving off toward the kids snaking their way inside that distance narrowed considerably. Trying to trip Cary one of the boys was just off the mark instead landing a vicious kick to his shin and dropping him to the ground with a howl. Looking at one another the boys were as surprised as any at what just happened. The boy who landed the kick backed away afraid someone may have heard and knowing a line might have been crossed that he didn't feel particularly well about, especially so since it was he who initiated its crossing. An equally nervous Jeremy rounded a couple of them up pushing them toward the other kids hoping to put as much distance as possible between he and the mistake they'd just left lying on the ground.

With Andy's help Cary stifled his cries. One of the lessons he'd yet to impart to his young brother was a wounded animal makes no noise lest it attract the attention of a predator. And whereas those posing an immediate threat were already fleeing the scene he knew there was every chance they could return. Besides, showing the hurt might only embolden them for the next confrontation. With his own history as a guide, he had no doubt there would indeed be another.

Helping him to his feet just as the last of the kids had gone inside they made their way down the slight incline toward the door. Standing and peering after them Miss McCall saw Andy holding onto Cary as he limped along.

"What happened?"

"He tripped when we were running to get in line," Andy answered.

"Yeah? Are you okay?" Leaning close to Cary to get a look at his face she was unconvinced.

Looking up at her and in obvious pain he was uncertain of her attention or how much he should say. Not wanting to contradict his brother he agreed, "Yeah, must be the new sneakers."

He regretted the lie.

With the holidays fast approaching Carl was still without a clue how he and Lily were going to manage it for the kids. Though they had the Christmas Club with the bank where a little of his pay was automatically set aside every two weeks it was a pitiable amount at this point adding up to still less with four children who were old enough to demand the impossible. And it didn't help that catalogs were daily showing up in the mail and landing in the kids' hands despite their best efforts to retrieve and discard them before they had a chance to see.

With the boys it was most difficult. They spent hours making lists to Santa Claus that would take from him half a year's wages, at the least. Clothing and other necessities still meant nothing to them as they pored over the pages compiling an inventory that began on page one continuing to the end. He mused they would gladly walk around without a stitch if it meant more and more toys. Cary was especially enamored of such accumulation still seemingly in the stage where he measured the quality of his life by all he owned.

With the girls it was easier. Even if they weren't fully appreciative of the economics of the Kane household they were old enough to know asking for anything unreasonable was just setting themselves up for a big disappointment. But while a perhaps more cognizant Beth asked little these days Audrey was picking up much of her slack. Largely forsaking the more expensive and frivolous items she was focused on as a young girl she nonetheless still had the expectation of a volume of gifts he found difficult to manage. With the gear of the average teenage girl being exceptionally expensive, and she demanding to be fully kitted, he could see them in the even poorer house, if such was possible. He sorely wished a little of each girl would rub off on the other.

Arriving at work for an early meeting he was glad for the release from his thoughts. They were beginning preparations for winter which meant a lot of tree pruning near power lines, dredging storm drains, staking the edges of back roads, parking lots and fire hydrants. New snow dumps had to be considered, old ones reconsidered, and for an hour it kept him focused elsewhere, lost in work a pleasant experience for his worried mind. These were problems he could solve, through hard work if nothing else, and they were common to him having been through so many seasons before.

Milling about afterward, coffee in hand, Big Earl approached. Formerly an enormous man he wasn't so big anymore, cancer taking care of that even if the moniker stuck. Though he'd beaten it the scars remained, his still lowering girth just the most obvious. Dispensing with work he was interested in social chatter, general events and family news. While in possession of many acquaintances he had few friends counting Earl among them, maybe foremost, and it was a place to where the man had worked a long time to get. Not many things in his life demanded order but for Carl not mixing work with pleasure was one that did and a separation of the two was important. Really it boiled down to the fact they inevitably bleed over and it takes just a single catalyst to spoil one, the other, or both. After so many years, and so many hard moments, Earl's help in keeping a wall between the two halves won his trust. It was no small feat, he was also Carl's boss.

"So what you looking at for the kids' Christmas?"

"I've been struggling with that one Earl, not much money this year."

"I hear ya."

"It's the boys really."

They spent time mulling over potential gifts, a tricky prospect when money and hopes are on divergent paths. With a boy of his own near enough ages with Carl's, Earl had a multitude of suggestions, most with a price tag to lament, before stumbling on an idea close to his own heart.

"You know Carl, I've been raising these dogs now for years and thinking I might stop soon. Fun as Hell but boy they take work. Anyway, I'm weaning some pups about that time so what about one of them for the boys?"

"I don't know Earl, I can't afford that."

"Naw, my gift to you, for the family."

"But that's a lot of money for you."

"Naw, I'd rather see it with a good home and some good kids than worry about the money. I always worked it that way and it'd do me good, really."

Stammering a bit he wasn't sure how to respond. It would be an awfully big surprise for the kids who'd often complained about not having a pet, especially a dog. They did try a cat for a short time but it was standoffish and, as a result, so too were the kids. Then one day, not terribly long after they got it and before a name was even chosen, it didn't come back home. Hardly anybody missed it, least of all Lily who never had been very comfortable with animals. He knew she would stand in definite opposition to the newest idea of a family pet with dogs tending to demand much more attention and she being home more than anyone. Their tendency to leave a mess behind would be another point to which she would object right away. If it wasn't the chewing, the food and water everywhere, the toys strewn about, it was the fur, the muddy tracks, the dirt leading from one end of the house to the other. He figured she'd probably liken it to having another child, something determinedly clear of her radar.

"Well, let me think about it Earl. I'll have to talk to Lily."

"Good, it'll have a fine home. Keep in mind they're real smart and all energy so it'll keep you on your toes. The boys'll have to have it outside a lot, give it a lot of exercise."

Some of Earl's past tales on the haps and mishaps of his dogs came to the fore of his mind. He thought it better if he just left it at dog rather than qualified any farther when he broached the subject with her. Then the more he thought about it, that one problem notwithstanding, the better the idea began to sound. It solved the dilemma of the big family present, an oddity that somehow crept into the holiday when he wasn't looking. It also saved considerable money not all of which need be spent on more stuff for Cary to accumulate or anything to further beautify Audrey, as though she were in need. It might just be the very thing, only Lily standing in the way.

Beth was dismayed to see Audrey following closely behind she and the boys on the walk from school. She thought these escapades had come to an end, that she'd been plain enough in her disgust with her sister. After all, she seemed to expend a great deal of energy avoiding her the rest of the weekend so something must have gotten through. It did admittedly please her a little though, to witness she the one who was silently trailing several paces, the queen reticent to speak. She figured she must have seen Chris talking to her and was after information, curious about what transpired between them. She'd be disappointed, there wasn't much to tell. He was apologetic, little more, about surprising her in the hall the previous week. It was enough, with that she was content. It may not change things, but then much of the agitation had been squeezed from her already. She had a real fear she was becoming apathetic and if not already, the destination was clearly in sight.

"What do you want Audrey?"

"What's the deal with him?"

"Who?" she asked wishing her sister would just out with it, the game growing tiresome.

"Cary?"

It took a moment for Beth to realize who she meant. Looking at him she saw for the first time on their trek home he was limping, quite noticeably limping. She shrugged her shoulders as Audrey pushed past glaring at her as she did so.

"Why are you limping Cary?"

"He fell at school," Andy hastily answered.

"The Hell he did. What happened Cary?"

Already telling one lie today, and in the universe it was told feeling it to a degree justified, he knew this was different, his brother's rules no longer applying, or at least shouldn't, where family was involved.

"One of the kids kicked me."

"Why?"

Beth stopped to listen. Glancing at her he felt a little more shy, always did when she was around, and though he may not have been able to explain his reasons well, at the root of it was trust. It wasn't that she'd ever done anything meaningful to hurt him, quite the contrary, she'd never done anything meaningful to help and thereby gain his confidence. He remained silent wishing she'd just keep walking.

"Andy, why?"

"It was some of the kids picking on him," he told her.

The girls hadn't been fully aware of what was happening to Cary. While Audrey was busy with her friends, Beth with herself and both busy avoiding one another the last few days, their attention was focused elsewhere. Now Beth's didn't stray from him as he cautiously looked from one sibling to another searching for where his eyes should fall or on whom. Contemplating the sweetness of his face and of his nature she recognized he was just a boy, a very young and innocent boy. It surprised her anyone would find him threatening enough to make a target. Then again, she often felt one herself through sheer neglect on the part of those around her, those closest to her, and having done nothing she could recall to provoke such inaction. Of course, her own sense of existence told her the virtuousness of the meek all but ensured they were the chosen prey of the strong.

"Well, did you hit them back?" Audrey continued.

"No."

"Where were you Andy?"

He didn't want to answer but his look was enough for Audrey to know he was there.

"And you didn't help him?"

He wanted to defend himself, explain he was in the process of showing Cary how to avoid just such an event but what could he have said, his best intentions were enough? He knew he let his brother down and probably would again. Shaking his head in regret of his own weakness was his admission he'd done nothing whatever to help.

"What's wrong with you two? Cary, you have to stand up for yourself. And Andy, you too when this crap goes on. Stick together and don't let these little jerks get to you. Why were they picking on you anyway?"

He tried finding his voice to tell her, to detail who started what and why. Yet in truth, he wasn't sure. He knew it started with his torn sneaker, that it continued with his winter boots, that it should have stopped now he had sneakers again, but that it didn't. Now it was his sexuality and his family's income, the supposed stupidity of he and his brother, their lack of friends, and his clothes, something to which he'd never paid much attention and didn't really know how. He was just a boy.

With everyone watching he felt nervous tears coming. Swallowing hard to keep them at bay it was of no use, they came in a stream of sobs as Audrey pulled him close.

"I don't know why they don't like me," he managed to answer.

"Oh, sweetie."

She squeezed him tight doing what she could to soothe his hurt yet knowing there was precious little she could to make it much better. He squeezed back just as tightly not wanting to let go hoping she would shelter him away forever, hide him from the pains he couldn't explain, the injuries he couldn't remedy, and his inability to comprehend either.

Feeling his pain Beth too wanted to comfort him and help all the grievous damage disappear for she saw much of herself in him and his experience. But in a real sense she was simply envious of his tears, her not shedding them in many, many years. It was a part of herself she closed off when she retreated from the world and she so often wanted to embrace them again yet her body seemed to have forgotten how, no longer able to register the pain sufficiently. In a significant way she had inured herself to the world starving her being of generous expression in the process.

As the tears came to an end Cary was insistent no one should know. Audrey's instinct was to at least tell their father about the abuse but with Andy backing him up she wavered. Hoping for some support she looked to Beth who only shrugged her shoulders, tacitly washing herself of the affair in Audrey's eyes. She in the end agreed to keep her tongue letting them know in future it wouldn't be so easy and with the further warning if the two didn't stand up for themselves she'd kick their butts all over town herself. It produced the intended giggles. With the hurt duly bandaged she took his hand and walked him the rest of the way home leaving Beth to slowly trail behind.

8.

Carl finally broached the subject of a Christmas dog with Lily. Spending a couple of days considering the best approach but coming up with nothing clever he decided to just lay it out for her. She immediately said no. When he tried to explain his reasoning she shut him up before he could get out even half a sentence. Never bothering to account for her inflexibility she waved him off every chance she could. It was clear there would be no discussion on the matter. Something was aggravating her so he knew regardless the subject he would have received the same response. Though undaunted, he judged it better to leave it until a little later in the evening hoping with some space she may see the benefit.

Descending to the basement he looked out the ice skates for the next night. Andy and he silently and independently conspired to keep the public skating idea a secret, his son wanting to be a part of something nice for Cary with his prolonged troubles at school, he simply wishing to do something nice for the family. His hope was it would include everyone knowing with the girls, and even perhaps Lily, it would be tough to get them on board. It was getting more and more difficult to have everyone together for an enjoyable moment especially with the girls getting older and seeming not much interested in family events. Though long knowing that time would come it didn't make it any less regretful.

What was truly distressing was he felt the same distance developing with Lily. Her seeming boredom with him was something that transpired as the years went on. From time to time he noticed it but it was more like the relentless creep of a glacier. Slowly eroding, chipping away, carving out its valley, a snapshot over time could quite plainly expose the changing landscape while standing next to it daily you'd hardly notice any marked difference at all. Yet her distance with the family was much more discernible, it was abrupt and painful, and it was unnerving him most.

Despite never being terribly close to her children he was never left in doubt of her love for them. He was now. She appeared to stop trying any longer, the feeble efforts she made over the last few days no more emblematic. He felt her heart wasn't in it, she simply going through the motions of being a mother without the emotions of being one. Spending most evenings after dinner camping out in their bedroom in quiet reflection her interaction, in those rare attempts, was forced and impotent. There was just something in the way she moved around them that bespoke a lack of interest in all of their lives, including her own.

Pulling several pair of skates from their pegs he examined the blades. The dull white boots of the girls' were still in decent shape, the threads strong, the leather sturdy. The blades however were covered with flecks of rust. Looking down the length of each he felt the edges with his thumb. Still sharp, but with additional oxidation there as well he knew they'd be no good without some attention. He and the boy's rather vintage skates were considerably worse. The boots were well worn having known several skaters during their time. The steel blades and towers were heavy with deterioration, the rivets barely holding in place. He didn't bother to test the sharpness knowing these too would need a lot of work before they'd be ready for the ice. He cursed himself for waiting so long into the week before checking. Now he'd have to squeeze in a trip to the rink during the day in hopes they had time to tend them. Moreover, he hoped the skates would still fit everyone because if he went through the trouble and expense of having them fixed up only to turn around and rent some then the cost of the free skate would become a bit prohibitive for their budget, let alone the fight that would ensue with Lily.

Piling them on an old table he made his way back upstairs. The thin daylight of the season had long left the downstairs of the house in darkness while everyone was occupied in their rooms, the lone exception Audrey who was out as always. With tobacco in hand he went to the stoop to roll a cigarette grabbing his flannel shirt on the way as a buffer against the evening which was surprisingly crisp and remarkably clear. Sitting on the granite step he felt just how cold it had become as the chill moved up his thighs to the rest of his body. Pulling the flannel tighter and buttoning it all the way up he took a pinch of tobacco, sprinkled it along the waiting paper and twisted tightly with both hands. The sound of dry tobacco breaking apart seemed to echo through the loneliness of the night. Striking a match he burned the first embers deep in his lungs, sighing as he exhaled the indulgence.

His thoughts returned to the dog as he lay back to gaze at the stars. One way or the other he was going to show Lily the rectitude of the decision even if in the end he foisted it upon her. He sincerely hoped it wouldn't come to that, but he knew risking a falling out with Lily was preferable to the disappointment their budget would effect on the children come Christmas day. There were too many of those days in the past and this was perhaps the first time he'd had what he considered a truly brilliant idea to make the season magical. And with some of that he was also hoping to perhaps dull the memory of a long successive line of disappointments.

Lily wasn't pleased at all; not about the dog, not about the holidays approaching, not about anything. And she was especially displeased with Carl, if for no other reason than he couldn't seem to sense her frustration. Through the course of the last few days she'd been trying the best she knew how to repair bad situations and involve herself in the affairs of the household but it seemed it was all for naught. If he wasn't quietly and passively undermining her then his solutions were dull with no attempt at elucidation whatsoever. The dog was especially illustrative of this state of affairs. Rather than find a way to get more cash to plug the widening hole in their budget he was flirting with the idea of adding another member of sorts to the household. Besides, if he'd thought much about it at all he would have known her feeling toward animals.

It was more than this that bothered her though. The endless cycle of subsistence living was dispiriting, exhausting. She'd known it since she was a girl and just old enough to understand her family was barely off the ground on the economic ladder. They struggled in silence, sought no help and received none. They never spoke of it as a family or, to her recollection, her parents from one to the other. It was a maddening acceptance of their situation with no realistic idea or action to change the circumstance. It was an oppressively hopeless atmosphere she'd longed to escape and when she met Carl she anticipated it would at last come to an end. He was the one suitor who stayed long enough to see the tumult beneath her superficially placid surface and not be frightened off. In those days he understood her, soothed her, sensed her with barely a word passing between the two. Or so she thought. But here she was, in the very same situation and still suffering in silence.

Subsequently she found herself wondering why she'd even accepted Carl as a suitor. He never really had any prospects coming from a family equally as poor as her own. In those days he'd just started working for the town depicting it more a short term necessity than a permanent means to an end. He held out hope he would be able to save enough money for tuition even if it was only to a small community college. Then as time went on he seemed content to have them stay where they were, no sense of adventure, no desire to explore the wider world, and all the while she feeling an overwhelming need to flee to the farthest corners. At the least she wanted to plant their roots elsewhere, away from the apathy and the lethargy she felt small town life bred into people but he was somehow comfortable, unable or unwilling to see the stagnation this kind of life would bring. More than once, even early on, she thought to slip out during the night as small hints of their future fortunes showed themselves. In the end, the birth of Audrey cemented her in place.

The evening wore on as Carl rolled a second and then a third cigarette. He at one point went back inside to retrieve a more substantial jacket to ward off the cold. It still bit, though the wonders of the night sky overruled any thoughts of retreating into the house. Every once in awhile a shooting star would streak its way through the dark burning out just as quickly as it appeared. He wished even one member of the family enjoyed this as much as he. To silently witness the universe compacted into his small window was pure magic.

The door creaked open behind him. Nothing was said, just empty silence. Turning to see the door ajar with not a body in sight he knew it was Lily, her irritated way of telling him the evening was late and perhaps it was time he should come inside. He hated to leave his corner of the heavens behind.

Returning to the confines of the house he noted the downstairs still cloaked in darkness. Knowing she must have gone back to their bedroom having come down merely as a summons he closed the door behind and creaked his way up the stairs. The children were still up, light pouring from beneath each of their doors. He'd lost all track of time but figured it couldn't be too late otherwise Lily would have told them it was lights out. Besides, Audrey hadn't come home yet and she was usually good about being in at a reasonable hour on a school night.

Entering the bedroom he found Lily brushing her hair in front of the mirror with her back to the door. Standing for an awkward moment he wondered if he was supposed to ask why she wanted him up here or if he should leave it to her to explain the reason. With nothing said and she scarcely glancing at his reflection he turned as though to exit when she finally spoke his name.

"Yes?"

"I want to talk to you. Come in here and shut the door."

Doing as she asked he was left waiting. Expecting she would follow it up and give him some idea of what was on her mind she instead sat quietly watching his reflection while continuing to brush through her hair. As the silence went on he had the sense this was about something more than the dog. Sitting on the bed he decided he had no choice but to wait her out.

There was much she wished to say, the tact with which to say it she found more illusive. A lot of that could be put down to their dwindling capacity for words, as acutely felt by she as him. Yet it was mostly due to her inability to articulate language that carried emotional weight. Baring much of her soul, even to her husband, was an alien part of her being. Once out there anything said can not be erased or explained away. Sometimes she felt it best to remain silent even though she recognized this probably wasn't one of those times. Even so, she backed away from her own sentiment offering instead a more mundane reason for summoning him to her.

"I think this dog is more about you than the kids."

The statement took him a bit by surprise. On the one hand it was because he'd expected much more and on the other because he hadn't a clue what she meant. Never wavering from her task in the mirror, not even looking toward him anymore, it took a moment for him to recover his equilibrium before responding.

"What?"

"I think this dog is about you."

"In what way?"

She paused, unclear as to what she herself was asking. "Why do you want this dog?"

"I told you, it's free and would be great for the kids."

"The boys maybe."

"No, the girls too. I think they'd love to have a dog."

She continued brushing her hair while he marveled there was any left with her strokes getting more and more vigorous.

"I've never heard the girls express any interest in a dog."

"No, I guess you wouldn't have," he trenchantly replied.

Stopping her brush in mid stroke she was stung by the caustic nature of his comment. Spinning around she dropped all pretense.

"This is about you."

He said nothing as she stared, daring him to respond. Reluctant to admit, he found the whole thing rather frightening, unused as he was to her addressing him so directly and with such intensity.

"How do you mean?"

"Why are we here Carl?"

The question seeming a little abstract, it caused him to despair what would come from his mouth next knowing there was no way to answer such a thing satisfactorily when you didn't comprehend it in the first place.

"Come on Carl," she continued, "why are we still here? Why do we continue to dig in the dirt year after year? Why do we get up every morning and do the same things over and over and over again?"

The inquisition was becoming more clear. Though the ideas were a bit disconnected from the present he understood the roots. This really was about their lives, not the holidays, not the dog, the kids and maybe not even wholly about money. He supposed it suddened upon him from nowhere, this vehemence, but in truth he had to acknowledge he saw it building deeply for some time.

"I'm not sure..."

"What you want me to say?" she interrupted, "Isn't that what you were going to ask? You never know what to say." Getting up from the bench she leaned over him and hissed, "I swear I know you better than you know yourself."

Wanting to retaliate she waved her hand to cut him off before he could utter a word.

"I don't care. I don't want to hear anything from you right now."

Pacing back and forth to compose her thoughts she was manic. He sensed some apprehension furrowing her brow, perhaps she too afraid of her next words. It was oddly attractive, the torment and the violence, her fever. His gaze was transfixed upon her anticipating a ferocious and chaotic storm to be unloosed, almost relishing the chance to see her emotional highs swirl about the room unchecked by her own constipation. Instead she abruptly stopped and faced him, the dark clouds still perceptible behind her eyes.

"We're here because of you. We dig in the dirt, we follow the same routines because of you. Our future is no different from our past or from our present. We face the same problems we've always faced day after day. It never changes, it never varies, it's always the same. And you know what? You never change, you're the same boy I met when I was a girl."

He again moved to speak and she again waved him off.

"At one time I thought there was promise in you, as a man. That you would somehow take us away from all this. Now I see you've just wasted our lives."

The words cut, the wound bled.

"What waste?" he interjected forcefully, "The kids, the roof over our heads, the food on our table, the clothes we wear?"

"Yes."

He was astounded, speechless, his thoughts scrambled. Did she really believe their lives were that devoid of meaning, that everything counted for nothing, even their own children? How could he come back from such a revelation? The whole affair suddenly ceased being attractive. Before a definite and unforgivable line was crossed in his mind he had to be sure.

"You really believe that?"

"What do you know about me Carl?" she asked by way of reply.

He said nothing, still standing on the ledge of her statements, daring her to push him off.

"You don't know anything. You think you do, you think you know all there is to me but you're lying to yourself. Do you honestly believe I wanted this life? That I wanted to spend it in the same damn town I grew up in, to live the same damn life my parents did? Do you even remember that we were going to get out, we were going to make our own way in the world?"

As he listened he was beginning to feel somewhat shaken by her composure. Everything she was saying was delivered with such calm he felt he was being introduced to a level of apathy toward her family he never really believed possible. At the same time she was harboring a bitterness toward him that, to his lament, he utterly failed to recognize simmering beneath the surface of her being. She was an alien creature standing before him dressed in her accusatory refinement.

"And I did all this to you?" he managed.

"Yes."

"And the kids?"

"Audrey."

Audrey, their first born, he reflected. She was reaching back to a moment when an untimely pregnancy turned everything in their lives upside down. This was her crucible, her cross, the exact point in time when her life was destroyed. It was day one of the rest of her wasted life.

"How dare you," he shot back turning on her. "How dare you turn this into a judgment on your own daughter. You want to know what I know about you? You're self-absorbed, you're pitiless, you're indifferent. You have no sense of reality. You sat there when I met you and sit there still getting all these romantic visions in your head of what your life is supposed to be like. Well you know what? This is your life, right here, right now, in this room. You're the one who's lying to themselves. No Lily, I know you all too well. I did until tonight anyway."

He stormed toward the door refusing to hear another word of her irrational speech. She caught his arm as he was passing.

"You listen," she demanded.

He shook his arm free, "No, you listen. If this reality is too hard for you then just move the Hell out of the way. I'm done talking about this and I'm done listening to you. Honestly, where's your damn head Lily?"

Her flame flickered out as he exited the room.

Tobacco in pocket, Carl slammed the front door behind him as he went out into the night. He was thankful he still wore his jacket, the rush of cold air rather like the shock of a slap to the face. No doubt the puddles would ice over this night, leaving their delicate patterns hollow for the morn. He walked toward town with no direction other than to seek out enough light under which he could roll himself a cigarette. Rarely feeling the dark pull of nicotine he sure did now. If he was a drinking man he likely would have sought a belt of the strongest liquor he could lay his hands on and not stop. Instead he halted under a street lamp and hastily rolled a cigarette. Noticing his hands were trembling, he was unsure if it was just the cold or the tattered state of his nerves. Either way, he spilled as much tobacco on the ground as he managed to get in the paper. Between the shaking and the sloppy roll it took three matches before he was able to keep it lit. They were the last three he had.

Lily didn't tarry long knowing almost immediately the dreadfulness of her mistake. Rehearsing ever and anon in her head, the dissertation she delivered nonetheless failed to capture what she was trying to communicate rather instead sounding like a eulogy. Now she was out and in search of him hoping she could reframe the discussion before it took permanent root. She didn't have to go far spotting him after a short distance, smoking and leaning against a lamppost. She first thought to approach quietly giving her time to read his language. It was habit and it was foolish, she knew his mood. It would almost be dishonest to sneak up on him when she knew more than anything she needed to be open with him in this moment more than most others she could remember.

It didn't matter much anyhow, in such cold air the sounds of the night reverberate for great distances and he knew the sound of his own front door. He knew she was behind him. She'd stopped a few feet away, still he feigned inattention. Closing his eyes he imagined her there, so slender, so statuesque, but now so hollow. He knew she'd come out without a jacket, still in her bedclothes and slippers, for he heard neither the swish of a jacket nor the shuffle of a shoe as she approached. He wanted to leave her there, standing in the cold, alone, but he heard her shivering. He silently took off his jacket and held it out, she accepted the gift and the invitation. Taking a final draw from his cigarette he put it out beneath his foot.

"Do you have another?" she quiescently asked.

"Out of matches."

"Hmph," she sounded, hugging herself and warming beneath the oversized jacket. "Carl, can we go back to the stoop?"

She stood patiently as he reflected, letting the question hang in the air. His inclination was to send her back alone. Practicality dictated otherwise as he had just given up his jacket and it hadn't taken long for the cold to invade his bones. The larger part of him wanted to demand it back, seventeen years of sharing buried the notion.

"I suppose."

The walk back was muted. They strode side by side, nary a glance between them, eyes gone to ground. The soft patter of her shuffle, the dull plod of his boot the only sound breaking the night. As they reached the house she slid from beneath his jacket and gave it back before disappearing inside for her own and a fresh book of matches. She turned on the outdoor light knowing she needn't ask, Carl would roll them both a cigarette. She noticed the shake of his hands as he worked the tobacco from the pouch. Guessing it wasn't just the cold she may have been partly right, but the chill from the brief walk worked itself deep, his back cramping as he maneuvered. When he finished she shut the light off again much preferring darkness if she were to part with still more of herself. They sat, her only hope she would be articulate enough to let go of her emotions without this time betraying herself in the process.

"Carl, I'm sorry."

"Yeah?" he contemptuously replied.

She knew she deserved little in this moment and was going to take anything he cared to give, good or otherwise.

"The things I said I didn't really mean. I mean...well, I just didn't say what I was thinking. It all came out and, what I mean is, it just kind of got away from me. I think it's..."

"It's ugly."

"I know, I know..." she trailed off.

They sat in silence for a long while, each drawing on their cigarette, alone in their own comforts but not in one another's.

"Carl, we've been living in silence for so long, for too long. And I've thought about leaving, more than a few times really. But I don't think I could do that. I just wanted you to know how frustrated I am because you don't seem to notice anymore. I know it's not Audrey's fault, not really your fault or anything else. It's just that I have to see an end to this, an end to the constant worry and not knowing if the next day is just going to push us over the edge. Some people can live like this, for a lifetime even, I just don't know if I'm that person. Do you understand what I'm saying?"

Unfortunately he did, and it didn't cheer him in the least.

"So what do you propose?"

"I don't propose anything, I just want you to know what I'm feeling."

"And that's it?"

She put her cigarette out on the edge of the stoop watching the embers fall to the frosty grass where they quickly extinguished themselves. She put her hand on his leg, absentmindedly rubbing his knee. He straightened it letting her hand fall to her side.

"Yeah, I suppose," she whispered.

"Well, it's cold."

Getting up he opened the door with she staring after him unable to make out much in the darkness other than a slight silhouette from the faint light inside.

"Oh, by the way, I'm taking the kids skating tomorrow. It might be a good idea if you came along."

"Of course."

She sat with her thoughts while he disappeared inside leaving the door open a crack. She wasn't sure she'd made anything much better but it was as close as she could get anymore. The dance with what she felt one could say without inviting scorn or recrimination was a particularly difficult one. And for someone who spent so much time peering inward she was all but blind. She was an addled, cluttered, hopeless mess and terrified others would see it too.

9.

Beth softened as the week wore on. The effort to keep up her antipathy, the since unspoken animus, toward Audrey had grown wearisome leaving her with the belief her energies could be better spent elsewhere and on other pursuits. One such was reading in her hideaway behind the house now the incessant rains had finally come to an end. It's where she spent the greater part of her evenings. With the leaves largely forsaking the protection of the trees by now the housecleaning became easy allowing her to quickly settle into a book. On the downside, that same foliage no longer provided her the protection from the world's eyes she'd come to enjoy, the house visible through bare trees and barren ground. Surmising it only a matter of time before her enclave would be spotted she tried to remain hopeful her siblings had enough respect for her space they'd leave her be. It was a great hope, one in which she didn't genuinely put much faith.

Nonetheless, she'd also done much reckoning with that time. The fascination with Chris died away, no doubt prematurely, and though the business between he and her sister precipitated the demise she came to recognize it wasn't necessarily the whole truth. He'd been like an unwrapped gift to her, one at which she'd spent days and weeks peering never once daring to tear a corner of the wrapping to peek inside. So full of mystery and promise, she would have preferred he stay untouched beneath the tree knowing always the disappointment when a gift fails to live up to what you've imagined. Sadly her sister's behavior and her own brief interaction with him tore away those corners to reveal he was just a boy, another ordinary and unremarkable person on the periphery of her life, and the dullness of an existence absent true sentiment continued to march alongside her.

Troubling her further was Cary and the subsequent interaction between all the siblings. It was something that stuck with her through the course of the week for many disparate reasons. Though not all of those could she fully fathom, among them was how easily and honestly Audrey soothed the boy's pain. It was almost maternal the way she so tenderly handled him while he during those moments was clearly reticent she herself continued standing nearby. It was bothering her, all of it. The relationship she shared with her sister certainly wasn't the one others shared with her yet that very lack of a relationship was itself replicated with them in every way. The perception of herself as a nonentity was real. And though she'd been putting no small effort into it over the years perhaps it was all a little too real. Her success was total, she'd achieved the goal, and now was left questioning whether it was the outcome she'd actually been seeking.

Either way, her senses were in flux, her thoughts lonely, and she wasn't fully comfortable with either any longer. Nor was she feeling much better about the cold as she'd been waiting a confounding long time for the boys to make an appearance in the exit of their school.

Carl left work early to get the skates tended to and, more importantly, to pick Audrey up from school. He was certain she would be the most hesitant to go along with his plans for the evening. With that in mind, his first step was to try to get to her before she disappeared with her friends. While the other kids could nearly always be found at home, other than meal and bedtime she could rarely be seen. He wondered that a single, solitary girl could be so busy in a town so small. If he'd been able to see her for anyone but his daughter he would've known right away.

Pulling in front of the building he saw her absorbed in animated banter with a group of other teens. Taking a moment to watch the interplay it reminded him of how innocent it all once was, even if it didn't feel so much so at the time. Never the center of attention like Audrey seemed to be, he and Lily nonetheless were much the same where their small circle of friends were both the beginning and end of the universe. Largely oblivious to life, especially the rest of your life, a daily existence was all there was and in some ways, he felt, all it should have been for somewhere in the gray matter you were cognizant on the far horizon another day would soon begin. He envied their indifference, he knew Lily did too.

He gave the horn a light tap calling her through the open window when she didn't respond.   Puzzling at his unexpected appearance, she bounced to the car conscious to maintain her own.

"What's up dad?"

"I'm gonna give you a ride home."

She glanced back toward her friends, "But I'm not going home."

"I think you should."

"Why? Is everything okay?"

"Sure, everything's fine. Just a little family time."

"Okay," she drew the syllables out.

Watching as she begged her goodbyes promising they'd all catch up later he wondered how everything had suddenly become so European. There were hugs, light pecks on the cheek, more hugs. He couldn't remember any of that from his own youth when they wore their standoffishness with pride. It was so adult. Despite his amusement, he felt it all looked a little contrived.

"So what's really going on?" she asked, barely in the car.

"Nothing," he replied starting to drive off.

"Wait, what about Beth and the boys?"

"Where are they?"

"Beth's probably waiting in front of their building."

"Let 'em walk then," he said smiling at her.

Baffled, she was expecting the worst and though not sure what that was, she was expecting it anyway. Looking at him earnestly while he kept his tongue she was convinced something was going on, and she was decidedly not one for surprises. Continuing her stare for as long as it took she knew eventually he'd have to talk. Everyone wilted under her gaze.

Feeling her eyes on him he appreciated her frustration with the silence and the unnecessary worry he was sure to be causing. It was regretful when he was only trying to strategize his way to the best possible light under which to put family time. But he knew she'd only beg off as usual rather than come with them if he couldn't field a compelling argument. With yet again nothing clever coming to mind and her steady gaze growing more uncomfortable on his skin he simply told her.

"We're going skating. The rink opens up tonight and I think we should go together, all of us," he said glancing at her. "It'll be some good family time and I want to do something nice for Cary."

"Okay?"

"He's having a rough time at school you know?"

"I know."

"So you should come out with us."

"I will."

"Okay then."

"Okay then," she repeated feeling some relief it was all he had on his mind.

Pleased to be checked by how easily she agreed and with all his nervous logic gladly left unused on the verge of his tongue he sped along a little more quickly warming further to the whole idea of family time.

Lily watched through the window as the car pulled up. She was nervous, unsure how Carl would react to her in the light of day and after many thoughtful hours had passed. Leaving early in the morning with hardly a word, it wouldn't have been altogether strange if circumstances were normal. Of course they weren't. As a result she'd searched his every subtle move, every gesture, for meaning before he'd slipped out the door for work. Finding nothing but silence she knew the rift was large. What bothered her more was the sense an unbridgeable gulf didn't scare her as much as she tried to tell herself it did.

Turning her attention to getting an early dinner started, busy work more than anything else, Audrey came in and after a brief greeting bounded the stairs. She continued her work keenly listening for Carl to come in behind. There was no sign of him. Going to the opposite counter she fluttered the curtains to peer outside trying her best to be inconspicuous. He was nowhere in sight. Walking into the living room she briefly glanced around then continued to the foot of the stair.

"Audrey, where's your father?"

"I don't know, he was right behind me," her muffled voice called back from behind the closed bedroom door.

Returning to the kitchen window she spotted him just as he was walking from the driveway and moving in the direction of town, probably off to meet the other kids as they returned from school. The circumstance now struck her queer that he would drive Audrey home but not the others. Then again, things were often happening around here she didn't fully fathom and, she was left to lament, likely much more for which she didn't even have the chance. The thought helped push from her mind the disappointment she felt with his not stopping long enough to greet her.

Carl went along thinking he'd meet the kids about halfway from home. It was an enjoyable walk. Taking his time, he considered the gardens of some of the houses, particularly the old man on the corner. Marveling over the twisted wreckage that passed as lawn ornamentation he was especially amused with the laundry detergent bottle wind chimes. He wondered if and by how much the intonation might change with various levels of liquid inside before realizing it probably wouldn't produce much more than a dull thud even if the added weight allowed them to move. Further on he stopped again to pore over the overgrown thicket surrounding Mrs. Jensen's home. By now little more than dull brown, matted and dead, he imagined turning over the whole thing and planting a lush green lawn with neatly trimmed hedges to ring the lot. Then just as quickly he decided the whole idea too prosaic, that type of manicure already making up most of the neighborhood. It was better to leave it be, a diversifying addition to the staid homes of its neighbors.

He continued down the street eventually spying Beth with the two boys off in the distance. Keeping an eye on them, he watched as the two boys were engrossed in their own conversation while she walked a few feet behind wrapped in her own thoughts, eyes seemingly pinned to her shoes. The boys clung close to one another, occasionally one laughingly pushing the other away. They paid their sister no mind, she the same. He stopped to let them approach remaining unnoticed for several minutes. When they were mere feet away they finally saw him, though it took a few seconds more for their minds to register. Spreading his arms the boys ran the last few steps and fell into them. Beth just stopped and watched. He smiled at her while they noisily carried on around him wondering why he was meeting them here in the street. Telling them to continue on home he walked over to her putting an arm around her shoulder and giving her a quick squeeze. He knew she wasn't one for too much sentiment but couldn't help himself.

"So how was school?"

"Okay." Then after a moment, "What are you doing here?"

"Just thought I'd meet you guys coming home. I want to take everyone skating tonight."

"Oh," she responded quietly.

"Are you in?"

"I guess."

Maintaining a slow, muted pace well behind the boys he was pleased to give her some company for the walk. She was as well. When they approached Mrs. Jensen's house he stopped. Turning to look it over she followed suit and the two spent some time quietly gazing at the yard.

"So what do you make of that?" she asked.

"I like it."

"Me too."

They continued down the block, glancing at the perfect lawns, many still in deep green despite the lateness of the season, a standing testament to the power of chemical induction. Neither of them cared to venture an opinion on these. So like one another, so formal in their greeting to the passerby, they remained virtually overlooked by the world as by the two of them. Arriving at the old man's house on the corner Beth was the first to stop.

"And this?"

"I like the wind chimes."

She considered his judgment, "Me too. But what about the car? He usually has flowers and stuff in there during the summer."

Agreeing it was a nice touch and probably made up the centerpiece, they spent the next few minutes looking over the whole affair picking out little details to one another that may have been otherwise lost. The old man's individuality was an inspiration to them both, recognizing his carefree exhibition an antidote to the reproductions they just passed. They also concurred that despite this it just wasn't in the Kanes to follow his lead. This was particularly true with Mrs. Kane who would probably die, or kill them outright, if they were caught trying to incorporate even a solitary detail into their own overgrown patch.

"So, is Audrey going?"

"Yeah."

He was tentative in his response, watching her reaction as he did so. She betrayed nothing as they carried on down the street. He wished the girls would someday see how important they were to one another, at the least find their way to a truce of sorts. But the enmity they shared seemed to grow as the years passed. It ran counter to how he always felt they would eventually find comfort in one another. He knew it was common for siblings to develop a rivalry. He also knew it was usually petty and superficial. Yet with these two the hate seemed to run much deeper. With both he and Lily being only children they were lost on how to help the girls navigate the world they'd created, to find their way to a respectful coexistence. Adding to that difficulty was neither of them could recall why or when it all started. No single event, no argument, word or even outside catalyst could be held accountable. It just was, always had been and, for all they could see, always would be.

"Dad, can I show you something?" she haltingly asked as they were nearing the house.

"Sure, honey."

Leading him through the backyard and up the hill in back they after a short distance came to her clearing overlooking the house and much of the neighborhood. It was tidy, leaves pushed to the side, what was left of the greenery and pine needles creating a dense carpet, bench set toward the back hiding it further from sight. It was a nice spot, a garden spot, with a commanding view. Impressed she created her own little space away from it all he rather liked the idea of using it himself.

"So you did all this?"

"Yeah, but please don't tell anyone."

"Not to worry."

They quietly shared the view looking out over their own backyard and those of the neighbors. Noting how shabby their own house looked from here he tried consoling himself with the thought it was just the back where he paid the least attention or, perhaps, just the fading light projecting irregular angles and shadows. Either way, he found it a bit discouraging when most things appear more attractive with distance. He was, however, charmed by his daughter taking time to share something that was clearly a precious and private space for her. Her reticence rarely worn thin it was a great comfort to know there were times when she felt a need for company and sharing, especially when it was with he alone.

Continuing to peacefully survey the panorama for several moments she made him repeat the promise of keeping it a secret before they returned to the house. Agreeing he would do so on condition he could sneak up on his own sometimes they concluded the compact with a smile and a nod. It was their binding secret.

Dinner was an accelerated affair with the usual pasta and frozen vegetables, more utility than anything else. It disappeared quickly, everyone excited in their own private way to be going out to the rink for a skate, the first of the season. For Cary it was a continuation of the roller coaster he'd been riding for the last couple of weeks. One day up, one day down, and tonight up again. Andy wanted badly for everything to be pure and simple fun, in many ways the absolution he craved after letting Cary down. Unable to shake the idea he somehow shared guilt for his brother's predicament, making it up to him became its own crusade. The girls were more tempered in their feeling, in some ways eager to be out yet still unsure how to proceed with one another. Reaching another stasis, it was perhaps dispassionate tolerance at best. Lily as well found her mood considerably heightened even if at its core it remained almost melancholic, an unabiding nervous tension. She all but prayed the night would prove redemptive; for she and Carl, for the kids, for her mind. Her conflicting reflections, determined to make amends, afraid she couldn't, fearful she'd prevent her own self from doing so, were driving her mad. It was concealed to all but Carl but he was determined the night was, and would remain, about the kids, the family. And for him the latter held dual realities, one with and one without Lily. He was unfortunately seeing virtue in both.

The anticipation afterward carried them outside where they quickly loaded the equipment and themselves into the car. With the four kids squeezed together in back, Lily and he up front, the boys were already playfully bickering over perceived violations of space. Audrey threatened to hammer them both if they didn't quiet down. Though it was a short ride, he lamented the day bucket seats became the norm in the front of the cabin.

In years past the six of them would have been seated comfortably, three abreast, and his eardrums would've received a break.

The rink was already packed with people when they arrived, small events in small towns annual milestones attracting the throngs like nothing or no place else can. And though the solstice was still a month away, here first ice marked the start of winter. Almost religious in nature, the adherents were gathered long before the doors officially opened coming to both mourn the passage of warmer weather and toast the arrival of the season's frosty brother. For the Kanes the ritual was more semiannual and Carl couldn't even remember the last time he had his entire clan alongside to celebrate. It warmed him. The boys, running inside stopping only long enough to grab a cup of free hot chocolate, soon got lost in the crowd leaving the rest to push their way through as best they could. Distracted by neighbors, acquaintances, and the occasional friend they managed to get past the gabbing hordes to the glass where they stopped to collect and count themselves. Spotting a contingent of followers lurking on the bleachers Audrey begged her goodbyes and ran to them, Beth and Lily staying close. Pausing to take a deep breath, the sweet aroma of coffee and chocolate mixing with the pungent scent of Zamboni exhaust, fresh ice, rubber mats and exuberant bodies, Carl was loving and welcoming every bit as it wafted through his nostrils and washed over his tongue. The taste was a memory of his youth, of play, liberty and enchantment, his dad, his friends, his adolescent skin, stronger legs and a teenage Lily. It was so wonderfully and sorrowfully bittersweet.

Wrapping her arm in his as he stood reminiscing Lily feigned possession for their benefit. Her countenance of grace, assurance, the presence of equanimity, was an impressive decoration for those who didn't know her well which was most, if not all. He couldn't help but betray a hint of satisfaction as she did so, an almost presumptive pleasure. They were a picture of strange equilibrium, self-evident faults erased, quality in elevation. It hid their anguish well, his sanguine thoughts remaining fixed.

Taking Beth by the elbow he led the three of them to the bleachers where they crowded in to put on their skates. He was fortunate, a friend from when they were kids and neighbors happened to be working at the rink earlier in the day when he brought the skates in for repair. He'd done so, even changing a few laces and buffing out what he could, for just the price of a sharpening. The girls skates cleaned up well, he and the boys adequately. It was a nice little savings, uncounted fortunes counting for something.

The boys were already on the ice, Carl wondering when they had suddenly become old enough to tie their skates tightly on their own. Looking to Lily, who gave him a faint smile as she bent over to lace her boot, he turned his attention to Beth watching as she very deliberately pushed each lace through its eyehole.

"You coming out with me?"

"Sure, dad," she replied without breaking her rhythm.

Extending the invitation to Lily as well they tentatively made their way onto the ice joining the oscillating crowd moving in its wide circle. While small groups of agile skaters were darting through and around the clusters of legs, center ice was clogged with parents prodding and holding up small children who in turn pushed traffic cones to keep their balance as they learned. A handful of older beginners were doing much the same, desperately hugging the boards in hopes of holding onto that last knuckle of their lives. Every now and again a splash was made when one of them lost their balance and crashed to the ice followed soon after with shrieks of laughter once confirmed the embarrassed party had injured little but their pride.

With the music playing loud and a wide grin painting his face Carl shouted out to his partners in turn. Both doing what they could to get their ice legs back, they were clearly enjoying the effort. He watched Beth's strides become longer, more certain as she made each lap. Lily, always a poised and gifted skater, held back allowing her daughter to first gain her confidence. Feeling quite pleased with her magnanimity she again reached out to wrap her arm in his. They smiled at one another, a small respite, and continued slowly etching wide circles around the ice.

Audrey, still pulling on her skates after abandoning her friends, watched from the comfortable distance of the bleachers. Laughing as the boys cavorted, delighted in throwing one another off balance, she was even more pleased watching Beth, her eyes following as she cleverly navigated the surface, lost in her own beauty. Though separate, content to skate on her own, she was still a smiling part of the crowd. It was a striking adornment.

Finished lacing she quickly caught up, mischievously toppling both boys as she went by. They convulsed with amusement, struggling to right themselves and catch up to her. Slowing when she got to her sister, she invited herself to skate alongside. Tracing a faint smile, she allowed the indulgence but before a word could be shared the boys caught up and plowed themselves into the back of Audrey's legs taking the three of them down at once. Shrieks of laughter broke out with the four of them, Beth helping the boys to regain their footing while Audrey chased them in circles around her.

After a few more revolutions Carl was in need of a break. Thinking it a further pleasure to get a coffee to share he suggested they return to the bleachers from where they could watch the children and give his weary legs a rest. It wasn't like when he was young and could skate for hours on end. All those little muscles had long since atrophied. Lily too was in need of a break. Her slender legs, unused to the effort, were beginning to tremble with each stride. She nonetheless embraced the exercise, despite the crowd, even now exhilarating in the cold air rushing over her face and through her long hair as they made their way from the ice. Reaching the comfort of a seat she stretched her legs to feel the gathering tightness while Carl went off in search of the line for coffee. Removing her skates to let her swelling feet get a taste of the cold air she didn't care it would only make putting them back on that much more difficult.

Beth was first to spot Chris skating with a couple of friends from their safe distance at the far end of the rink. Wrapped tightly in conversation he hadn't yet noticed she or her sister skating side by side on the same ice. Taking small glances in his direction she tried hard to keep her family life in the right perspective though as ever it was proving onerous. Audrey, still beside her, noticed him shortly after. Seeking to keep the distance where it was by stepping up the pace, she hoped Beth would match her stride. She remained oblivious, slowing to a glide, unwitting even to herself. Turning to face her Audrey regarded her troubled features, a darkness descending behind the eyes. Recently becoming more and more acquainted with this mask she turned back to leave the ice for the comfort of her friends and the space between.

No one took notice of Jeremy and his cohorts stalking the boys, gliding amongst the crowd unnoticed and some distance behind. Seeing the Kanes come in they'd been biding their time with no small debate as to how wise it would be to confront them here. Impudence ruled the day, the weaker boys caved, and for once Jeremy let mob rule, uncertain himself how much stomach he had left for the game. Almost feeling a sense of liberation for vacating the leadership role, thinking he may at least rest his head a little better at night, he glided to the boards where he leaned to watch otherwise declining to take part.

The game went on without him. Tracing a wide arc, one of the boys came swiftly from the side while another came from behind. Coordinating the attack to simultaneously wipe out both boys there was no defense, the first ramming himself into Cary, the second sweeping Andy's skates from beneath him. Careening into the corner, the momentum carried the boys together bouncing them hard off the boards. The commotion drew Beth's attention. Unsure what was happening, she had a vague idea it was coming from the direction she recalled last sighting her brothers. Looking close she could see they were sprawled on the ice while another group of boys were quickly skating away in her direction. As one moved to squeeze between she and the few feet separating them from the boards she slammed her body into his without much thought. With his speed and her relative size it was a decisive blow, his skates lifting from the surface as he careened backwards, his body hitting the boards and his head the ice. Calmly skating away to give aide to her brothers she never glanced back.

While hardly anyone had seen what happened to the boy one exception was Lily. Unaware anything had occurred with her own boys, she sat watching her young daughter intentionally and viciously collide with the kid and skate off with scarcely a look back. There was no remorse and no pity, it was just a cold, clear, unthinking act of violence. She was horrified, and awestruck. Never before witnessing something in her own family of such breathtaking calculation it scared her leaving her for the moment little more than an unblinking bystander.

Another exception was the group of kids who were following the now injured boy as they made their escape. Staggered by the savage impact, they first turned their attention to their fallen friend but after picking the dizzy boy up turned their attention to Beth as she helped Cary off the ice. Screaming epithets they brought every part of her under scrutiny; ugly, grotesque, shabby, a slut and a whore, gross and untouchable with bad clothes and worse hair. Their anger not yet satisfied they went after Cary and Andy as well; stupid, poor, queer, base, miserable and moronic losers from dubious parentage and a still more dubious and impoverished family tree. It was unmerciful, incessant, and it was eternal. Taking it all in Beth quietly removed her skates putting back on her shoes. With everything in order she stood, turned, composedly walked toward them and was in the process of pulling her fist back when her mother grabbed her hand stopping it before she could bring it forward and beat the kid.

"You're embarrassing me."

Walking up Carl barely heard the words from his wife. Looking around and seeing Audrey helping the boys on with their shoes, Beth in an icy exchange with her mother, he was left with no idea as to what was happening. Taking the coffee from his hands Lily threw it in a nearby bin and pushed him along angrily grabbing Cary by the arm as she went by. The laces she was tying yanked from her hands, Audrey stood up looking over to Beth who looked away, her gaze meeting Chris' as he stood on the ice watching. It was another resplendent sixty seconds in her life.

10.

Lily watched the rain come in flooding torrents. A tropical wave had come up and spread itself widely throughout the region bringing more soaking rain and unseasonably warm temperatures. The winds accompanying the gale shuddered the bare trees and invested itself in every cranny of the old home's exposed quarters, whistling as it escaped the confinement and spread its draft inside. On the hill in back the evergreens gave a great whoosh as they swayed with each gust, their soft wood twisting and creaking as they bumped one another. Occasionally she could hear one of the branches snap and fall to the ground with a mighty crack and thud sending a startled tingle up her spine to the nape of her neck. It was an impressive display and one on which she'd rather not stand witness while waiting for Carl to return with the car.

With the weather what it was he drove Audrey and Beth to school rather than have them risk the walk, Cary and Andy electing to stay home after being given the option. Since it was Friday little harm could be done and perhaps a long weekend would improve their perspective. He decided to stay with them telling Lily she could have the car for work. It only made sense since she had no paid time off and they couldn't stand to lose even her modest sum for a few hours work. At least that's what he told her. In truth he wanted time to think; about her, the boys, the family and how it all fit together, or didn't. Not a word had been spoken, from anyone, over what happened the previous evening. He was still unsure of all that had gone on after arriving late on the scene with coffee and being thrust into the middle of an ongoing fight. Ordinarily he would have chosen to stand his ground but with confusion holding court retreat was the only option. He felt sure of only one thing, Lily retreated long before he got there pushing the rest of the family through the doors with scarcely a glance or a word.

Pulling into the driveway and taking a last look at the dashboard clock he knew he'd cut it close. Tardiness for work wasn't something with which she willingly flirted but he felt the urgent need to stop for coffee and time alone before continuing home. The thought of spending even a moment in the company of his wife was an added inducement. Before passing judgment he required knowledge, of her and the whole night's affair, and was sure if he didn't take the necessary space to gather and reflect then he would make a snap decision of no good to anyone. Even if after all was done he would have proved to be right it would forever sit foul in his mind as rash.

Coming in he put the keys down on the small entryway table and continued upstairs without taking the time to remove and shake out his coat or wet footwear. She expected as much, waiting for his footsteps to fade before leaving the kitchen and exiting the house. Caring little if the rain matted her hair or sopped her clothing she didn't bother with her umbrella instead tracing a path to the car while the rain put down its steady drumbeat. Watching the dark house from behind the blurry windshield she breathed for what felt the first time that day.

Carl stood in the doorway to his bedroom and just looked. The bed crisply made, her dressing table laid out as though ever and always unused, an area rug covering a severe bald spot in the worn floorboards. It was sterile, foreign and cold. Reflective of his mood it was incongruous, an illusory scene. Everything seemed just out of focus, troubling his mind as he tried embracing the idea two bodies ever warmed the room at all. And as the house sighed with every breath from the storm outside he felt more alone.

"Dad?" Cary poked his head from his room and wandered down the hall, repeating it again when his first attempt failed to stir his father from meditation.

He looked down at the boy, remembering why he was here at all. Andy came out of the room and joined them in the hallway. Taking a long moment he regarded his two sons.

"So, shall we get some coffee or what?"

"Can I have one too?" Cary asked, his expression hopeful. He'd never been offered a cup of his own only begging and accepting a swallow when he could.

"Sure you can," he answered winking at the boy.

The three made their way to the kitchen, Carl trailed by the boys, boisterous as they strutted the way trying hard to walk like two cocksure grown men. They sat upright in their chairs, feet dangling but moving little as Carl went about preparing their cups and waiting for the kettle to boil. Once in awhile he stole a glance over his shoulder, the two quietly watching his every move in anticipation of the steamy brew. They delighted in the resonating tinkle of the spoon as he stirred in a healthy amount of sugar for the boys and put a full cup in front of each before taking his own to join them. Andy sipped first, finishing with a satisfied moan, Cary following with his own flourish. He let them enjoy the moment while he watched the rain batter the window in great sweeping cascades, the electricity blinking intermittently, the boys gasping in amusement each time. Taking the cups when they finished he gave a quick rinse otherwise leaving them in the sink unwashed. Feeling it an appropriate moment, one in which they could dispense with the impediment of age and relation and talk like men, he asked them what happened at the rink.

Recounting what they could from their unique points of view neither were fully aware of what really happened with the other it occurred so fast. Next thing they knew Beth was leaning over Cary, Andy doing the same after he regained his footing, the both of them picking him up and supporting his weight. Making their way back to the bleachers they saw one of the boys being helped from the ice and then next they knew the rest of the kids started yelling and teasing they and Beth while Audrey took their skates off. That was it until he arrived on scene and Lily whisked them all away.

Two things initially struck Carl as he listened hoping to glean a little sense from their tale. The first was he couldn't see how Beth was all mixed up in this other than assisting Cary from the ice and that certainly wasn't worth the other kid's attention. Yet when he got there much of their scorn was being heaped on her even as Lily was turning her around trying to push her toward the exit. The other thing that struck him was the rather circumstantial confirmation of his fears as they related to Lily. It wasn't anything the boys said, it was what they didn't say; not once did she at all help. She wasn't on the ice after they'd gone down, she didn't help them to their seats or to remove their skates, she gave no comfort whatever, and when he arrived he could plainly see for himself she was doing nothing to defend her young children making instead what sounded like a nonsensical statement of her own embarrassment.

That in particular was what he was having a tough time believing and in a very marked way it unnerved him. The fact she would stand by and watch her children be tormented and abused without coming to their defense in a mad rage was deplorable enough. The idea she may have been more embarrassed than furious was simply intolerable. It was causing him to fight hard against her rise as a pariah in his mind but each time he tried to weigh the other side he couldn't find one. Plumbing her depths all these years he never thought they could be so deep or quite so dark. He felt he'd always been forgiving of her eccentricities even softening a bit after her stark outburst a couple nights before. Yet if these facts proved true then she was well beyond his scope of discovery, and well beyond the sweep of his reality.

He kept these murky thoughts well hidden from the boys as they continued filling out the event with minor details and meaningless musings of their own. The last thing he wanted was to pollute their esteem with such speculation when clearly they hadn't heard a word their mother said to their sister. Trying to keep an even disposition and allow the topic to fade he then realized perhaps he was simply learning something they'd already known of and become accustomed to with their mother. It wasn't enough they didn't recall or question her lack of intervention on their behalf, they clearly had no expectation. Nothing was amiss, nothing strange about her complacency, certainly not enough to raise questions. This was their relationship with their mother, this was their mother. He had an inkling through the years, even giving it voice in the last couple of weeks, but he supposed he'd been hoping it wasn't quite this ugly.

Still, they were assumptions and he owed her the benefit of the doubt, at the least. He tuned back into the conversation just as it began to peter out, the boys recognizing his mind had drifted elsewhere.

"So wait a second Cary, let's go back to the beginning, why are these boys still picking on you?"

Cary looked at him for a moment, turned away, and then back again. It was a good question, a reasonable question, one he and Andy had been struggling to answer for the last couple of weeks. He considered a few seconds more.

"I don't know dad."

Searching Andy for the answer, he simply frowned and gave an indicating nod toward Cary letting him know anything to be said would be done so by he alone. This was his tale to tell, as little or as much as needed. Carl understood, and waited. Cary would begin to talk eventually, he knew the boy needed to unburden himself and it was unlike him to hold things in for long.

"Well, you know it started with my sneakers," he said after awhile, "but they just haven't stopped doing it dad. I don't know why, they just think it's funny I guess."

"And that's it, that damn pair of lousy sneakers?"

"Yeah, I guess."

Though he kept it to himself, Cary really felt part of the answer was about something more. A couple of weeks before, having finally grown tired of always playing by himself, he decided to join in with the other kids playing soccer during recess. He learned quickly, surprised he was actually pretty good at something athletic. As time wore on some of the other kids noticed it too and were pleased to welcome him on their team. He was a natural playmaker, a gift bestowed on those who learn to share early in their lives, but it took the shine from the usual playground stars, children accustomed to the worship and adoration of others. Sharing was not a part of their lives, with him anyway. He felt the tension building with some of the other kids so he took a little off his game in hopes they'd be pacified. They weren't, and the day he ripped his sneaker was the moment they chose to vent their anger on him. He ever since regretted abandoning his self play in favor of joining the others, a mere two weeks of joy hardly worth the persecution he'd endured since. Yet explaining that to his dad, even Andy, wasn't easy so he maintained his silence.

Fidgeting in his seat Andy had his own ideas as to what was happening to Cary and much of it was built around his feelings from when in the past the ridicule was being more stridently pointed toward him. Though he'd kept his tongue then, no one save Cary wise to the incidents, he wasn't going to any longer.

"Dad, are we poor? I mean really poor?"

Such a simple question it took Carl off guard in its frankness. He knew from where it came, he traced it often in those uncomfortable moments of reflection and self doubt. He knew his past, he knew his present, and he had a very good idea of his future. He was okay with that and mostly lain it to rest with the realization he was as much as perhaps he would ever be. For his children though he hoped there was somehow more, that they could avoid the certainty of being poor as an inheritance, its lurking presence a drag on their blossoming future. Now it was plain an awareness was pushing its way in and he had no idea how to stop it, or how to answer the question with anything but another of his own.

"Why do you ask?"

"Well, the kids pick on our clothes quite a bit."

"They're picking on you too?"

"Yeah, well, mostly before."

"What do you mean before?"

He looked uneasily at his father knowing he was about to let go of a secret shame he'd been carrying.

"Well, the kids were picking on me last year just like Cary. It's just they were mostly picking on my hair 'cause you know, mom was cutting it and it didn't look so good."

Cary, suddenly feeling self-conscious about his own hair, rubbed his hands through the back to see if there was something wrong he'd never before noticed. Despite everything seeming okay it was a nervous idea there was more to his look that put him out of place than he'd considered.

Andy continued, "They picked on my clothes a little bit. They were kind of new just not the right kind I guess. I think they get after Cary more 'cause he's wearing them now and they're not so new anymore."

Carl studied their faces, looking over their hair and what he could of their clothes, and he understood. For that instant he could see the way others saw them, how they may perceive and how they might react to them. They looked poor, they were poor. He wondered too about the girls. Was this what turned Beth inward, causing her to hide in her own protective shell? Audrey seemed fine, able to get along and always looking good while doing so. Of course, beauty transcends and she has that in abundance, he thought, while the boys weren't blessed with such obvious and solicitous attractiveness. Of course, they were just boys anyway.

Picking over the question again he thought how best to answer. He couldn't escape it, his sons deserving a forthright response to such a candid question. After all, he wanted this discussion to be amongst men so it was imperative he hold up his end.

"Yeah, Andy, you could say we're poor, leastways working poor. Now why didn't you tell me they were doing this to you last year?"

"I don't know, I guess I just didn't want to. It pretty much stopped anyway."

"But now they're doing it again?"

"Yeah, not really the same kids though."

"Besides the boots they're giving you a rough time about your clothes too?" he asked looking to Cary.

"Yeah, sometimes."

"And hair?"

"No," he quickly replied feeling the back of his head anew, "not yet."

He thought for a moment, "Are they calling you boys poor?"

"Yeah, sometimes, quite a bit," Andy answered while Cary was nodding in agreement.

"You think that's why they pick on you?"

"Yeah, I think so."

"Cary, you think so too?"

"Maybe."

Carl stood up from the table and slowly walked about the kitchen. It was an awful idea to wrap his head around, the kids being badgered simply because they were poor. It bothered him too that he didn't know the full extent and the boys hadn't come to him earlier. Especially Andy with it having gone on last year and he left ignorant all this time. He took pride in his close relationship with his sons often holding it in sad compare to his daughters with whom he was ever left wishing the same would be true. Now it seems he'd not been as close as all that after all. It hurt him a bit.

"Hey dad, what does working poor mean?" Andy asked after he and Cary had been puzzling over it awhile.

He had to pull his thoughts back together. "It's uh, well, your mom and I work very hard but we just don't make much money."

"So how's that different from just being poor?"

"Well, I guess in reality it's not much. I mean, we work for what we have, nobody gives it us. When we want something we have to work hard to get it so I guess it's just that we're working poor."

He knew he was doing an awful job explaining the concept. Though it was just a label it was invested with all kinds of meaning, most unarticulated but understood. Trying to then explain it to the boys in language divested of that meaning thus made simple was beyond his ability. This became ever more clear by the confounded expressions the boys wore. He started to speak again then decided to leave it there, he would only confuse them further and it really wasn't the most salient point on which to hang the conversation.

"So, what are we going to do about this whole thing?"

The boys shrugged. Though the question had long been defined, the answer was proving more difficult to find. The gimmicks Andy used in the past were showing themselves to be little more than mere tricks simply forestalling the inevitable.

"Do you want me talk to the school?"

"No dad," Cary shrunk at the idea, Miss McCall already being overly concerned with his well-being and afraid further attention would only increase the wrath.

"Andy?"

"No dad, I think it'll probably just make it worse."

Carl knew they'd react this way yet felt he needed to ask the question anyway, a parental duty if nothing else. It didn't make things any easier, in fact it made things a long way harder.

"Okay, but promise me that if this continues you'll tell me. And not next year," he warned looking intently at Andy, "you'll tell me when it happens."

They readily agreed feeling they'd avoided a situation that could get a whole lot worse if the school was involved. Carl was a little ashamed hiding from the boys the conviction if it did happen again he would be going to the school regardless of what they thought. His hands were otherwise tied. He couldn't be there beside them and there was no other place for them to go. Beth would have to be more vigilant when she was walking them to and from school. Perhaps she could also find out for him who these boys were since it might be a good idea to confront their parents as well. Though that type of thing always felt a little dicey to him, they were usually not too receptive to the idea of their kid as a bad actor in the community. Greeted as an indictment of their parenting skills, it was.

"Now, how about some peanut butter sandwiches?" he asked trying to be enthusiastic. It wasn't easy. With all due respect to Mr. Carver, he thought, a peanut is little more than a peanut when you're a Kane.

When they finished their sandwiches Carl pushed the boys back off to their room to play and wile away the afternoon hours. He could tell they were unhappy with this hoping instead to have a day's worth of man time with him. But there were other issues he needed to sort out and Lily was the top of that list. He was yet unsure what he would do when he had time to confront her figuring the moment would show him the way as long as he ignored his faulty instinct and embraced his logic instead. He was still struggling with the notion she deserved the benefit of the doubt when there was so little of it left in his mind. However, he'd always believed himself a judicious man and reasoned she, and their marriage, warranted something.

Turning his attention to small meaningless tasks around the house none of them consumed much of his time. It wasn't the point, wiling away some of his own hours until Lily came back home was.

Lily arrived to work on time, just, and out of sorts. After a sleepless night the upset of her morning routine simply heaped more misery on her wretched self. She couldn't concentrate, everything she did a series of false starts while she worked out what she was doing at a particular time or place. Her coworkers noticed it too. Stacks of files were still piled high on her small desk as she sat and stared into space, unhearing and unminding. Every once in awhile she'd rise from her chair, take a small batch and approach the file cabinets only to place them back down again as though she couldn't quite work out where they belonged or why she had them in her hand at all. They whispered about it at first realizing soon after it was unnecessary to take such precaution when she was oblivious anyhow. They finally summoned one of the doctors to speak with her. Insisting she was fine, everything was fine, she refused the rest of the day off when it was offered. From that point she tried being more conscientious of her duties but it remained absentminded at best, her coworkers following every step to right her mistakes. She never noticed, the slop swishing around in her head diffusing all focus. After a short time of this they finally prevailed on her to go home and rest assuring her she would be paid for the full shift. She reluctantly agreed knowing home was the last place she should be at this moment.

Picking up her belongings she was thankful she had the car having almost forgotten until the jingling keys in her purse sent a reminder. Walking through the parking lot, caring little to dodge the raindrops, she got behind the wheel and then simply sat staring through the steamed windshield. She had nowhere to go, no one to see. An overwhelming insignificance blanketed her.

It was something she'd felt many times through the years, her life somehow irrelevant. It purposefully took root at the fore of her consciousness when her parents died, still young and within weeks of one another, leaving her with no family but the most distant relations. She felt so singularly alone at the time, anchorless, fluttering in the breeze, scared in a way she'd never before been. Carl was there, Audrey just a baby, so she initially tried to compensate by throwing herself into this new substitute family for the next couple of years. It didn't seem to take, even with the subsequent birth of Beth. Unable to focus long enough the bonds had no strength, no meaning for her. It was the legacy of her parents, the emotional disconnect of her first family. Though stilted, she had comforted in its knowing, an accustomed security in silence, even if it left her impaired, forging new bonds simply beyond her grasp.

It was now more evident than ever, the cold shoulder of an isolating social irrelevance new company for her thoughts. Over all the years she formed not a single friendship of any significance. Wanting to blame Carl for this as well she knew in reality the circumstance was of her own making. A caregiver and companion, mother to their children, there was little else in her adult life. She had no hobbies, no outside interests and, save for her part-time job, no outlets and thus no real chance to interact meaningfully with others. Brooding alone in her room at night she vowed every next day would be different. Then it would come and she'd still make no effort. She sensed her life had become a series of tomorrows while she waited to die. It was an awful thought, but she was desolate.

Starting the car she drove for hours with no particular direction, no destination in mind. She couldn't return home, not for a long while yet. She needed the time for retrospective, to make sense of what lay in the past. She also needed to understand what lay ahead, her night terrors, where she was alone and falling, having become her waking terror. And despite the ever present desire to just leave it all behind, the extra money she couldn't spare on the gas she was now using served to temper the romantic thought of driving forever.

11.

The weekend rolled coldly into the Kane house. Lily didn't return home until the late hours of Friday night, early Saturday by Carl's reckoning, at which time his mood could be found somewhere between indignation and concern. Yet he'd long given up the idea of speaking with her over the situation when finally and silently she crept to bed. His instinct told him a late night discussion would lead nowhere productive, a night's sleep, fitful or otherwise, preferable. She wouldn't have spoken with him anyway. Her thoughts not yet fully formed, she was desperate to avoid the same mistakes of the recent past by blurting something out in a moment of pique.

For the boys, however, it was mostly hours of concern. It was unlike their mother to be absent from them for so long without her hiding away in her room or sitting alone at the kitchen table. At one point they sought an answer from their dad who offered no other reason than she had gone out and all was otherwise fine. They knew better, she didn't just go out, her lurking presence a fixture in the house at all times except when she was off to work. Though the raging storm of the day had mostly passed they began wondering if perhaps something had happened, an accident or some such thing that could explain her absence for so long. After awhile they reasoned it was highly improbable, an ordeal surely would have followed. Whatever it was, it was altogether new and disquieting, an unwelcome deviation from the normal to which they'd grown accustomed.

Audrey and Beth weren't so oblivious to the reality of it all. With the weather remaining on the foul side Audrey chose to stay home that night and spend most of her time upstairs in their room with Beth. She didn't mind, the uneasy truce and the early laughs of the previous night's skate enough to calm the angst of spending too much time with Audrey. It proved itself enlightening as well, her sister divulging what she saw from her own perspective arriving late on the scene at the rink. Beth was so distracted by the derision from the gang of boys, her own satisfaction at getting a measure of vengeance for her brothers, the presence of Chris, removing her skates and Cary's well-being she never noticed her mother at all, until she stepped in her way.

"So she just stood there?"

"Yup."

"The whole time and not a word?"

"Nope."

"Until she told me I was embarrassing her?"

"Yup."

"Dad must be pretty upset about that."

"I think so."

She thoughtfully studied the matter for a few minutes while Audrey spent her usual time in front of the mirror fussing with her hair. For a moment it distracted her and she watched, the long strands framing the gentle and refined features of her face. Caught staring, Audrey simply smiled at her and kept on trying to undo the day's poor weather. Her thoughts turned again to the evident rift between her parents. It wasn't altogether a surprise her mother did nothing to intervene, it was about what she would have expected. In her mind she'd proved ever unreliable and unmoved since she could remember. Yet there was always a hint of expectation that under duress her mother was capable of rising to the test. If nothing else she always projected an air of strength, a calm port in a forever stormy sea. Acutely aware they were poor, just getting enough food on the table a challenge, her parents always managed nonetheless and she gave some of that credit to her mother. Sure, she wasn't much of a breadwinner but she was collected, her dad too earthy, too connected to manage the finances in the cool, rational way they demanded. In that sense they were a good team, their skill sets making for a complimentary union.

Still, she couldn't deny she often wondered about the attraction her father had for her mother. She was every bit as beautiful as Audrey, especially so for an older woman, but unlike Audrey it was a shell with no underlying warmth. Despite the problems she had with her sister she was at the least an engaging personality, even enthralling to most judging by their reaction. With her mother there was none of that and you could feel people conspicuously shrink away when trapped in her company for long. She mused it was like the thousand yard stare, her attention never quite focused on the people or events before her. Surely her dad must have seen and felt it after all this time, even if he was blinded by her physical attractiveness in the beginning. Her emotional emptiness, feigned moments of happiness, the restrained alienation, were so transparent anyone would have noticed by now.

She surely did. She couldn't remember a singular moment of comfort when in the company of her mother, ever. The vacuousness with which she approached motherhood was damning, the evidence littering her childhood from skinned knees to a soul numbing lack of affection. And it always seemed more pointed at her as if there was something she'd done to deserve an especial and individual scorn. Growing in her childhood consciousness she sought to dismiss the idea she was singled out, that the emotional distance was shared equally among her siblings. To an extent it was true and she saw it frequently yet she'd never been able to shake the idea she was held to account more often than the others and markedly more so than Audrey for whom her mother held a particular, almost deferential, regard. It was all so very odd, her childhood repeatedly distracted by the brooding thought growing up Elizabeth Kane was nothing to envy.

"So where do you think she is?" Audrey asked breaking the spell. She was still brushing the last of the knots from her hair as Beth glanced at her reflection.

"I haven't the faintest, and I couldn't say I care," the last words coming without discretion.

Audrey kept working letting the statement go unremarked. She'd have been more inclined to put up a fuss over such ideas before last night but now she had come to the uncomfortable realization her mother was probably every bit of not much. It hurt her to see the boys and Beth under fire, her father trying to make sense of all that was happening, she doing the same, while her mother stood by on the fringe as mere witness, an embarrassed one at that. Besides, she knew Beth's ragged and unpredictable emotional states so raising an objection would only provoke an unnecessary response. Better to let things lay as they were, the morning likely to shed some rational light on their mother's absence. That said, she was willing to take one chance as the moment seemed right, rarely having presented itself before.

"Come sit over here a minute," she asked.

"Why?"

"Just do it."

Beth hesitantly got up and sat in front of the mirror. Audrey went behind and started to brush her hair, taking it in handfuls starting with the roots and working to the ends. She never said a word, not once glancing at Beth's reflection in the mirror as she deftly worked through the little kinks and knots, the tangle of split ends. Finishing each section she held it aloft for a brief moment before letting it fall back to her shoulder and begin work on the next. Every brush stroke took the moisture of the damp, chill night from her hair leaving a long voluminous mass that fell nearly the length of her arm and torso. So used to the heavy and shapeless chaos roosting atop her head the weightless luminosity Audrey produced with a few simple strokes was a delightful and startling revelation. Her hair was beautiful, it charmed her.

Audrey continued to work silently through every strand delicately untangling each snarl so as not to do any damage. Every once in awhile she took a pair of scissors laying nearby and clipped a small piece, a dead end or a hopeless snag. Completing the full orbit, and with Beth's head clasped in both hands, she pointed her toward the mirror.

"Beautiful," she proclaimed.

Beth demurred at first, but glancing at her reflection again she couldn't help trace a wide smile. It was lovely, even elegant. Reaching up she ran her fingers through lingering to stroke the ends and feel the softness.

"It is," she agreed moving her head from side to side to get a full profile view. Like Audrey, it framed her face perfectly drawing attention to features she'd never much noticed before; naturally arched eyebrows, soft jaw line, almost dainty nose.

"See how beautiful you are?" Audrey said standing back to admire her work.

Beth peered at her sister's reflection, arms crossed, ever present flirtatious smile playing on her lips.

"Stop it," she snapped hastily standing and going back to sit on her bed.

"Stop what?"

"Just stop it. I don't know what game you're playing now but just stop it."

Audrey saw the darkness behind her eyes return as Beth stared her down, a certain hate filling the rims. Being captivated by the moment, connecting with her sister in a way she'd never done before, she realized too late that her push was too far. Feeling a brief impulse to strike back and castigate her, to continue with the familiar, she knew she couldn't, too much time and energy already squandered. There was also the urge to for once know something of her sister without the pettiest of squabbles or she herself getting in the way.

"Beth, you are beautiful you know."

"I'm not you, I'll never be you, so stop trying."

"I don't want you to be me, I want you to be you."

Beth turned her back and started rubbing her fingers together as she so often did, hunched over, picking her way through each worn nail. Watching her Audrey could feel the subtle fluctuations of her agitation while she searched her mind for a way around. It wasn't often she sensed her emotions so strongly, even less so when she even cared. It was a minefield she avoided, emotions both high and low filling her with discomfort, a sure sign of a discontented and maladjusted soul to her thinking. Then as the chafing silence continued she thought to ask the one question she'd often wondered but always dismissed, frequently through lack of interest one way or the other.

"Beth, why is it you don't like me?"

She didn't flinch, maintaining her reserve, picking through each nail, letting the question linger. She calculated her continued, unmoving chill would extinguish Audrey's curiosity and put an end to the conversation before it had a chance to gain legs as it had ever done in the past. She knew her sister's flaky nature, her lack of attention and lack of regard would soon cause her to look for amusement elsewhere. And still she waited, her sister's resolute focus keeping company, and for a rare time she began to feel the one unnerved.

"Why do you care?" she muttered.

"Because you're my sister."

She flitted through all the past hurts Audrey caused, the small insults, the criticism, the endless parade of fabricated attention and caring. It all added up and yet still fell short and she knew why, she'd always known why.

"Okay, I tell you what, I'll answer your question if you answer one of mine."

"Fine."

She turned and faced her, "Why'd you kiss him?"

Taken completely off her guard, as much by the question as wondering how in the world the girl knew and didn't give it up until this point, Audrey wanted to pretend ignorance. It would have been a hopeless gambit, she knew it full well. A fair question, it was one she needed to answer if they were to finally get past this crucible in their relationship. It was also a small weight she was tired of carrying.

"Because I was trying to convince him to talk to you, to get to know you and like you."

Beth watched her, looking for any trace that might betray the girl's intentions as they were and not as she was presenting them to be.

"I thought it would make you happy, strangely enough" she continued.

Beth moved to put up further resistance, to show the preposterousness of such an idea, but stopped herself short. Over the years she'd watched her sister tease, torment, and cause immeasurable harm to people and always with a lack of certain malice as if she weren't fully aware of her actions. An act this callous would have been done with forethought and though she thought low of her sister, in more candid moments she knew she was incapable of action this low. Besides, she was too tired to carry this on any longer.

"It's the truth Beth. I know it was stupid but I did it."

She nodded and looked away.

A little baffled at how easily she accepted the explanation Audrey saw it fortuitous enough to let the subject lie adding nothing further that may only complicate things. But after subduing long enough her impatience for the answer to her own question she quietly repeated it.

"So why don't you like me?"

Beth evaluated how best to approach the matter. Though in possession of the answer, she was not in the best way to articulate it effectively. Never dreaming she'd be in this conversation, that she'd ever let herself be, it was proving illusive. While preferring to keep her pain close this was prying it loose and yet, as uncomfortable as it was, she'd agreed to the bargain.

"Audrey, has mom ever told you she loves you?"

She thought for a moment. It was a familiar notion that bounced around in her own head often enough and in odd moments through the years she pondered it but like much else dismissed it as meaningless, just not in her way to express such sentiment. Of course she must love them, that was part of the job, she was a mother, she's their mother.

"No, but I know she does. Don't you?"

"Yeah, I know she loves you."

"And you."

"I know she doesn't."

There was a sadness to her response.

"Of course she does."

"No she doesn't, she loves you."

Audrey puzzled over the statement trying hard to consider what Beth was saying. Despite her understanding of the idea, she'd only ever studied it from her own perspective, the only one with which she was acquainted, or ever bothered to be. Still, not everything was making sense, her allegation simple enough but with no relation whatsoever to the question.

"What do you mean?"

Beth hesitated, "You asked why I don't like you."

"Okay."

"There's your answer."

"You don't like me because you think mom doesn't love you?"

She was a bit dismissive, the whole thing sounding ridiculous, the silly girl not liking her over and after all these years because she thought her mother didn't love her.

"No, because mom loves you."

For a moment she felt like she was on shifting sand, Beth playing with words again and losing the logic. Yet even if she couldn't parse it all out, she knew.

"Look at me for a minute Beth. You don't like me because you think mom loves me, and only me, no one else including you?"

She nodded and looked away again.

"Why? I mean, why do you think that?"

"Have you ever noticed the way her eyes follow you when you're around?"

"No."

"Well they do. She watches everything you do, she's enamored with you."

"Enamored?"

Beth sighed, uncomfortable in the conversation.

"Mom never looks at me that way, not any of us. She only has that look for you. Ever since I can remember she's looked at you that way and paid no attention to me. It's like I'm just a border in her house, barely an acquaintance."

"Beth," she started moving toward her.

"Don't. I don't need your sympathy, and I certainly don't need you to play mother to me. You asked the question and I told you the answer."

"Even if that's true, why do you hate me and not her?"

"I do."

That much was true, Audrey thought, her feelings quite clear when she earlier made it known she didn't care what had become of their mother. Still, she herself was being held to account for the actions of another and as disturbing as Beth's perception of that other's actions were, she wasn't in any way responsible so shouldn't wear the same yoke of punishment.

"That's still no reason to hate me."

Beth knew she was right of course, this had nothing to do with her and was between she and her mother alone. It didn't diminish the real harm Audrey had done her over the years but she was reluctantly aware most were little more than adolescent sibling wounds, the kind time and adulthood tend to forgive.

Remaining quiet, Audrey allowed her to work through her thoughts knowing the portent. She also had many of her own through which to work. For once, for this sliver of time, she was feeling a kinship with Beth, a shared destiny in family. They had a history after all and it wasn't so divergent or as indifferent as she believed for so long. Except the union, if it were to be, was being uncomfortably built on a lack of expressive love from their mother. It was forcing her to begin a reevaluation of much of what she assumed growing up in the Kane household. Perhaps what she failed to see over the years was a choice made because it had real and distressing significance.

Looking at her sister, sitting ever so still, crowded and brooding, she knew the significance was real. Quietly sitting on the bed and putting her arm around her she felt her stiffen at first then relent, the effort accepted for at least a few moments. It was gratifying, no scorn, no rejection, Beth feeling the inclination for neither. They remained like this for a long time, silent, alone with their clamorous thoughts, awkward, self-conscious, secure, content, understood, conflicted. Eventually Beth gently pushed her arm away and stood with her back turned and head low. Audrey studied her, so young, so unhappy.

"Have you ever said anything to mom?" she whispered.

"No."

"What about dad?"

"No, he wouldn't understand."

She felt uneasy saying it knowing her dad had always made far more effort to know her and especially of late. He was also far more in tune with her than anyone else in the house even if he didn't himself fully know. He was, in truth, the only person she could almost say she loved.

"Well, maybe he would, but I couldn't tell him that."

"Yeah, maybe."

"And don't you tell him, or her," she whirled around as she spoke, panicked with the familiar thought that in letting her guard down and admitting these things her sister would in turn use them, intentionally or not, to do her further harm.

"I won't," she promised seeing the alarm in her sister's eyes.

12.

Carl left Lily laying in bed Saturday morning and crept downstairs, dawn breaking with a fresh blanket of white, the first snow of the season. He started the kettle in a stupor, too tired to sleep any longer, too awake to embrace the dullness of his mind. The chill in the air did precious little to waken his bones, his knees cracking as he went to the window. An arctic air mass had forced it's way in from the northwest pushing the tropical moisture eastward while nipping at its heels enough to make a couple of inches. He could tell it would be gone by day's end, the slushy mess already falling from the trees and wires with the weak morning rays. It was a small wonder nonetheless, the first real sign winter's grip was at hand. He loved this time of year, the in between waiting over, icy mornings and frosty evenings, oversized coats and wool sweaters, hats, gloves, duck boots and cold so fresh your every breath hung in the air long enough to be sure you were still alive. He embraced it all and, despite the weight he was carrying, could barely suppress the twinkle in his eye a first snow delivered.

The whistle of the kettle broke his transcendence. He turned to see Beth pulling it off the burner, a wide yawn punctuating her effort. Wordlessly taking a couple of mugs from the cupboard she spooned a heap of coffee into each. He sat at the table where she put a mug in front of him and sat down with her own, stifling another yawn.

"Why are you up so early dad?" she asked while gently stirring her coffee, careful to deaden the sound of metal spoon on ceramic. She hated the piercing tinkle first thing in the morning, her nighttime ears still keen. A plastic spoon would be real nice at these times, she thought.

"I was gonna ask you the same thing."

"Eh, couldn't sleep," she trailed off with another yawn, "you?"

He caught the bug, trying to speak as he did so. She understood the gist of his unintelligible mutter, the same for him. They stared at their coffee, each trying to shake the webs. She was in no hurry, clutching at the blessed numbness of her waking mind and its fight against the encroaching tide of full consciousness. She chanced to glance out the window, seeing the snow for the first time and, craning her neck, took a quick survey of the yard.

"Would you look at that?"

"Yup, a couple inches. It's already melting though."

She turned back, "Yeah, I can see that. So's mom home?"

"Yeah."

"Where was she?"

He searched for an answer, one that would satisfy his own self and put her off. It was too early yet for dialogue. It was also too early for his inert mind to circumvent the question.

"I don't know," was all he could manage.

She watched him stare deeply into his mug, perhaps in expectation a better answer could be found somewhere at the bottom. He looked so poignantly feeble, the collar of his pajama top poking from his flannel shirt, the puffy crescents beneath his eyes accentuated with his head slung low, the sturdy frame in the bones of his hands culminating in the permanence of the soil beneath his fingertips. It was stirring and whether moved by the scene in front of her, the burden she'd unloaded the night before, or a combination of the two, she wanted nothing so badly as to absolve him, to hug him and tell him everything was just fine, everything would be just fine. She did the best she could, reaching out and squeezing his hand.

"It's Thanksgiving on Thursday."

"I know," he answered squeezing back.

Lily hardly slept most of the night too but, as uncomfortable as it was, moved little through the hours so as not to alert Carl to her wakefulness. She felt him stir one final time and disappear downstairs as the sun was rising. Still doing battle with her own worst thoughts, she drifted into a restless coma, a paltry substitute for peace but about the best her fatigued self could hope. It didn't last long, the short pierce of the kettle and clink of the spoons enough to fracture her brief respite. Continuing the fight for a while longer she surrendered in the end, even broken sleep impossible. Rising and donning her robe, she made her way downstairs.

Sometime during her transient slumber, when the dreamlets flit through the mind in their truncated abruptness, she failed to notice Beth waken and join her father in the kitchen. If she'd known she would have stayed in her room. It was one thing to invite the inevitable with Carl but she was not yet ready to face the questioning looks of her children, especially this one.

Hearing her coming, both Carl and Beth pulled their hands away then tried to hide their shame from one another for having done so. But at the root of it they knew whatever this was about and whatever may come there was a shared feeling Lily's emotionless bearing played a role. To have her witness even the most distant of embraces and familial affection was unnecessary, or so they felt. And with no idea to where she'd disappeared during the previous day they knew nothing of what to expect from her now.

Coming into the kitchen without a word she put on the kettle. Doing her best to ignore the two at the table while not appearing to intentionally do so she busied herself with preparing a mug taking enough time she could have counted the crystals out by hand. The water still not boiling she went to the window, her first glance at the weather outside. It wasn't what she'd hoped, wanting instead a day dark and brooding to match her mood. She watched as a couple of noisy blue jays flew from branch to branch looking for a fresh perch free of the falling wet snow. They never settled for long, the next more enticing than the one before. The whistling kettle brought a welcome disturbance to the laden stillness. Hoping Beth would have left by now, she stirred her mug and went to the darkened living room to sit on her own, sipping as she went.

Beth knew her disappointed intentions but wanted to stay a moment longer. She looked up at her father as her mother left the room, reading his passing thoughts. He was tired, the stress tracing each radiating line from his eyes to his furrowed brow. She drew his contemplative gaze and told him what she could with her own, that everything was going to be just fine. He smiled at her and nodded. He knew she was right, it was the road there that was unwelcome at the moment. She got up from the table and left resisting every urge to actualize her hate and strike her mother as she passed by on the way to her room.

Carl sat alone for a time working through the muddle, hoping to find the path least clogged with brambles. There wasn't one, doubt pervaded every turn. Of only one thing was he sure, he needed to get this over with and quickly. With that he pushed himself from the table and joined his wife in the living room, buoyed by the reassurance from his daughter.

"Where were you last night?"

"Driving. Thinking," she answered, never breaking focus from her hands clasping the mug of coffee.

A literal path it was to be, "So what happened at the rink?"

"You know what happened."

She assumed he did, having spent all day with the kids and with plenty of time for them to regale him with every nuance their perspectives offered. It was an unkind thing, she not around to defend herself. But she knew she did that to herself, disappearing for so long, still confused whether it was with intent or simply out of the need for privacy with herself. Either way, she saw little need to flesh out the details, for the moment.

"I know what happened to the boys but not much else."

"There's not much else to tell."

Listening to her evade her own account he couldn't help think she was behaving much like you'd expect a troubled child. She never met his gaze, staring incessantly at her hands instead, her voice low, stern, barely more interested than a monotone. It was an abject display, one on which he was having trouble finding a handle.

"Okay, let's try this a different way, can you tell me what happened at the rink, as an interested parent?"

"I told you, there isn't much to tell."

"Oh, c'mon Lily, you can do better than that," he stood over her scolding.

"Don't take that tone with me."

Backing off he sat in the chair opposite, feeling foolish. She was still disarming, even in her childlike obstinacy, and it annoyed him, not because she could do it but, rather like Pavlov's dog, he was so well-heeled. It was a true struggle for him to swallow the apology fighting to escape his lips.

Searching his mind he looked for another way around. There wasn't one, or at least one he was able to find before they were interrupted by the boys creeping down the stairs. They moved slowly, eyes wide in the shadow, inspecting the two of them as they made their way off the final step. With Cary still lingering at the bottom Andy edged toward his father and whispered a good morning. He quietly returned it while the boy was scrutinizing his mother, uncertain whether to speak or slink away. Before he had to decide she got up and went to the stair, intent on her room. As she gained the first step Cary reached out hugging her tight. Her eyes glistening in the dull light, she looked down at him, he up at her.

"You're okay," he said burying his head in her robe.

She brushed his hair with her hand, "I'm fine."

He let her go and she hurriedly climbed the rest of the stairs. He watched her ascent before turning his attention back toward his father and brother. Doing so he noticed the snow through a crack spread in the window curtain behind them and his eyes widened.

"Snow!" he exclaimed rushing past and pushing the curtains open.

It wasn't much but it covered the ground and that was all that mattered. Joining him at the window Andy and he together marveled at the sight. Debating whether it was enough to slide on, to make a snowman or have a snowball fight of one thing they were sure, it was enough to make snow angels. There was always enough for that no matter how little snow fell. Carl listened as they imagined all they would do, plotting the course of their day, carefree in their singular purpose.

"Not before breakfast boys," he winked, "so let's get you something to eat."

The twinkle was back in his eye, the flourish of the first snow reinforced by the boy's exuberance. He herded them into the kitchen, Audrey sneaking behind. She pulled Cary into a bear hug, he shrieked, she laughed. Andy came to his defense but she tickled him until he fled to the other side of the table. Carl chuckled, noisily taking the cereal bowls from the cupboard, the silverware from the drawer, Beth joining him having followed Audrey down. The clamor and chatter echoed through the house where, reaching the upstairs, it died away, lonely.

Carl saw the boys outside after they had breakfast and changed into their clothes. It was a chore getting them to don the winter gear, especially Cary who had a new aversion to boots. Despite the appropriate weather at last, his reticence was built on the permanence of ridicule. The moment was fleeting, his boots crunching the wet snow just outside the door an auditory reminder to his soul. Hitting the yard the boys took a giant leap and fell to the ground on their backs each working a snow angel so perfect it was an envy to the heavens. Carl watched from the stoop until they chased him back inside with a barrage of snowballs, the last ricocheting off the closing door and breaking apart in the living room. It was indeed first snow.

He returned to the kitchen where he put the kettle on for the three of them, Beth and Audrey still at the table chatting. He quietly moved about, surprised the two had conversation at all, let alone such that wasn't dripping with sarcasm, spite and disgust. It was a day brimming with firsts, he mused, blithely ignoring Lily's retreat which was still scratching at the back of his head.

Their talk died away as he put a mug in front of each and joined them at the table. They sat, staring at the coffee, he feeling a bit of regret he broke up their discussion, they lost in their own thoughts of their mother's withdrawal. Audrey only knew she'd returned, Beth having time enough to tell her that much after she awoke and before they all gathered downstairs. From there she knew nothing, neither where she'd been nor that she'd already had an exchange with their father. Looking at him and marking his tired visage, she covered his hand with her own, obliged to help.

"Dad, I think you should go talk to mom."

Beth got up from the table, speciously watching the boys from the window. The scene was suddenly nauseating. She didn't know if it was Audrey's actions, their discussion the night before, the overwhelming urge to hit her mother or the discomfort of her father. What she did know was she wanted her mother gone. Carl watched her, her feelings barely disguised, knowing there was a part of him sharing that grief.

He sighed, "Yeah, I'm just giving her a little time."

"It'll be fine," she said tapping his hand.

Beth smugly rolled her eyes, having earlier and in her mind more meaningfully dispensed the same encouragement. Carl noted it as well and thought how funny it was that identical words or actions can convey distinctly different messages depending on who delivers them and how invested they are in the recipient. In this case, fairly or not, he had little faith in the message, or the messenger.

"Well," he answered pulling his hand back, "I better go then."

Slowly and deliberately climbing the stairs he made his way down the hall to their bedroom, hesitant in his mission, wary of his likely reception. Inching his way in when he reached the door, the room cloaked in darkness, the curtains still drawn, he found Lily laying in bed, her back to the room. Creeping inside a few inches more he stopped and loitered near the door, fearful she was asleep. He could hear her breathing in the stillness, not quite shallow enough for his wife who was ever gentle, remarkably tender and feminine as she slept. It was the same with everything she did. In truth, he believed she was the most feminine woman he'd ever known, a sure part of the attraction.

"Close the door," she ordered, breaking his regard.

He did as she asked, shutting out what little light remained. His eyes not yet accustomed to the gloom, he could scarcely see her shadow as she sat upright. Still waiting near the door he slid down, using it to prop against rather than make any move toward her.

"So," he whispered in the dark, "are we ready to talk?"

"I guess," she answered softly, all she had to offer at first. But with the silence multiplying she sought to fill the void, "What are we going to do Carl?"

"I'm not sure I follow," he replied, the question sufficiently broad from his view of the last few days in the Kane household.

"I'm not happy, you're not happy. We're struggling."

He took it in for a moment, "Well I was happy up until a few days ago."

"No you weren't," she corrected, "you were oblivious." She paused to collect her tired wayward thoughts, careful to parse her words. "You live through routine, it's who you are, and the routine of this family gives you comfort and as long as it's not upset too much everything is alright with you. You have simple needs, but that's not who I am."

"Okay," he replied blankly.

"No, it's not okay," she warned him, "nothing is okay."

He felt uneasy, her thoughts incomplete, almost randomly general. "Well what gives you comfort then?" was the only question that came to mind.

"I don't know, but it's not this."

He searched for a certainty on which to balance the conversation but found nothing. Over the last few days her erratic demonstrations, in his case remonstrations, had come with increasing frequency. Worse still, they all seemed to search for and then miss the mark which made it all the more confusing. And in direct point of fact she was, in his estimation, the one who lived for routine, her life a rote rehearsal while she waited for something. Just what it was he wasn't sure but she always seemed to be in anticipation. Besides, this wasn't the conversation they were supposed to be having and he was beginning to get impatient.

"Lily, I'm not understanding."

She was sure he wouldn't which is why she'd been putting this off for so very long. It was difficult to explain what she had little understanding of herself. Her mind was conscious of a larger burden she carried but the details of that burden eluded her, for much of her life for all she could recall.

"Okay, take the rink the other night, I didn't know what to do."

"Then why don't we start there and you can tell me what happened?"

"No, you don't understand," she responded earnestly, "what happened doesn't matter. What matters is that I didn't know what to do, so I did nothing." She hesitated then whispered, "And I hate you for that."

He gasped, catching an acerbic retort just on the edge of his tongue. He swallowed it bitterly, the taste like bile. Reminding himself again of her capricious behavior of late he knew the better course was trod lightly.

"Well, let's start with that – why?"

"Because you always know what to do."

"Not always."

"Always. And I get pushed into the background. Always."

He found her self-pity loathsome. She was taking an unfortunate event in the children's lives, an ongoing one for the boys, an improbably embarrassing one for her, and was not surprisingly again turning the spotlight on herself. So often she climbed that cross he wondered she didn't just stay up there. Perhaps, he thought, it was time he finally nailed her in place.

"Lily, I'm still not following."

"Whenever the kids have a problem, large or small, they come to you. They don't ask for my help. When I try to offer it's like they're suspicious of me, like I'm going to do them more harm than good."

"Don't you think you kind of conditioned them that way?"

"No, you did, always swooping in and making everything seem so much better."

"And that's not good?" he questioned smartly.

"Not when it's at my expense, when I'm trying to be the one that helps."

He considered this for a moment. "But Lily, you never want to help. It's like you've always got one foot out the door around here."

"Only because you're pushing me out."

"I don't know, you've at least got your hand on the knob."

They tasted the silence, alive with the unspoken. Each retreated to their corner to consider knowing the import of their next exchange. It was as uncomfortable a moment as either could recall living through together.

"Carl," she quietly confessed, trying to ease the tension, "I don't know what to do."

"About what?"

"This. Us. Everything."

He sighed unevenly, "Are you leaving?"

"I don't know, sometimes I think it would be for the best."

"For you of course."

She was stunned by the remark, thinking he'd finally understood what she was saying. "How dare you, no."

"Oh, this isn't about you?"

"Have you heard a damn thing I've said?"

"Apparently not."

"Yeah, apparently not, as always," she nearly shouted. Calming herself, she followed in a low voice, "I was embarrassed."

She felt him move to speak a couple of times only to cut his own words short.

"Sometimes I think to leave because I'm not good for the kids. It's like at the rink. I wanted to help and I wanted to say something but I didn't know how. I didn't know what to say. And then I suddenly felt embarrassed. And not just for them but for me. For a moment I saw them the way others see them and it's not fair. I want to be a good mother and a good person and see past it but I just don't know how." She paused, then continued, "And I don't even know how I got here. It's like I've been asleep for so long and now all of a sudden I realize where I am and I don't like it. And I don't even know how I got here. One minute I'm a girl and the next I've got four kids and I'm old. And just so very tired. And lonely. And I don't know how I got this way. And I don't know what to do," she trailed off.

Despite her scattered thoughts his mind first stuck on the loneliness. It was a deep regret, he knew she was lonely, had been since they met. He remembered how his comfort at first seemed to do her good bringing a sparkle to her eye, then it was just as quickly gone again. He knew the birth of Audrey and the death of her parents had shaken her, yet was sure her withdrawal started long before then, maybe even before they began making their lives together. The coming of Beth seemed to renew her vigor, give her a sense of purpose, only that too faded away. From then on she seemed to settle into a sort of resignation, an apathy he fought but to which he in the end became accustomed. Finally in time he forgot how to comfort her, and gave up trying.

Then his thoughts returned to their children and her embarrassment. He too saw for a fleeting moment what others saw when they looked at the kids, perhaps even themselves. It disturbed him as well but in the end there was no question of looking past for him. There was nothing for which he felt ashamed, nothing for which he should, and nothing for which she should either. Despite the open wound he was having a hard time finding sympathy for her, at least on this.

"Do you understand Carl?"

"I guess."

"So what am I to do?"

"I don't know." He pushed himself off the door and sat cross-legged, staring into the emptiness. "Do you regret it all that much? I mean us, the kids?"

"You asked me that the other night." She thoughtfully considered her words, "Look, I think the best I can say is yes, there are things I regret. I don't want to be poor. I'm so tired of the struggle, so very, very tired. And I'm embarrassed - for me, the kids, for you. I want everyone to have all the wonderful things in the world to make their hurt go away but I can't give it to them. And I'm tired of being angry at you and blaming you and not even knowing why or how to stop feeling that way. And sometimes, all the time really, I regret me. I so want to be funny and pleasing and captivating and warm. And I want to be a good mother, but I don't know how to do any of those things, and I hate me for it. And I hate me for feeling ashamed." She began to trail off again but before doing so she quietly added, "And that's why I hate you sometimes, you're all those good things without even trying."

He watched her through the darkness.

"And so do I regret us? No, as hard as it is I think it would be even harder to leave. I just want the shame to go away. And I want you to help me."

She began to weep, ever so softly, the cool and composed years of existence broken. He wanted nothing more than to sit opposite her on the bed, take her hands in his and let her cry. She needed it and in many ways deserved it, his failure to be a good friend, in spite of all his virtuousness in her eyes, and his walking away from her through the years helping build the mess he saw in front of him. But he couldn't, she needed to find her way alone. The miasmic wall she'd built around herself would have to come down brick by brick and only she could do that and not just for herself, for their children. It was her duty to them, he could be of little help, and if she failed even then he knew there was little he could do. He was just thankful she was still here.

13.

Sunday came into the Kane household riding a cold north wind. It was late November, just days before Thanksgiving, and Mother Nature extended her icy grip on the landscape. The snow failed to completely melt away instead leaving delicate traces deep beneath the grass and tucked in corners where the weak autumn rays failed to reach. Now unpleasant, it was no good to play in, not worthy of admiration. It was little more than the initial layer of permafrost, the first to acquaint itself with the land, the last to bid its farewell in spring. In its essence it was tolerated, little more.

Still reticent, Lily moved about the house with purpose, when she did. She otherwise took care to avoid the accusing stares, the bewildered and questioning faces with which she was sure the children would greet her if she tarried too long, or even looked up. She was not yet ready to explain anything to them, unsure as she was in her own wisdom and in her own self. They stayed clear as much as they could, observing her discomfort with stolen glances from afar. That was true of everyone but Cary.

He'd heard her come in during those early morning hours, he being the only one for all he knew. Too young to fully understand the idea of her not coming back of her own accord, he'd tossed most of the night in worry something more awful had come of her. So it was with immense relief that he heard the front door open and recognized her footsteps through the living room and up the stairs. He could finally put his head down, sleep would come. But it remained elusive, an uncertain anxiety stealing the blessed dreams he thought had been granted with her return. In those troubled hours his mind remained overwrought with concepts he couldn't explain, of foreboding changes, fears of loss. As a result he'd done his best to keep her in his view, to know her every move, since she'd come back home.

Lily felt his scrutiny. She heard his footsteps on the landing when she was in her room, caught him peeking from his own when she went downstairs. Everywhere she turned he was there, if not seen then felt. It was welcome. His greeting the morning before, the benevolence with which it was delivered, the genuine comfort he took from knowing she was well, did more to console her spirit than she could have imagined. Probably more than he could have imagined as well for she had come within a breath, a misplaced word, an ill-conceived moment, of walking from the house hoping never to return. To where she would have gone she didn't know. Of one thing she was sure, none would have missed her, or so she believed.

She heard the return of his stocking feet stop just outside her door as she folded laundry, an absentminded chore easy to pass the time while Carl was out getting some groceries with what little money was left in the late month's budget. He seemed to be tracing a wide path, coming from his room and returning, briefly listening by the door as he passed. When he'd shuffled off to his room again she crept over thinking at first she'd surprise him, give him a playful fright, but when within a few minutes he was back waiting outside where she imagined his ear pressed lightly against the wood she thought better of the game instead cracking the door a touch as he walked off. She heard him hasten the pace back to his bedroom. Swinging it wide she peeked her head around just as he turned the corner.

"Cary?"

There was no response. "Cary?" she repeated.

"Yes, mom?"

She could see he was just inside his own door, his shadow a betrayal. "Can you come here a minute?" she asked, pretending a serious tone.

"Okay."

He crept from his room and made his way toward her, denying eye contact as best he could. She invited him in to which he agreed, reluctantly.

"Where's your brother?"

"He went with dad."

"Oh? Why didn't you go?"

He deigned not to speak. Sensing his unease she let it go unanswered. "No matter, I wanted to talk to you anyway. Go ahead, sit there on the bed."

He climbed up, legs dangling with no hope of reaching the floor. He couldn't recall ever sitting up here, leastways since being much younger when it was still okay to cry out with nightmares and rush headlong into their room. He missed those days, a lifetime ago he felt.

She didn't know how to begin, making amends not something to which she was terribly accustomed. She was also little practiced in having meaningful conversation with her children, any children for that matter. She decided to start slowly, ease into it gently.

"So, are you okay?"

"Yeah, I guess," he replied, thinking she meant in the immediate here and now.

"Well that's good then."

She watched him for a moment, keen on assessing his reaction. There was none, he simply sat staring at his feet, swinging them back and forth. Suddenly and strangely self-conscious, she turned away and began to fuss with the laundry, folding and refolding the same shirt, the same pants, before satisfying herself and picking up another garment. She wondered if he noticed her discomfort, if it made him want to leave, if he was puzzled, speculating, sitting in judgment. It was unpleasant, it was silly, she knew it was both. But the more she thought of it the more true it became and the wider the gap between them and before she could fill it she was left with several piles of neatly folded clothes and an empty basket. She turned it upside down, folding her arms on top, leaning heavily, and hesitated.

"Can I help?" he asked, seeing anything but his stocking feet for the first time.

She recomposed herself, trying her best to push the peculiar thoughts away. "No, no, I'm done." She turned to face him, "You sure you're okay?"

He smiled at her, "I'm fine mom," then asking, "are you?"

She returned his smile, "Yes, I'm fine."

"Good."

They sat quietly again, he swinging his feet, she fidgeting with the buttons of her sweater as she knelt in front of him. She went to start again but failed to find her voice, her odd mood stealing the words before they could settle. Sensing another difficult lull developing that could take away her resolve she at last confided in him.

"You know, I'm sorry about the other night."

"Don't worry mom, you're home now, right?" he inquired thinking she meant the immediate night before and frightened she wouldn't be forever, or even for very long.

"Oh no, not about that. I mean, I'm sorry for that too, especially since it made you worry. No, I meant for, well, not being much help the other night at the rink."

"Oh." He looked down and started swinging his legs again.

As she watched him, her discomfort blunted by the apology finally delivered, the unnatural youthfulness and timidity of the boy worried her. Looking and acting so awfully young she wondered how he was ever going to stand up to the world and demand his own, take what he was rightfully due. More than that, how was he ever to climb from the humble beginnings of being a Kane and shout to the world that he was here, and he mattered? She just couldn't see him leaving the entombment this little town imposed on a certain percentage of its population, most often the poorer among them. She'd been watching for years the more affluent, more mobile young residents leave for more lucrative endeavors with a little push and seed money from mom and dad. They went far and wide, leaving their mark, diffident of their small town roots. Then as they got a little older they'd return with their own children having married someone exotic, someone who grew up out there and found their hometown quaint, just as they now did. Filled with this misguided nostalgia they'd lead their young families through the small haunts they remembered as a child and as a teen. It was all innocent fun, so many years ago, and the tour bus would plod on and they'd leave thinking what a wonderful time they'd had of it all. And all the while it was people like the Kanes who were for generations left behind to ensure they had their Frank Capra moments by keeping the general store open, the sandwich shop serving their BLT, hot coffee and muffin while they pretended not to recognize the person behind the counter who was either too kind or too ashamed to point out the error in front of their handsome smiling children. This is what she feared as she watched him swinging his legs, knowing he just didn't have the conceit to be recognized, and to tell them all to go to Hell.

"Well," she started, finding her voice again, wary of continuing for both their sake,"what do you say we leave this laundry here and go downstairs for a cup of coffee, just you and me?"

"Okay," he answered enthusiastically.

He was glad the conversation with his mother had come to an end. It seemed an unwanted subject, she no more comfortable delivering the apology than he was in its acceptance. Besides, he'd survive, had much worse to now, and so would she. He was just happy everyone was treating him like a man with all the coffee they were offering of late. Pretty soon he thought he might demand it as a part of his breakfast, the start of a definite morning routine, or maybe even after dinner. It was still a little bitter to his taste but with enough sugar it was as good as anything he could imagine.

Carl and Andy arrived back home early in the afternoon stirring Beth from her slumber. She'd been alternating between reading and sleep, a good measure of thought distracting her from both. It was an adventure story, heroes and heroines, travel and travail, death and glory. It wasn't her usual fare but in going into it that was the point. She didn't imagine there would be much depth, and there wasn't, so she could read along with little effort and even less consequence if she found her mind drifting from the page every now and again. Unfortunately what it did have was an exotic locale from an author who, despite many faults, was quite magnificent in her ability to transport the reader halfway around the world and make them believe it was the most wonderful and fascinating place they could ever hope to see and more so since so few had. Dangerous in its innocence, resplendently rundown, abandoned and united, it had appeal, it was sexy, and it was reinforcing her desire to flee, to there or anywhere. Reading it she felt so very small.

Wandering downstairs she was ill-tempered yet hopeful her father brought something home to fill the hole in her belly. She hadn't eaten much over the last day, hiding in her room preferable to a chance meeting with her mother. There also hadn't been much in the cupboards when she found her way to the kitchen in the late night hours. Reaching there now her hope was little effected, the couple of bags meaning necessities, nothing more. There would be no snacking unless she was willing to cook something and by unwritten Kane rules that meant making enough for others to enjoy as well. Turning on her heel once more she climbed the stairs trying to find a measure of content in the return to elsewhere.

Stepping around the clothes strewn about she cut a path to her bed, the idea of continuing to hide doing her outlook few favors. Adding to the misery she felt she was on the verge of bed sores, every corner of her body aching from laying so long. There was little choice, her mother suddenly more active as they moved deeper into the day and she with nowhere to go. Making herself as comfortable as she could she picked her book up again trying to find where she left off. Before she could delve back in there was a gentle knock at the door where, opening slowly, she watched her dad poke his head around the edge.

"Can I come in?"

"You already have."

She scolded herself, the snark unwarranted. She really needed to remember who the enemy was in this farce and reserve the persecution for them alone. He ignored it anyway, surprisingly light in his smile and step. She felt less badly now, his mood not quite the antidote she sought.

"I brought something for you." Sitting on the bed next to her he pulled a large fruit and nut chocolate bar from behind his back. "Don't tell anyone."

She took it thanking him and attempting to look pleased. It was a poor fit.

Watching her struggle to neatly tear the wrapper he noticed her hair. "It looks real pretty, what did you do?"

She ran her fingers through surprised to discover from Friday it still had life and, especially startling, had so even though she hadn't showered since. Whatever her sister had done she would have to pay much closer attention in future because it really was nicely buoyant and resilient when you considered.

"Thanks dad. Do you want a piece?" she asked finally finding it open without losing any of it on her bed.

"Maybe a small one, just a couple of blocks," he replied in a hushed tone as though the secret between them was of dramatic importance.

"Okay," she whispered dryly, mocking him less with intent than disposition.

She handed him the two blocks, broken yet still secure in the gold foil. They contented themselves with the sweet treasure, she gobbling it down before it had the chance to tickle her tongue, he reducing it to its essence of raisins and almonds before swallowing. She could hear his suckling noises, drawing the chocolate from in and around a nut, smacking his lips together before the final crunch as he broke it apart. Though his mastications were annoying, and completely uncouth, she refrained from rebuking him.

"It's good," he opined.

She nodded. It was almost too good, her hunger greater than her empty stomach could reasonably accommodate. Wrapping the foil back around the bar she put it on the edge of the dressing table and slid back toward the wall. Despite what she saw as an obvious ploy for her time, her dad's company wasn't altogether unwelcome even providing a nice break from her own head and besides, she was curious how his talk with her mother had come off. She surmised rather good based on his elevated mood though she knew full well an act, a well-crafted one, was frequently so much more convincing than reality that the pretenders themselves often had trouble distinguishing between the two. Sharing a room with Audrey it was a lesson she knew well.

"So, how did it go with mother yesterday?"

He finished chewing. "Well, with your *mom*," he didn't like Beth's calling her by the objective, "it went okay I guess. I think she's just, you know, a little overwhelmed right now."

She thought about it, her mother a little overwhelmed, and wondered how? She worked part time, her duties with the children ending in the morning, dinner being the exception, and then she was sitting alone in the kitchen or off to her room for the evening. She neither listened, conversed, played, soothed, tended or had otherwise anything whatsoever to do with them. The same was likely true of her husband, the lot little more than cogs in a machine, albeit a broken one in her estimation. So with all that, or better, without all that, how could she possibly be overwhelmed? The question was really more analytical, in some ways amusing, than much else for as hard as she tried to get her anger up in the end it fell flat; she just didn't care. If her mother was overwhelmed with what little she had to do around here then she couldn't possibly be of less interest to her. On the other hand, as she thought about it, what was of interest was how her father ever found the fish a suitable mate.

"So dad, how, or why, did you ever meet and get married to her?"

"Don't forget, without her you wouldn't be here," he smartly replied.

"Please, I would've just squeezed out somewhere else."

He chuckled, "Yeah, maybe."

"Or not at all. Either way's good."

His levity vanished, "Don't."

He stared intently at her, she looked away and began playing with her fingernails. He found it odd how she always went to the fingers, something Lily used to do all the time, still did, only now she thought it was in secret. Becoming cognizant of her tells she tried hiding them when she could. It only led to more, her stiffness as the tension built the most obvious. He supposed you couldn't hide a thing like that, nervousness and stress will naturally manifest itself in some other way. It has to, otherwise it just builds and builds until it consumes and leaves nothing but a smoldering black hole where your life used to be. Now that he thought about it, he better let Lily know it was just fine with him if she wanted to chew her nails.

"Well?"

"Oh, right, how we met. Well it was right here of course. Our dads, your grandfathers, used to be friends. Your grandmothers too but really it was between her dad and mine. He used to come over and have a few beers, sit by the fire. Dad always had a fire, right deep into the fall really. Boy," he leaned back on the pillow with his arms folded behind his head, "I used to love that. My room was the one your mother and I are in so I was right there next to the backyard." He paused as if considering for the first time, "You know, I guess I've never left that room. Anyway, he'd always send me off to bed early and I'd lay there listening to them talk. I was just a kid of course. But it was nice even if I couldn't understand all they were saying. Well, as I got a little older I didn't have to go to bed so early so I'd sit there with them, just drinking pop of course." He winked at her but she failed to notice. "And then eventually I saw her, your mom. Do you know she'd been coming for years and I just didn't know? Really.

She was coming and just staying in the house with your grandmas and not saying a word. You'd never have known she was there. I suppose I must have seen her at some point and not paid any attention but you know for the life of me I don't remember. She does. She says I saw her but heck, I was a goofy kid anyway."

Beth wanted to rush him, get the story moving to the more interesting parts, she just couldn't bring herself to interrupt. He was rapt with his own story, dreaming almost, and in its way it was enrapturing to her as well because she'd heard so little of him as a boy. Kind of queer she thought, most kids can recite their parent's tales of what it was like to be young as if they were memories of their own. She laid down next to him as he continued, the warmth as soothing as his voice.

"Well, when I finally noticed her, when I remember noticing her, we were sixteen and my goodness was she beautiful. Sad to say but that's all I remember seeing, she just looked so, well, stunning really. We were all sitting by the fire and she comes walking up and stands there just staring at it, doesn't say a word. I look over at dad and he says to me to offer Lily a seat. Here it was I thought she was some new girl in the neighborhood or something, kind of brash you know, just walking up like that, but he knows her name. Anyway, that's how we met, right here."

"Lust at first sight then?"

"Hey, that's not fair, I'm just telling you how we met."

"Sorry," she murmured, herself offended by her own worst tendencies. "So how does that lead to getting married?"

He pondered the question for a moment, aware her opinion of Lily already low and not wanting to subtract further. It was a hard question to answer, not just because of her other failed suitors, in truth a failure pinned on her, rightfully or not, but because the story of his own past had been changing with the increasingly strange statements coming from Lily herself. Whether she was rewriting her history, his, or theirs, he didn't know. Perhaps she was just fleshing out their story, bringing the uncomfortable facets he'd forgotten back into focus, that his own history wasn't quite as he remembered it and by deduction neither was theirs. Somehow he didn't think that was the case. He had a nagging suspicion she was rewriting it to suit some need of her own.

"Well, after that night I kind of chased her a bit. Of course I tried to be cool about it, not sure if I was or not. But I started making sure she was coming over and then tried to look nice and all and went in the house to make sure she came out by the fire. But you know how it is?"

Sadly, not quite, she thought as he spoke.

"So I started getting her out on other nights, mostly just walking and talking. Neither of us had much money you see and being a small town, well, I don't have to tell you. So we did a lot of walking, I did a lot of talking. She never said much on those walks. It was so hard to get anything out of her even if it was about nothing at all. She was kind of like you, you know?" he looked over at her mistakenly grinning as he spoke.

"You can leave any time," she responded coldly.

"Aw, don't take it like that."

"Like what? Insulting me as I lay here indulging your tale of impending fatherhood?"

"What does that mean?"

She groaned, never an answer, an explanation, just another question. Even if her own were more rhetorical statements than actual queries it didn't matter, it was the intent he should have understood. She tried to let it go but could feel the warmth of the moment slipping away. She mourned its passing, even as she pushed.

"Come on dad, you've been married seventeen years, Audrey's seventeen. It isn't like your anniversary's nine months before."

"What, you think that's why we got married?"

"Isn't it?"

Sitting up and feeling twice stung, he lashed out before he collected his thoughts, "You know, sometimes you are just like your mother."

She pounced on the confession making more of it than the intent allowed. "So she's of the same opinion then, since we're so alike?"

He was struck dumb. His miscalculations of his daughter, their talk, her capacity for verbal violence, bleeding evident. He stormed toward the door, turned to speak, thought better of himself, and left the room closing the door roughly behind.

She watched it for a long time afterward hoping he would come back through giving her a moment to explain, to apologize, anything. He didn't come back, the door remained closed, nothing but silence on the other side.

She really was her own worst enemy, the impediment to her own happiness, and she was every day becoming more aware. She rolled over and faced the wall, suddenly cold.

14.

By Wednesday night the Kane household was ready to let go a collective sigh of relief. They had survived the week, ready for a long Thanksgiving weekend and the chance to recover some energy for the final push through the holiday season. Never an easy time of year, they recounted their losses, of family and conflict, of finance and security, of needs yet unmet and wants left unfulfilled. It was time to reflect on the year past, grow morose for the one to come. Worse still, it was a season that provided daily reminders they lived in a land of plenty as every house on the block blossomed with brightly lit decorations beckoning with warmth and the sweet smell of delicacies, friends, new and old, loved ones, and family. But in a world that seemed to want for little they were ever left wanting for much. It was with near empty cupboards, an all but barren tree and empty promise they decorated the house and rang in the New Year. Still, they had each other for another year and that counted for something.

It did most for Carl who was busy much of the week brooding over his battles with Lily and Beth, both losses of one degree or another in his mind. With Beth it was plain, she'd scorned him in a place he was oddly vulnerable and with a malevolence he hadn't anticipated. Yet he should have, so like her mother he had little reason to be surprised. It was nagging him and for the very reason he considered his troubles with Lily a loss, both were introducing an uncertainty to his life from a corner he thought secure. He was used to a level of ambivalence from the world at large, even from Audrey at times, but these were people who had a vested interest in him, and he in they, for it was family, the only possession to which he thought he could lay firm claim.

Occupied with these reflections he stepped outside for his late evening cigarette, Lily busy making an apple pie and preparing the turkey for the next day's meal. Normally refreshed by the rush of cool air on his face, the last days of nervous tension had left him feeling perpetually cold, an ache introduced to the marrow. He shivered as he stood watching the darkness, the icy mist of his breath suspended, enveloping him, the blue smoke of his tobacco swirling and forming a corona with each exhale. It was quiet, his only company a small animal poking around in the leaves on the other side of the road. He was otherwise alone, himself his sole companion.

And so his mind wandered, forgetting the cold, forgetting the morrow, the petty squabbles, the childish rants and the darkness. Unfettered and free it carved its own winding path through his psyche connecting the disconnected, scratching the surface and plumbing the depths. He thought of books, of grasshoppers and farmers, postcards and Chicago, optimists, Hitler, the illiterate, the infirm, the old and the young. He thought about music for a time puzzling over the mathematics involved, pyramids and the supreme balance of geometry, and questioned what the Hell quantum physics was anyway? He imagined how the land must have looked before man, the enormity of the fish, the grandeur of the trees, the sheer size of mosquito swarms feeding on critters in the swamps of Pangaea with no hand around to squash the little bastards dead. Speculating about Christians he wondered if the person who made the nails that hammered Jesus in place knew how they were used? Perhaps he believed they were destined to build shelter for the poor, a wide shelf, sturdy furniture, or construct a brothel to serve weary soldiers on the march. Was he horrified and saddened to know or could he have ever known? Would he have cared anyway, looking to the sky only to decide whether or not it was good beach weather? And why should he care? Did it alter his reality, was his perspective changed one bit as he used those earnings to buy bread for his family, pay tax to the Romans, or invite a whore to share his bed? Why should it, did he not wake to the same aches he had the day before, the same hunger, the same wants and needs and unfulfilled dreams? And what of the Atheist, was he feeling as lonely today as the first person who proposed a divine guidance once did? Were they both dreamers or were they pragmatists, the smartest of their time or the dumbest? And did they feel as lonely as he did now, standing on his stoop, shivering alone in the dark without a clever answer to offer himself, his sole companion?

He bid the animal still rustling in the leaves across the road a good night and returned to the house, a sniffle tickling the end of his nose. Hanging his jacket he wandered into the kitchen where Lily was pinching the lid on her apple pie. She looked up briefly and smiled, returning to the task without concern. He put the kettle on, a bit late for coffee but knowing his mind would have no rest regardless. Besides, if it was going to aimlessly wander it may as well have a stimulating companion. He chuckled to himself thinking that may be the cleverest thought he'd had all night.

Sitting to sip his coffee, still deeply considering his own loneliness, he failed to notice a concerned Lily pause to stare at the ever so slight tremble in her fingers, a disconcerting reminder of the anxiety through which she was living. He couldn't have seen that Andy and Cary were upstairs busy puzzling over their ability to make it through the previous three days at school without incident and, though elated, growing more disconsolate the further they questioned their good fortune knowing retribution was sure to come. Nor could he have known across the hall Beth was stuck in her own maze, alone, still seeking the appropriate apology to offer her father, her inability to find the words and stubborn defiance blocking every turn. And making her way home, tracing a slow path to the front door through the cold, Audrey embracing the rare gift of a moment to herself, away from her life as a whirlwind of necessity and action, of constant display and coquettish performance.

Lily set the timer for the oven and left Carl to himself. It was some time before he recognized his coffee had cooled off, that he was alone, the steady beat of the analog timer like a metronome, his leg keeping an unconscious beat. Bemusedly reacquainting his mind with the surroundings he reached for the tobacco drawer and, despite the chill, returned to the stoop for a smoke. He saw Audrey standing at the end of the walk, seemingly oblivious to his presence, in quiet reflection, watching her own breath as it escaped her lips in wispy vapors.

"Isn't it an awesome sight dad? Millions and millions of stars snaking their way to oblivion. And we're just one in a variety, of no particular importance, our lives as obscure and meaningless as any other, a singular nothingness."

She stretched her arms to the heavens, whimsically spun on her heel and strode the path toward him. He watched her approach, dumbstruck by the acuity of her observation. She sat down on the stoop, inviting him to do the same, aware she'd just thrown him off balance. It pleased her. He clumsily started to roll his cigarette, neither of them with a desire to chase the darkness by turning on the light. As he finally managed to pull it together she shamelessly snatched it from him.

"Now roll one for yourself," she directed brazenly putting the cigarette between her lips.

"Give that back, you don't smoke."

"No," she laughed, "but I'm going to have one with you anyway."

"But your mother will kill me."

"Maybe, but right now I'm the only woman you need to worry about."

There was some merit in that, he observed to himself. With reluctance he rolled another and put it between his lips. Looking around to be sure there were no lurkers behind the windows he lit a match, first lighting hers then his own. They together took the smoke deeply into their lungs. With certainty he observed this was not her first cigarette, she took no precaution to pretend it was. He resolved it best to just ignore the fact.

"So why are you home so early?"

"I don't know. I guess I just wanted some time to myself."

He took another puff. She did the same, trying to blow smoke rings as she exhaled but with no particular success. He shook his head and looked away.

"I didn't know you liked to look at the stars."

"Sure," she said.

"Well how come you never sat with me before?"

"You never asked," she replied simply.

"Well, still."

"Dad," she playfully nudged him, "I know this is your alone time."

"I reckon."

They leaned back, quietly watching the stars. He thought again of her keen observation on the universe, the singularity of a life. It was akin to his own thoughts on countless nights as he alone pondered the sky. Only now he wasn't feeling so isolated, nor quite so cold as before.

Audrey leaned forward, "So you see right there, just poking up over the hill?" She pointed to the horizon, the amber glow of her cigarette leading the way. "Well that's Andromeda, the constellation. The galaxy is part of it too of course."

"You know the constellations?"

"Sure."

"I never did learn those."

"It's easy. Well, not always. Some nights like this one it gets hard because there are so many stars out."

"You'll have to teach me sometime. I can't do more than the big dipper."

"Sure. But just so you know," she reduced her voice to a whisper, "the big dipper isn't a constellation."

"No?" he questioned with a titter, "shows what your dad knows."

"Aw, you know lots," she laughed as she put her arm in his and snuggled into his shoulder.

"Yeah, maybe."

They finished their smokes in silence. She pulled away to snuff hers out before wrapping both arms around his and leaning on him. He enjoyed the warmth.

"So what are you going to do about Beth?" she asked glancing up at him in the dark.

He sighed, an unfortunate return to the problems waiting on the other side of the door. "So you know about that, huh?

"A little, but I don't need to know much."

In truth, she didn't know much, she had simply lived in the house long enough to intuit.

"Yeah, well I still don't know what to do."

"I think you do," she gently chided.

"What makes you so sure?"

"Because I know you, and I know her, now anyway. Took me a long time but I think I know a little something."

"Then please illuminate me."

"Well, I know there's no one in this house she has more affection for than you. I know that what you think of her means more than she's willing

151

to admit. I know she's an exceptionally stubborn girl. And I know she's upstairs right now tormented by whatever happened."

He sighed, "Then why do you think she lashed out at me like that?"

"Are you sure it was you she was lashing out at?"

He thought about it for a moment.

"How'd you get so wise?" he gave her a little nudge, marveling at how exotic and unpredictable was the young woman nestled into him.

"Aw, dad, you already knew all that. You just have too many things going on at once. I think you just need to pick them off one at a time."

"So are you gonna help with your mother next?"

"That one's all yours," she chuckled.

They stood up and readied themselves to go inside. He'd all but forgotten the cigarettes they just shared but remembered at the last.

"And not a word to your mother about me letting you have a cigarette," he said shaking his head, obligated to show he still disapproved.

"Not to worry, dad, I'll make sure I cover my breath so you don't get into trouble with mom."

"And hey, how come Beth has such a hard time with your mother?"

"Well, that's not really for me to say." She paused briefly, "But dad, be patient with her. It took a long time for me to learn that lesson. And you know she isn't going to be all hugs and kisses when you go up there so don't expect a whole lot. Just let her do what she does."

It was sage advice.

Lily was sitting at the kitchen table when they entered. She looked up and smiled while they wondered if she'd been listening in on their conversation. In the event they needn't be concerned, she was wrapped in her own thoughts unaware they were even outside. Audrey casually made her way to the cupboards to root for something to eat, and incidentally to cover her breath as promised. She found only Saltines, the usual fare, but tonight of no great consequence. Carl smiled back at his wife and made his way upstairs to the girl's room where he gently rapped on the door.

The aroma of roasting turkey saturated every corner of the house from early morning on Thanksgiving day. It was a scent to which Carl had never accustomed despite how fond he was of the taste. There was just something about baking skin and scorched flesh in such prolonged concentration that lay foul in his mouth and nostrils. It also tended to sting his eyes until they teared uncontrollably in an effort to sooth the irritation. As a result he spent most of the day outside doing odds and ends around the house. Busy work as usual, he accomplished little in a measurable sense but was able to wile away the hours with ease.

It was early afternoon when he heard a car pull up out front. He listened, not expecting guests and thinking it was another turnaround with their dead end location, until he heard a door close, the car still idling. Moseying around the side of the house he took a peek. He didn't recognize the vehicle, nor was anyone in sight. Reaching the front door he was met by Danny Senior coming back out.

"Ah, Carl," he gave him a couple pats on the shoulder as he hurried back to his car, "just stopped for two ticks, must be off. We'll be back later, me and the boy, so get that fire stoking out back. We'll bring some beer too." Then as he climbed into the car, "Oh, my missus will be coming, can't say for sure about Lois though."

With that he was gone, a confused Carl, unable to get even a word out, watching long after the car disappeared from sight. Thinking the whole thing queer he went inside.

"He dropped off a pie and a bottle of wine, a little Thanksgiving gift I guess," an equally perplexed Lily explained.

"And that was it?"

"Yes. Also that you had to get the fire going out back."

He smiled, she too, a little nostalgia at just the right moment.

He returned outdoors, glad to finally have work with purpose. His first chore was to resurrect the fire pit which had lain unused for a number of years. Really it meant little more than gathering the rocks that once circled the burned out hole. With that done the boys joined him in time for gathering wood, mostly kindling, before it gave way to play and they were off again. Piling up what he had alongside the old pit, including some larger logs he dragged out of the woods, he wasn't sure if the wood was dry enough knowing only it was plenty dead so he hoped it would do. If not the night's fire would be little more than burning branches and twigs, a poor substitute for the roaring warmth he remembered. Satisfied he'd done what he could he surveyed the work, only the chairs left to pull out of the shed. Audrey sauntered up and stood next to him, inspecting the work.

"Nice," she commended having looked the whole thing over. "We need to do this more often."

"Yeah," he agreed on both counts.

"Dinner's ready."

"Yeah?"

They turned and wound their way to the door kicking up the last of the leaves as they went and reminding Carl he intended to gather these few stragglers to fill a couple more bags to put around the house.

"Nice work with Beth by the way."

"Oh, you two talk?"

"No. Started to, then she fell right asleep, first time this week I think."

"Good." He was pleased, especially so since his presence was greeted rather coolly.

Thanksgiving dinner was delicious. The turkey moist, magnificent as it melted on the tongue, a rejoice for the palate, the potatoes light, the squash smooth, even the turnip sweet. Looking around the table at the quiet faces, their mouths stuffed to overflowing, the boys with an eye on the pies, he was delighted. His family together, friends to come, it was the rare day that seems to come together when you need it most. He mused it was the reason why everything was so delectable, an acrid taste reflected a sour mood while a cheerful and pleasant mood made food all the more enjoyable.

He knew he wasn't alone in his good feeling. Lily never raised an objection when he poured a glass of wine for the girls. She'd even been the first to propose a toast, to everyone's health, naturally. Though she and the girls weren't mixing much, neither were they avoiding one another in the same way they had over the past week. Of course his real hope was that it would last beyond the meal or even the day, but for now he was satisfied. If this was as good as it would get then it wasn't so bad after all. As to the boys, they were oblivious to everything anyway with only one thought on their mind, pie. It happens they used their lack of wine as an excuse to wangle a second piece after dinner. He was fairly confident they wouldn't have the room so saw no harm in consenting to the deal.

With dinner over, the table cleared, their stomachs settled, they sat down for coffee and desert. Lily was a little peeved when she discovered Danny had dropped off another apple pie. As hard as she tried, baking was never her strong suit in the kitchen, if she had one. Carl tried to make light of it by mixing the two up so they could have a taste test. Only the blind, and not even they, could fail to tell the two apart, her's always a little flatter, lumpier than an apple pie should be. As to taste, let's leave it that she was always well-intentioned when she baked. In the end it backfired, he and Audrey the only two votes in her corner. He suspected the boys didn't fully understand the point of game they were playing with their mother while with Beth, it was about the score. Lily goodnaturedly brushed it off pretending to revel in her two votes after unsuccessfully lobbying to have a vote of her own count.

It was around six the two generations of Whytes showed up at the door. Carl had the fire well-stoked by then, the logs proving to be more than ready for the burn. They came with beer as promised and another couple bottles of wine for the women. Before long the two sexes segregated with the men gathering in chairs around the fire, the women sitting in the living room raising a toast to the holiday season. The boys, curious as to the goings on and the novelty of having guests, especially so many, were dividing their time between listening from the top of the stairs and watching out of the window in their parent's room. Beth, squirreled away in her room with another book, was back to the more serious fare which was to her liking. Audrey went out for the night gathering with friends, new and old, those on break from college, those yet a few months away, and those who'd never have the chance to go.

"So," Carl Senior invoked as he raised his beer, "as promised, a toast to your dad. Jim, may God rest your soul, I'll be seeing you soon – let's hope not for a few years yet though."

The three of them drew heavily on their bottles and sat quietly staring at the flames. It was a somber moment, Senior and Carl considering the loss of a best friend and father, Junior out of the sense the moment transcended him. In the end mirth returned when Senior belched deeply and it was met with a loud pop and ember from the fire whizzing past and dying in the grass.

"Oh, talking back are you," he accused as the three laughed.

"This is nice, real nice," Junior piped in as the laughter faded away.

"Yup, Jim and I did this for years. Course, don't know where he kept getting all the wood from, surprised there's any trees left."

"Yeah, I think he acquired a lot of it here and there," Carl added conspiratorially, "he was a crafty son of gun."

At this Senior launched into a series of stories about Jim on some of which Carl could offer a new and different perspective and many others of which he'd never before heard. Most were humorous, some heartfelt, all were entertaining. Listening to him Carl had forgotten what a natural storyteller he was and how adept at delivering a punchline. It was little wonder he'd been so successful in business, his gift of gab and engagement so real. He had a way of making the most preposterous believable and of engaging you as though you were the most important person there was and, in fact, in that moment, to him you were. It's what made him special.

Inside Lily was nervously entertaining the two ladies, one of whom she knew only from having to pay a bill and the other in whose company she hadn't spent any meaningful time since she was a girl and a young woman. Though it was work she was enjoying it nonetheless. Reticent to speak on the more personal subjects she instead became an attentive listener. When the conversation turned to the mundane she would chime in with a quip, an anecdote, a fleeting thought, but as the wine flowed her range of topics became more expansive, the lowering of her inhibitions commensurate with the declining levels in her glass. It had been a long time since she'd imbibed, a very long time, and she was thrilled.

"So when you were a teenager, what did you think of Carl when you first met him?" Senior's wife, Cora, asked keenly interested in reminiscing throughout the evening.

"I don't know. He was cute. He was interested in me. He wasn't the white knight but he was attentive."

"Oh c'mon," Lois remarked, "wasn't he sexy?"

"Yeah, I guess, in his own quiet way."

"He was a good looking boy," Cora assured her.

"Yeah, I guess."

"And still is."

The three sat quietly for a moment, Lois feeling timid at Lily's straightforward, sterile answers while Cora was on the other hand remembering how peculiar she was as a girl. So stunningly beautiful yet so introverted you could almost imagine her collapse unto herself like a black hole. Never one to remain quiet and ever ready to cut the discussion to size she continued.

"Well, you certainly loved him."

"I think so. Yeah, yeah I did."

"Did?"

"And do, I guess. I mean, how do we know?"

"Easy. Imagine yourself and your life without him. If it hurts then that's probably a good sign."

"Yeah, just imagine what your life would have been like without him all these years," Lois added trying to step back into the conversation.

"I can, and I do. Frequently in fact."

The ladies were startled with her plainspoken revelation, Lily not caring as she stared at her mostly empty glass.

"Well, doesn't it hurt?" Cora asked.

"Sure it does. But does that mean it's love?" She paused, "Maybe it's just fear."

"Fear?" Lois questioned.

"Yeah, you know, maybe I'm just used to him, that's all. Imagining life without him, walking out that door, maybe it's just fear, of the unknown, of not knowing who I am. So I stay."

"Well that's not too encouraging," Cora suggested.

"No, I suppose it's not."

Lois went to the kitchen and uncorked the last bottle feeling they'd all need another glass or two if they were going to navigate such a thorny path and if she herself was to continue enduring the night. She was reluctant to come at all not knowing much of Lily other than the general feeling of discomfort she aroused in people about town. She had this odd reputation as being cold, aloof, disconnected, which was rich for a woman so poor. Despite the beauty she still possessed, and she was sure if she searched the house she'd find an aging portrait, she was bereft of much else in her estimation thus far. She returned to the living room filling all three glasses and stepping back into the conversation where it left off, neither Cora or Lily saying anything in her absence.

"So are you saying that you've thought about leaving?" Cora asked.

"Sure, doesn't everyone from time to time? But I don't think I would."

"Don't think?"

"Yeah, don't think," she answered knowing Cora was after a more positive affirmation than she was willing to give. "It's just we don't talk anymore and the stress of living so close to the edge with money is killing me. You know, I remember sitting here in this same room when I was a girl and listening to you and mom and Nancy gab half the night and here I am still. And I'm not like mom was, I had dreams and aspirations, and they didn't include staying in this town."

"You don't think your mom had dreams and aspirations too? You don't think she wanted to leave this town? Did you ever actually listen to her when you were here? If you had you would know she did. But you know what, she loved your father and, more importantly, she loved you. I know she was scared of the edge too, just like you, but she never showed it and never talked about it, she was too proud for that. And you know why, because she loved you so much."

"Well she sure didn't show it."

"Maybe not always in a way you understood or may have wanted but believe me, you were the world to her." She stopped to collect her thoughts. "Listen, your mother gave up all of her dreams when you were born, your dad too. They knew regardless of anything else, their obligations in life changed the day you came into the world. Rather than focus on themselves everything they did was for you. They weren't the luckiest people in the world, never had the gift of money or education or any of those things, but they had you and that was enough. The fact she stayed should say something."

Lily swirled the wine in her glass fighting the emotions thoughts of her parents evoked from loss, to pity, to anger, to the bereavement of being left alone in the world.

"Now," Cora continued, "I can't sit here and talk to you about what goes on in this house or even what goes on in your own mind because I don't know. What I do know is you have four kids and a husband who depend on you so you better think long and hard before saying such things."

Lily stayed still for a moment, then muttered "To thine own self be true."

Lois, who'd shrunk from the conversation in discomfort, was nonetheless watching the two of them spar from the relief of her own distance. There was some amusement in it, no doubt aided by quickly downing her newly poured glass of wine and the dent she was putting in another, yet there was something tragically morose and unhappy about the woman in whose living room she was sitting for the first time. She realized there was no arrogance to her, no indulgence of her own beauty, just a lonely reserve seeming to spring from the disconnect she had with her own history, her future, and her own skin.

Outside the jocularity subsided, the tales at an end, the flames mesmerizing as they do late into the night and after a few beers. The wood nearly at an end, the evening was at a close and Carl felt indulged, with stories, friends, food, alcohol, warmth and a new formed memory. He couldn't recall an evening as fine as the one he just experienced and returned to an earlier thought, these days seeming to come along when you need them most. He was most appreciative.

"So, Carl," Junior broke the silence, "I've got two things for you. First, I want to apologize for my behavior at the office a few weeks ago."

"Don't worry about it Danny."

"No Carl, I do worry about it because it was uncalled for. I see that now. You know, sometimes you just get wrapped up in the dollars and cents and kind of forget. But no excuses, I'm sorry. Now, second, I have a proposal so hear me out. I need some general help around the place, on the weekend, Saturdays, maybe Sundays if you want, and I'd like you to maybe do some work. You know, only if you want to, no big deal if you don't. I figure I can give you a fair wage and I know you're handy with the vehicles and the grounds and such. So, what I'm thinking is we put half toward the bill and the other half to take home, you know, so you don't feel like you're just working for that."

Carl looked over at Danny Senior who suddenly sat upright from his slouch and keenly focused on his boy. Thinking at first Senior put him up to it the more he watched the two the more he realized this was a concoction of Junior's alone. It probably explained why he'd come over tonight with his father which he'd found strange ever since it was mentioned earlier in the day. He imagined Senior was probably as equally confounded when his son wanted to tag along to the Kane backyard and the raising of a toast to a man he barely remembered and certainly never knew from anything other than a delinquent account number.

"Well, I think that's a winner. What do you think Carl?" Senior asked eagerly.

"I think you're right. When do you want me to start?"

"Well how about next weekend? You know, spend this weekend with your family as you should and then we'll talk next week and come up with a plan."

Danny Senior sat beaming, heartened his boy was helping an old friend. Taking the last gulp of his beer he stood announcing, "Well, that's it for this old man, I gotta get the missus and find my bed before it finds me."

"Yeah, me too. It was a great night Carl," Junior said extending a handshake he readily accepted, "We'll talk next week. And we gotta do this thing again, maybe in the Spring when it's a little warmer."

"Sure thing Danny." He in turn extended his hand to Senior, "Sir, always a pleasure."

"The pleasure was mine, all mine. It's been a long time and I think I really needed a night like this, the cold be damned." He took Carl's hand in both of his own whispering before he let go, "They're never too old to learn and thank goodness for that."

Carl and Lily bid their guests farewell, both feeling light on their feet. They had tales to tell one another, news, of the mundane and otherwise, but they kept it to themselves. For just one night they seemed to want to keep private their thoughts, embrace the evening for the release it was, the catharsis for which they were in such dire need.

Upstairs the boys had fallen asleep on their bed, the laughter, the deep voices, the tales from around the fire the last they heard. Each taking one and cradling him in their arms, Carl and Lily brought the boys to their own beds. Carefully tucking them in they gave each a kiss goodnight lingering at the door to be sure neither had stirred.

15.

December came with no measurable snow, a huge disappointment for the boys. The brief tease a couple weeks before raised hopes the storms would soon begin. What they had instead were days of sunshine and unseasonable warmth. It was back to medium jackets and sweaters, no need of hats and gloves. For Cary his frustration was somewhat tempered by the ability to continue wearing sneakers while he remained sour on his boots. But in the end he would in a second have traded that comfort for a good dumping of snow. It wasn't simply there was so much fun to be had and after all, if it was going to be cold, as the season should, then it might as well snow, it was this time of year came with the hope of a snow day, a great big storm powerful enough to cancel school and give free reign to kids all over town. It's one of the thrills of youth.

The respite was, however, good news for Carl and Lily. With he starting his new part-time job in a few days and the warm weather cutting down on their oil use the coming holiday no longer felt so crippling. It was the first time in years and it energized them, she in particular. She was more active around the house involving herself with the boys, spending evenings away from her room, even getting an early start on the gifts and cards. She put up what meager decorations they had trying her best to infect the house with a festive mood, irreverently nagging Carl to cut a tree down so she could finish. If you could, you would have said she was excited, and she may have agreed.

None of these were sentiments shared by Beth. As the anticipation of those around her grew she was sinking deeper into despair spending more time alone in her room, avoiding the smiles and the laughter. To her it rang hollow, a forced illusion. The semblance of good will was nothing more than a bubble that would soon burst once the Kanes came to their senses. And so she waited for it, after a time even wishing for it, but nothing changed. It went on for interminable day after day.

Sadly, her absence passed largely unremarked, seemingly lost on all but Carl and Audrey. They tried to get her out and more involved, even for the smallest of moments, but she dismissed them and often with a mere wave of her hand. She stopped joining the family for dinner taking her meals late at night instead. She left early for school, forsaking her obligation with the boys, and returning early only to climb the stairs once more. It was beginning to look like she was determined to spend the rest of the season in her room behind the pages of a book and otherwise alone.

Carl blamed the situation on himself, his apology not strong enough. As expected their talk that night was brief with no hugs and kisses, no reciprocal amends. It was all very one-sided with he doing the talking and she listening sullenly. Despite what he knew he'd hoped for more, and he blamed himself for that too. Standing in front of her he wasn't entirely sure why he was apologizing. He'd done nothing other than venture to share a little of himself at her request and his reward was she turning the affair ugly. He'd heard the accusations before, mostly while Lily was pregnant and just after Audrey's birth, but never accommodated them well. Coming from her he accepted them less. So in hindsight he wondered if she sensed his heart really wasn't investing the words, his actions more an obligation as a father than real warmth as a dad.

Either way, a midweek call from Earl announcing it was time to choose a pup provided what Carl hoped was an answer. Although he had set himself to the surprise, constantly imagining the faces of his children and the joy of Christmas day, he was inspired to include Beth in the decision. He hoped besides getting her out of the house it would give them a chance to talk out whatever was still laying between them. And if that didn't work he thought she may at least be relied upon to help him carry the ruse until Christmas morning since keeping a puppy quiet for an entire night was an obstacle he'd yet figured out how to overcome.

It was no small task. All but physically dragging her from the house he managed finally to get her into the car, his pleading and cajoling giving way to a command. It was an unexpected wielding of authority he rarely used and quite frankly thought lost. Though suffering a tinge of guilt, he was determined to tell her nothing of the secret letting her find it for herself, the decision as to which puppy for she alone. He contented himself with this small pleasure for the short drive, her resentment at being dragged out completely lost on him. She made it known the moment they pulled in the drive stopping just before the open door of Earl's small barn.

"What are we doing here?" she demanded without looking.

"I need you to help me make a decision."

Exiting the car he cheerfully smiled and disappeared inside. She remained, seething at the idea he drove her out in the cold to a stranger's house for some decision on which she remained unknowing and totally ambivalent when she could be trying to stay warm in her own bed with a drab book in her hands. It was yet another moment to hate, her hour glass filling rapidly. But before long a chill crept in, her immobility no help as she sat shivering in the dark. Cursing him for pocketing the keys she got out to follow closing the door quietly behind. Leaning against the car she continued the debate with herself, feeling completely ridiculous to be entering the game, when she heard what she thought was the high raspy bark of a puppy. Cocking her head to be sure, she slowly crept up the ramp peering just around the corner of the barn door and there they were, some half dozen black and white puppies cavorting, bouncing and flopping, their fat little tails wagging, shaking their entire bodies and taking their awkward selves down.

"What's all this?" she asked excitedly rushing inside.

"Your decision," Carl laughed.

"We're taking one home?"

"Well not yet, for Christmas. It's our secret though," he said putting a finger to his lips.

She arched an eyebrow looking at him, "And who else knows?"

"Yes, your mother knows."

"Good." She knelt down amongst them, stroking their fur as they raced by chasing and biting one another. "So can I hold one?"

"Course you can, that's why you're here ain't it?" Earl answered.

She reached down and nabbed the first puppy that came running by holding it out to peer into its eyes. Suddenly it licked her nose, the tongue longer than she expected. Giggling at the kiss she put it back and corralled another. Squirming around, much more restless than the first, she picked up a third and more patient pup marveling at its pudgy face, stubby whiskers and white stripe with black freckles running from the snout to a sharp point on the crown of its head. Flipping it over to rub its belly it right away began growling and barking, pawing at her hands and nibbling her fingertips whenever it could get its mouth near, fighting her the whole way.

"They're all so beautiful," she exclaimed putting it down again.

"They sure are," Earl chuckled, "but this here is my little darling, Rosebud. Come over and meet her." He bent to stroke her fur, one of the pups trying to climb over the edge of her bed looking for attention of its own. "She's a superb mother and been a great companion. She'll be the last. I am gonna keep one of the pups for the boy though. It'll be good for him and Hell, what's a boy without a dog?"

"A very unlucky boy," Carl answered. "So you said you're giving them all away?"

"All but one."

"How come? I mean, that's a lot of money lost isn't it?"

"Naw, it ain't lost."

Earl pulled him outside, away from Beth and the dogs. She could hear their hushed voices, a monotone of basso, but paid no mind. She was charmed with the half dozen puppies clumsily climbing over her like she was a jungle gym. Rosebud kept a watchful eye from her oversized bedding beneath a couple of heat lamps Earl rigged up on the edge of an old stall. Ears flicking from time to time as she listened to the two men outside, she seemed otherwise unperturbed by Beth's presence alone with her. Content to lounge, she was perhaps grateful for the break.

Almost immediately as she studied them Beth could see which was the alpha, the beta and the omega. It was an attitudinal thing, borne of instinct she imagined, with no clear relation to their size. Spending most of its time chasing the other pups around, nipping at their heel and yipping in their ear, the alpha's need to herd appeared strongest. It was intent on collecting order from the chaos. The beta was close behind, watching and trying to mimic the alpha's every move yet at times getting lost in the chaos as well and reacting rather poorly when it did. The object of its frustration was most often and what Beth naturally assumed the omega, now hiding behind her while she blocked the beta's advance. It was all rather comical and she couldn't help but laugh at its fussing each time she thwarted the attempt to get past. She finally picked up the beleaguered omega holding it close and it was decided.

"Dad, this is the one we should take," she declared as the two men came drifting back inside.

"That's great honey," he smiled weakly, "but we ought to be going."

"Can't we stay just a little longer?"

Trying to pout when he didn't answer she as quickly gave up. It was a fake at which she wasn't particularly adept. Giving a final sigh she made her way back to the car leaving the men to exchange some last words. Climbing in, Carl let out a deep sigh of his own.

"You know, I don't really feel like going home yet so what do you say to a cup of coffee?"

She nodded noting the enthusiasm had gone from his voice. Watching him slumped in his seat as they drove back to town he was distracted, out of the moment, lost in the sea of elsewhere. The cars piling behind, he didn't realize how slowly they were creeping along the road until the lights of a frustrated driver started to flicker. Rather than speed up and pay more attention he pulled to the side letting the long line pass. He was in no hurry, she sensed it was as if he wished time to slow around them so he could parse through whatever was troubling him. Hoping it had nothing to do with the puppy she remained still, hesitant to say anything lest the promise of a Christmas dog be jinxed. Despite being overly rational a bit of the superstitious had edged its way into her mind.

The silence continued as they sipped their coffee in the cramped shop. She accepted his offer of a muffin, taking it as one often does when a rare treat is given though she had no appetite for it, the plate setting untouched between them. She wanted fewer people about so they could talk but the place continued welcoming refugees from the cold. Their boisterous laughter and smiling faces as they rubbed their hands together and called out the choices to one another from the menu hanging behind the counter annoyed her, even more so when they jostled the table trying to navigate to a seat of their own. To her the whole scene was playing inconsiderate, another universal injustice, when her father was yearning for little more than a moment of peace. She found herself wishing they'd all drop dead, the owner locking the door and allowing them to freeze on the step outside.

Feeling a break would never come and tiring of the wait she finally reached out and took his hand.

"Dad, what's wrong?"

He composed himself, drawing his nowhere focus near, meeting her gaze, "He's dying."

"Oh no, how?"

"His cancer's back. It's terminal."

She cupped his hand in her own feeling the rough skin, not knowing what to say. The difficult necessity of death had left Beth untouched in her young life, the impending no different. She didn't have the language to console, nor could she have known there was none. All she had to draw on were the comforting speeches of an actor or the soothing words of an author. She was wise enough to know the difference so said nothing.

"He's got a kid, a young kid. You know, he's ten years older than me. He and his wife tried for so long to have kids but nothing happened. Then one day it did. I remember he was worried about it, and this was before his first bout with cancer. I think he was afraid as old as he was that he might not be around. And now he won't."

They sat for a long while, the shop finally emptying, neither of them paying the least attention. It wasn't until an offer was made to wrap the muffin to go they realized it was closing. Asking her to keep silent on the night they made their way home as slowly as before.

Sitting in the dark picking loose paint from the windowsill Beth wondered if there was lead in the old chips she was discarding on the floor. With every appearance of belonging to the original construction she thought it was quite probable yet couldn't care less, the long strips peeling so nicely from the shriveled wood. Besides, she reasoned, if ignorance was bliss then she could stand to lose a little brainpower. Moving her finger up to the windowpane she scraped frost from the corner where the putty had long ago cracked and pulled away from the glass. It was the same all the way around, every pane wearing an icy draft where the gaps appeared. She watched a droplet of water gather and trickle from where she left her print, making a few inches before freezing again.

It was the same every cold night, always had been. As much as she loved the cool breezes in summer, she hated having the bed near the window in winter. Despite an assortment of towels pressed into the corners to blunt the worst of it a good rest was nearly impossible, most nights spent shivering the last few hours when it was at its coldest. It was a seasonal condition, one that seemed destined never to change. Nothing with the old house ever did. Certainly not the outside where the same color faded, the same clapboards remained broken, the same missing roof slates remained, well, missing, and the same windows failed to keep the warmth. It was really no different on the inside. The furniture never changed, either in fact or in place, the same wallpaper hung in every room, sometimes torn, the same faucets dripped and the same damn blankets kept her cold at night. And considering it all, she realized even the people never changed, in fact or in place, the same persons haunting the same places throughout the house almost like clockwork. There was a melancholy to this sameness, an infinite sadness of drab, and she was tired of taking it in alone.

Remembering she still had an untouched muffin she carefully halved it and went across the hall. Knocking quietly on the door and peeking her head inside she found the boys laying on the floor, pens in hand and catalogs spread before them. They had been wishing like mad, their long lists a compendium of the impossible, an effort so earnest she had to laugh.

"Do you honestly think you're going to get all that stuff?"

"No," Andy huffed defensively, "we're just messing around. What do you want anyway?"

"Just thought you guys might want this," she said pulling the muffin from behind her back. They jumped up, greedily reaching while she held it over them, "Uh-uh, I'll give them to you."

Eying the two pieces to be sure they were close to even she handed Cary the one she believed slightly larger figuring he deserved it if for no other reason than her conviction Andy cheated him every chance he got. Sitting on his bed she glanced down at one of the lists.

"A pool table? Seriously?"

"Yeah, so?" Andy managed between bites.

"So nothing," she replied searching for the balance between teasing and indulgence, "if that's what you really want."

Looking again at the lists they compiled she for a moment felt the urge to get down herself and start flipping through to create her own ultimate wish list. She'd never done it before, her pragmatic side always getting the better. But then, knowing what she did, the puppy was probably as good as anything she'd ever find between those pages.

"You know boys, if you could have just one wish for Christmas what would it be?"

"Snow," Cary answered immediately.

"Snow? Out of everything you want snow?"

"Yeah, because then school would get canceled."

Clever thinking in its own way, she thought. "What about you Andy?"

"Well, I can't say a pool table now," he scowled at her, "so I'd have to say, um, a sled."

"A sled? All you want is a sled?"

"Sure, if Cary's getting snow I want a sled."

Amused their answers were as shrewd as that she couldn't help question where the dreaming had gone and after countless days of compiling lists? Still, it was nice, their ideas refreshingly simple.

"What about you?" Cary asked.

Evaluating the possibilities they were endless. She flirted with saying a puppy yet she'd given her word to say nothing even if she doubted they'd make any sort of connection. She might wish for new books, new clothes, a new bed, maybe even an entirely new room if it were possible. Hell, in the whole world and with money no object she might as well go for a new house and away from here. But it was too cynical and didn't really fit the rules of the game.

"Okay, I think I'd wish for an electric blanket."

"Pfft, that's boring," Andy declared.

"Why? Cary gets his snow, you get your sled, and I get my blanket to stay warm."

"Yeah, makes good sense to me," Cary agreed.

Debating the merits of their choices they ribbed one another, each trying to poke holes in the others' reasoning, before Beth decided to go back to her room after hearing Audrey come home.

"Are you going to start walking us to school again?" Cary asked as she opened the door.

"Yes, I'll walk with you to school. If that's what you wish?" she teased.

"No, I want snow!" he yelled out as she closed the door behind, their laughter carrying her across the hall.

"What was that about?" Audrey asked pulling off her sweater.

"Nothing, just a little game."

"Yeah?" she replied looking pleased.

Audrey moved around the room getting herself ready for bed while Beth sat on her own to watch, everything her sister did a lesson in anarchy. Flipping her shoes off and not paying attention to where they were sailing she knew she'd end up complaining within a couple of days when she couldn't find them beneath the mess. The same was true of her sweater, her socks and the contents of her pockets just as it was with the hairbrush for which she was now searching in frustration.

"It's over there on the nightstand, under your shirt" Beth snickered.

"Well what the Hell is it doing there?"

Sitting in front of the mirror she began to work out the knots of the day, her efforts becoming more frantic the more they resisted. "Damn this dry air," she cursed finally, "I give up."

Beth looked away as she stripped down getting into her bedclothes.

"So what was all the laughter?"

"Just wishing."

"Wishing?"

"Yeah, if you had one wish for Christmas, what would it be?"

"And?"

"Well, Cary wants snow, Andy wants a sled and I want an electric blanket."

"My, what a practical lot you all are."

"Maybe. What about you?"

"One wish?"

"One wish."

"To be away from here," she answered without hesitation.

Lily found Carl bundled up on the stoop struggling to roll a cigarette. She took the pouch from him and rolled one for each of them. She could tell he was watching her intently as she generously sprinkled tobacco along the paper, moistened the edge and wound each of them tightly. Taking a box of matches from her jacket she lit them handing his without a glance and taking a puff of her own.

"Well don't be so surprised, do you think you're the only one around here with stress?" she grinned.

"I guess not," he replied taking a drag and holding the cigarette out in regard, "and to judge from this I'd say you got more stress than me."

Although she felt that was probably true, at the least sure she endured it more, she could tell he'd been deeply troubled since coming home with Beth. She wondered if the girl had done something to upset his mood in such a way. But he'd been bursting with so much anticipation before they left she thought it improbable. As vexing as the girl was of late she could scarcely imagine anything she could do to drag him so low. No, it was something altogether more substantial.

"You know, Earl said something to me tonight. He picked it up somewhere but felt it was truer and smarter than anything he could say on his own. He said 'We're born alone, we live alone, we die alone. Only through our love and friendship can we create the illusion that we're not alone'. He said that as we were leaving. It's kinda shaken me up, you know?"

"Orson Welles."

"Huh?"

"It was Orson Welles who said that."

"No kidding."

"But it's 'the illusion for the moment that we're not alone'." She could tell the subtlety was lost on him so she continued, "You see, for the moment means it's temporary, transient, not a permanent state of feeling or being. The illusion doesn't last a lifetime, you're still alone through almost all the hours of your life and when you really think about it, since we experience life in our own heads, it may none of it be real, just an illusion. You see?"

"When the Hell did everyone around me get so damn smart?"

She chuckled, "Maybe we always were."

"Well then you all should have stopped being so deceptive and joined me out here."

"Right, somehow I don't think you would've liked that. So why did he say it anyway?"

He took a deep breath, "He's dying. Maybe a few days, a few weeks, he doesn't know."

"Oh Carl, I'm so sorry."

She knew he counted on one hand the number of friends he held close and, though she'd only met him a couple of times, Earl was one. It was an odd friendship cultivated and nurtured almost solely through work yet it counted no less. She knew the esteem he held for the man was indefinite, the loss to be felt profound, and the mourning already begun. She clung close to him.

"He just told me tonight. He hasn't told anyone."

"But his family knows, right?"

"Yeah, they've known for a few months but that's it, now me."

"Doesn't he have a young boy?"

"Yup."

She thought about the boy, wondering what must be going through his mind. Lucky enough to hold onto her own parents until she was an adult, as a child, a young child, she just couldn't imagine.

"Why'd he wait so long to tell you?"

"He was afraid, wanted to be sure while they ran some tests and sent him to specialists and such. He didn't want to run the chance they'd find out at work and fire him so they wouldn't have to pay. But it doesn't matter anymore, nothing they can do."

She nestled closer resting her head on his shoulder. They remained quiet, ignoring the cold, sharing their warmth. For a moment they felt fortunate to be together, to be alive, to have the days still spread before them. She retreated to thoughts of her parents, the day she lost her father, the day a few weeks later when she lost her mother. She'd never felt so alone, even in all the years that preceded it when she despaired of being unloved and the years since when she feared the touch of loneliness tapping her shoulder nearly every day. He reflected on their children, his own mortality, and the things he'd yet to share with them. He thought of Earl and his boy, the time that would be lost, the memories they'd never again create, and questioned how much the boy would know and remember as he grew to a man and had children of his own. Looking to the stars it was too much for him to consider in the moment.

"Well, Beth chose a dog," he told her.

"That's good," she said stroking his hair, pulling a strand over his ear, "was she happy?"

"I think so."

They continued quietly watching the sky, the chill coming closer and drawing them closer. A shooting star came streaking over the edge of the far horizon burning itself out almost as quickly as it appeared.

"Did you make a wish?" she asked.

"Yeah, for another one of your cigarettes before we go back inside out of this cold."

She ran her hand through his hair, twisting the end on her fingertip.

16.

Beth did as promised and started again chaperoning the boys to and from school. No longer in a rush to distance themselves from her they were pleasant and the conversation light. Full of drama, humor and events of the day their tales regaled her the length of the journey home with one or both taking the lead role. She played along gasping at the right moment, laughing at a silly joke or just affecting interest. It made the walk easier and far more enjoyable in the dipping temperatures, the storms still at bay while they remained trapped in a cold vice. She was remembering daily her pretend wish for an electric blanket by the time they reached home, a cup of coffee for the three of them an adequate substitute for now.

Life was getting better for the boys in other ways as well. It was around this time Carl came home with chocolate advent calendars and though deep into the month it didn't take long for them to catch up. Depicting Santa and his workshop, elves hard at work making toys, a roaring fire in the hearth, an equally ferocious storm raging through the curtained window, the novelty was delightful even if the chocolate was not. Wafer thin and tasteless, it didn't need to be much else with the sentiment on the box and their enthusiasm investing it with a sweetness the makers overlooked. The first gift of the season, it was their great hope for more, an icon over which Cary prayed for snow, Andy a sled, and both for continued peace from the thugs at school.

They couldn't understand why but the night at the skating rink seemed to mark the low point of their problems with the other kids. From then on it was sporadic and minor incidents, little else. Andy was back playing with his group of friends inviting Cary along when he felt his brother was spending too much time alone. A chance at some company it gave him a sense of belonging he hadn't often felt and for that he was grateful. But that was the extent of all they offered. Under no illusion as to how quickly they would scatter at any sign of trouble there was no sense of protection. Almost never feeling safe anymore, a condition that simply couldn't endure, he at other times found himself wanting to be alone. He knew his problems were his own and at some point would have to be his own agent of change so to hasten this he put himself out as bait in these moments welcoming a chance to have a final confrontation that may once and for all end the situation. There were never any takers.

It was a peculiar development neither of them could fully understand. They noticed Jeremy fading into the background, even at the rink, despite having started it all. And while the rest of the kids split off and went their separate ways he was these days almost as alone as Cary. He in turn found his hatred of the boy ebbing the more his role diminished. Though he'd never openly admit it, there was an occasional feeling of pity for his enemy when he watched him pacing the playground on his own, none of his former mates paying any mind. It was strange to Cary how little separated the two boys when you stopped to look.

"So why do you think that is?" he was asking Beth as they walked, hoping her experienced counsel might help him better understand.

"I don't know, maybe it's just cutting off the head of the snake. The little jerk's on his own so without him to stir up trouble the others don't bother."

"But why?"

"Cary, I honestly don't know, I'm not there with you," she said trying to be gentle despite her impatience as they rounded the last corner. "You should probably ask dad because I'm not really the best person to be giving advice."

The boys kept to themselves the rest of the short way, her perceived lack of consideration and guidance a great disappointment. Walking ahead scuffing their feet they kicked up clouds of dust in the cold, dry air forcing her to adjust her scarf to keep it from her lungs. It was all she could do to stifle the urge to scold them thinking sure they were doing it to her with purpose.

Arriving home they were surprised to see their father's car in the driveway, the boys running inside breathlessly calling to him. When there was no response they continued the hunt upstairs while she, hearing movement, went to the top of the basement and called down. It was only her mother starting a load of laundry. Reporting the last she'd seen he was out front, Beth noted she was of little help as usual and went out in search. Yet rounding each corner of the house she still found no sign of him. Stopping in the backyard and looking around she began to call out hearing only her own echo in return. Giving up she was about to go back inside when she caught a whiff of tobacco smoke on the wind. Knowing just where he'd gone she walked the hill in back popping her head over the ridge to see him sitting on her bench.

"Why didn't you answer when I called?"

"I knew you'd find me."

She sat next to him looking out over the neighborhood. It was an ugly scene, dirty little houses shuttered against the cold, their backyards a quilt of dead and dying vegetation. There was no sign of life, any life, through the skeleton of hardwoods, their fleshy remains scattered beneath the view. Even the hill opposite offered no diversion for the despondency of the land, the parched khaki meadows suffocating under a frost, evergreens dominating the jagged elevations standing stark against the light blue sky. As reluctant as she was to admit, and hoping for the quick passage of winter, a fresh coating of snow would go a long way in tidying up their perspective.

"So why are you home so early?"

"Just had some extra time to use up at work."

It was a partial truth, the least important. Earl told the rest of the crew that morning including his own bosses. He kept Carl by his side while he made his way through the offices finally calling in and setting the rest down at lunch. When he'd gone for the afternoon Carl couldn't face the rest of the day there without him. For that there would be more than enough time ahead. For now he just needed to continue imagining the place unchanged.

"So you like the dog?" he asked.

"I sure do."

"You think the boys'll like it too?"

"Of course they will dad," she encouraged him. "How's your friend?"

He shifted, sitting on his gloved hands trying to warm them. In his state of mind it was a frustratingly dumb question, akin to asking someone rolling on the ground in agony if they're okay, but he understood the point. Fobbing it off with a shrug he looked into middle nowhere with interest.

"Well, not that it matters much, I'm sorry for getting so angry at you. It really wasn't very fair and I just, well, you know, don't know when to keep my mouth shut."

"Funny how that is," he chuckled, "when you don't say much anyway."

"Yeah, imagine if I did?"

"Yeah," he agreed, "but it's kind of been bothering me a bit, why did you?" he asked looking her direct, his mirthful smile gone.

She glared back focusing on each eye trying to divine the answer for which he was seeking. His unflinching stare, pupils mere pinpricks in the cold gray of his iris, told her he wasn't seeking further words of apology. Nor was he going to allow her the satisfaction of an evasion she so famously and often employed. Weighing the consequences of one answer over another with precious little time to think, she turned icily away.

"So?" he asked again.

"I wasn't mad at you."

"I kind of figured that. Then who?"

"Well I was kind of mad at myself mostly."

Although he didn't doubt what she said to be true, it was insincere, more of her tendency to give only measured responses. He was too tired, the same frustratingly indirect game he'd played with Lily for a lifetime.

"Why are you always so angry at your mother?"

She kept her back to him. If forced into this discussion in which she thought there could be no good outcome then she would do so in protest. At least he would understand it's on his shoulders and not hers once she gave the answers he seemed intent on hearing.

"Because, I hate her," she doled the words out slowly.

He quietly took them in allowing her the space she needed now they'd been spoken and there was no going back. She put her hands between her thighs rubbing them together as though she were cold. He suspected it was a rather poor substitute for the chance to pick at her nails.

"Well, I guess it runs in the tree," he observed finally.

"If you even say I'm just like her I'll walk away from you for good."

He knew she meant it, regrettably for the obvious truth of which she was in denial.

"Look, your mother never trusted her mother's love either. I'm not saying you're like her, just that I think I know a little of why you're so mad."

"You don't know anything."

"Then tell me something so I do."

She turned to face him. "Okay, I'll tell you something, if I could I'd nail her to that damn cross she's always climbing on, so how's that?" she furiously snapped before turning around again.

He remained still, absorbing the anger, puzzling and almost amused at the allusion she chose to use. Her breathing heavy, he watched its escape in short vapory bursts, her chest heaving erratically. He knew then that a reasonable discussion about the nature of their relationship was impossible, her animosity ran too deep.

"You know what's worse," she said more calmly, "is I have my nose stuck in it every single day of my life. At least she was alone when she was growing up, but I'm stuck with Audrey."

"I don't follow."

"Why am I not surprised," she lamented, "everyone's eyes are forever closed. Look dad, she's always been in love with Audrey, from the day I was born I saw it. And there's never been a place for me in this family. The boys are the boys and they don't care anyhow but for me she always made it known that I wasn't Audrey. And do you know what that's like? Do you know what it's like to not be good enough just being yourself? And then to be told you're an embarrassment?"

Sighing, he sat on his hands again, the chill coming down as the sky darkened in the falling light. He could see streetlights popping on one by one through the town and lights appearing in windows as people arrived home from work. He thought how warm they must feel in their nicely trimmed homes, Christmas lights twinkling, tinsel and candy canes, a stack of gifts growing ever larger beneath the tree while he sat with a broken girl in the frozen winter air.

"I guess all I can say is the embarrassment wasn't over you, it was over herself, and so all I ask is you give her a chance. I'm not expecting any miracles, I just want to see you happier."

She wasn't sure what, if anything, she accomplished by sharing her thoughts as there were no expectations against which she could measure, the whole affair a confusing torment. As to her mother she doubted any chance would be given, a miracle the more realistic hope if she was her father. For herself it was more a matter of time, a counting of the days until she could escape.

"Dad, have you ever thought of just leaving?" she asked quietly.

"God no, where would I go?"

"I don't know, Chicago maybe. You always liked it there."

"No. I've dreamed of other places, maybe Chicago, maybe somewhere warm, an island in the sun, but not without you guys. Do you?"

"Constantly."

"Where would you go?"

"I don't know, and I don't care, as long as it's away from here."

"And leave your old man?" he sniffed.

She was unamused, frowning as she turned to face him, his chanced levity lost. He was the only reason she was here, the certainty of which she knew he was aware, otherwise she would have run long ago. At best it would be to a much happier place, the land far away, at worst to join the chemical tribe, the state of blissful oblivion. Either would've worked just fine.

"Look," he said gently, "you should dream of leaving, you're young. I'd think you were a little strange if you didn't." He paused, "But for now let's just keep this your place away because as long as I know you're no farther than up here I can always reach you when I need you. And you know, without you here I'd have a hard time staying too."

They sat talking for a long time afterward, she giving him a chance to remember his friend, he allowing her the space to collect herself. Putting his arm around her they left the bench searching their way through the trees. Darkness was descending quickly, the path home illuminated by a near full moon shining brilliant in the arctic clear. When they reached the backyard they stopped to gaze at its halo carving a wide circle. It was a sure sign the dry air would soon depart, the cold vice loosening its grip, a flood of moisture to beautify the earth soon to follow.

By the next day Lily was nearing panic. The days before Christmas were growing short, the final gifts still undecided, tawdry knickknacks all there was to fill the void beneath the tree. While the boys had about all they were going to get, most of those remained hidden in her closet. It was less a feint to keep the magic of Santa alive, that time had passed a couple of years ago, as it was to keep curious fingers from spoiling any surprises. As for the girls, little had been done. Audrey, persnickety even when receiving a gift, required careful consideration and though she'd been searching her mind she was without inspiration and soon found herself consulting the same catalogs she conspired to discard. Beth was more difficult yet. Caring little for the gifts your average fourteen year old would be wishing she was completely bereft of ideas.

"Books," Carl suggested sipping his coffee, "and an electric blanket."

"An electric blanket?" she asked looking up from the checkbook she had been trying to balance.

"Yeah, I got that one from Cary."

She rolled her eyes, "So what books?"

"Hmm, I'll have to get back to you on that."

She turned her attention back to her work. Still on familiar ground, the ease of his money from the part-time work with Danny not yet evident, the Christmas Club dollars meager, it was the usual game of shifting money from one place to another, robbing Peter to pay Paul as it were. It was the burden she despised the most and the one she procrastinated on the longest. Knowing the moment she sat down with the checkbook was the moment any good feeling would disappear to be replaced with an angst and grieving that would take a full night to get over she put it off as long as she could. And that too was part of the game, avoiding even thoughts of the chore as much as possible the only way to function without medication.

"And what about this damn dog?" she asked forcefully, slamming her pen down as she did so.

"Calm down. What about it?"

"It's like a whole other person to shop for. And what the Hell am I supposed to get for it anyway?"

"Don't worry," he said lightly tapping her hand, "I'll take care of it."

They'd spoken little of the dog over the last few weeks, her indignant reservations just below the surface and he unwilling to scratch. The subject had settled into an uneasy calm though he'd long suspected the closer they got to Christmas the greater the likelihood she'd have something more to say on the matter. Either way, the path was clear and there wasn't much she could do to alter the fact, the Kanes would have their dog. That Beth was so enamored of the puppies when she had the chance to play with them was reason enough if there had been any doubt, which there never was in his mind.

"This isn't going to work," she said slamming her pen down once more and getting up to put the kettle on. "We just don't have enough."

He sat quietly at the table, well used to the outbursts when she set to balancing the checkbook. She moved abruptly around the kitchen preparing her mug, fulminating about the state of their financial affairs and her tattered nerves, snippets of anger exploding in theatrics largely incoherent. For such an otherwise reserved and emotionless being she poured an awful lot into these tirades he determined, ignoring the part where she passively blamed him for it all. When she was somewhat more composed, the rattle of her spoon on ceramic the only sound she made, he reached for the tobacco.

"Come on, I rolled us each a cigarette."

She scowled at him then relented, another part of the game being played.

Stepping outside they stood on the stoop wordlessly leaning against the posts. It was too cold to sit, the stillness of their inert bodies soaking it like a sponge. Another clear night, the visibility of the stars washed out by the brightness of the moon, its ghostly halo vanished, it seemed one of those rare winters when the promise of snow was given empty. And without its moderating temperatures and insulation around the base of the house it would be a more expensive one for the Kanes to absorb.

"So how are you going to hide this dog from the kids?"

"Earl's going to bring him by in the morning."

She took a draw from her cigarette, "How's he look?"

He thought about it, "Haggard, but he seems okay. You know he came in again today, says he'll keep coming in."

"Why?"

"Well, I was thinking about that. He says it's like we used to joke, about having to work until we dropped dead, that folks like us can't afford a retirement. What I really think is that it's his way of holding on as long as he can, kind of denying what's going to happen."

Peering into the night, the pale light of the moon throwing shadows, she thought how this time of year really was the time of the dead. It wasn't just the lifeless vegetation, the absence of most insects, the birds gone leaving but a cackling few while the remaining and smarter animals were in some state of hibernation, it was the passage of much more. The streets were empty, the laughter and smiles packed away, the stagnant odor of vehicle exhaust and burning wood replacing the fresh aroma of a life in bloom. The dry air caused your skin to die and flake off, your hair to grow stiff and weak, your mood to numb and become apathetic, your own depressed sleep long and wasted, the insipid hours passing slowly. And the cold, the ever invading, clutching, unending cold so much, she imagined, like death's cold, indifferent embrace. When she died she wanted it to be in winter.

Putting her cigarette out, the checkbook suddenly felt a bit less menacing. It was aided by a thought she'd been actively forcing from her mind for days; with Earl gone Carl would be the likely choice to take over his position. It would mean quite a bit more money and she suspected it's why he took Carl around with him when he told the news and for all intents said his goodbyes. He was the hand-chosen successor. She admonished herself leading the two of them back inside.

"So tell me what's going on at school," Carl asked sitting down with the boys in their room, the Christmas lists they continued poring over well-hidden from his view.

He felt he'd given them ample space over the last couple weeks to sort through the problems on their own and while he initially thought no news was good news, as the days wore on their silence was becoming more disconcerting. He found himself imagining the situation worse, their hush a ward to his going to the administration or the kid's parents. Looking for small changes in their personality and demeanor or less enthusiasm for joking and playing he found nothing. They acted the same as they always did, and he didn't like it.

"Nothing's happening," Andy replied, Cary nodding.

They'd conspired to remain secretive on the goings on at school for nearly the same reason their dad suspected, a fear he would stir the pot by going to teachers, parents or even the kids themselves. While it was calm and there really wasn't much to report Andy saw little reason to muddy the situation and Cary agreed, even if the waiting had him on edge. Either way they together felt no good could come from getting him involved or in some way opening the invitation so they ignored Beth's advice to seek an answer from him. But ever weak in the face of an adult, especially his father, Cary then went on to explain the same confusing situation he'd described a couple of days before.

"She says it's like cutting off the head of a snake," Andy concluded when Cary was done.

"Yeah, could be," Carl acknowledged, "so the other kids that were with this boy aren't picking on anyone else instead?"

They shook their heads.

"Well, it is kind of peculiar but I guess you should be thankful."

Thinking about their account he reflected on the bullies he'd met as an adult and how the effect on those around them was no different though the methods changed. The physical antagonizing was all but gone, a fistfight a rare thing indeed, but the taunts and the verbal aggression remained, perhaps even more damaging with age. Less and less among equals as you grew older, it frequently involved a power relationship instead. And this he thought was worse because schoolkids continue to grow, they become smarter, they change, and they at the least go in different directions when they leave school having the chance to put it all behind. Yet as adults you don't often have that luxury. You're set in your career, your home, your family, its well-being put more easily at risk, escape increasingly difficult and when it involves a boss to a subordinate can be devastating. He felt lucky to have had Earl all those years.

"Did you get picked on in school dad?" Cary asked.

"No."

"Did you pick on anyone else?" Andy followed.

"Goodness no, son," he laughed, "I don't think I have it in me. And I don't think it was quite the same when I was growing up. We were all kind of the same, you know? I mean, we had people with more money and all but I don't think the differences were as great, or at least we didn't make them out to be. You just didn't act that way if you came from a wealthier family. I think it's changed."

"What would you do if someone did?"

"Well, I wouldn't have let them do it, not again," he confessed.

"Would you hit him?" Cary pressed further.

"If need be, yes, I would."

"You'd really hit them?"

"They'd be singing with the chin music I'd play on them," he grinned as the boys laughed at the colloquialism of his boast.

"But why do you think it is that they're leaving us alone and Jeremy's on his own?" Cary asked remembering the point of the whole conversation.

"Well, I don't know. Maybe he tried bullying them or they got tired of his antics. It could be the kid has something going on at home. You know, that's where it usually starts with kids your age. Or maybe they realized you aren't such bad kids after all," he smiled.

"Fat chance of that," Andy noted.

"Now, now. Look, just ignore them and don't worry about it. If it starts again you know how to handle yourselves. But if it does start again I want you to tell me, you understand?" he said sternly.

They nodded.

"Good. Now get back to those wish lists," he winked.

Leaving the room he wondered if his advice was the best he could have given or if it was what they really wanted to hear anyway. The idea of them in a fight was troubling, yet the idea of the teasing starting again more so. He hoped they understood he just wanted them to earn their self-respect and defend one another, take pride in themselves and in their family and, admitting to himself, all he really wanted was for they to never feel embarrassed of themselves or each other.

17.

With Christmas a couple of days away Audrey found herself home more often now there was less to do outside the house. Occupied with entertainment duties, the demands of the holiday and forced family time, her friends were at their own homes welcoming guests from all over which in turn wiped her social calendar clean. She took it in stride seeing a rather fortuitous chance to spend more time with herself and build on the relationship she was sharing with Beth. Be that as it may, with the boys excitement she regretted the former was unlikely until the post-Christmas exhaustion slowed them down. Yet their energy was at the same time a ready excuse when she needed a break to seek refuge in her own room and when you consider the inordinate amount of time her sister was spending there by herself it helped make the effort toward the latter more simple.

"What the - !" she exclaimed rushing in slamming the door behind and leaning against it where the boys were left screaming and pushing from the other side.

Beth glanced up from her reading, another trifle of a book she could easily forget knowing anything more would be a loss after listening to the parade up and down the hall for most of the night. Looking back down she returned to a spot at random, where she left off or picked up irrelevant.

Feeling she'd finally beaten them off, their screeches echoing down the stairs, Audrey released her grip on the handle and sat on the floor in front of the door still keeping her weight against it in case of their return. She thought it probable since she wound them like a top chasing and teasing much to their mother's chagrin. It was unlikely she would stand them carrying on like that for long, her mother's patience about on par with theirs, but for the moment she herself was safe, the tornado of their hysteria wreaking havoc elsewhere.

"So what are you reading?"

Beth flipped the book over, unsure of the title herself, "My Salad Days."

"Any good?"

"I honestly couldn't tell you," she answered closing the book on her lap.

Audrey put her ear to the door listening for movement outside. "Think it's safe?"

"Yeah, I think so."

Beth accepted the interruption with some relief, her tired eyes and boredom signaling another pleasureless nap to come. With the indifference of her book she'd been nodding on and off only to be awakened shortly after by the clamor from outside the room. This had been going on over the past few hours and though she knew it meant a sleepless night ahead it mattered little, the last day at school before the holiday break a breeze.

Audrey got up from the floor and kicked her shoes off before sitting on her bed. Beth watched as they flew to the far corners of the room getting lost in the wreckage. It was like a ship at sea being tossed and smashed on the rocks, the flotsam a myriad reminder of a life borne of chaos. It was little wonder she perceived her sister's mind a tumultuous muddle of incongruent and inconvenient thoughts, the anarchy of her action could produce little else. Still, it was a wonder, so unlike her own neat and balanced self.

"So why do you keep reading it then?"

"I don't know, I guess because I started it," she supposed. "Probably not a good reason though."

"No, probably not."

Audrey got up from the bed and sat in front of the mirror picking through her appearance. She hated winter and all it stood for, the cold, the chafed skin, the bad hair, the shapeless clothing. There was nothing delicate about it, the low light casting harsh shadows across a barren land, the long nights as empty as the short days, and little she could do to maintain the delicacy of her features. Looking at herself in the mirror she caught glimpses of an older woman. Not bad, but not where she wanted to be.

"So what did you mean when you wished to be anywhere but here the other night?" Beth asked.

Audrey didn't answer right away, continuing to stare at her features. She noticed a patch of dry skin flaking off near her ear, a sure sign of her skin's poor health. Sighing at the troubling reflection she licked the tip of her finger and rubbed the spot, a temporary solution though it would at least be from her mind.

"Come here and sit."

Beth surprised herself by getting up and sitting in front of the mirror without putting up much of an argument. Perhaps the spirit of the season had in some way worked itself into her. More likely, she reasoned, it was just the monotony of her evening.

As she faced the mirror Audrey pulled the hair away from her face. Twisting and holding it at rest on top of her head, she took her other hand and moved Beth's face from one side to the other.

"Okay, now face me."

She started rooting through the clutter on the dresser knocking several bottles harmlessly to the floor. Finding her makeup bag she dumped its contents on the bed picking up the eyeliner as it fell out on top. Before Beth could raise a complaint she pulled the cap off and, holding her sister's head steady, started applying it to the lower lids.

"You're not going to make me up like a little China doll," she disapproved, a protest light enough that Audrey kept working carefully without pause.

"Don't worry about it. Wouldn't suit you anyway, your features are too refined."

Finishing with the upper lids she dug through for her mascara and gently worked the length of each pair of lashes, the task made more difficult by Beth's continuous blinking. Scolding her to sit still she found herself doing the same when she tried to apply lip gloss having to first deny then explain the difference between it and lipstick. Thinking she might finish with an eyebrow pencil she decided against it, her sister's brows defined well enough, sculpted into an almost natural inquisitive arch.

"So why did you wish to be anywhere but here?" she asked again as Audrey brushed out her hair, misting each tress with water.

"I don't know. I just don't like winter I guess."

Laboring in a circle Audrey pulled each strand, marveling at the length. Culling the knots, she regretted how wonderful her sister's hair if only she took the time to care for it. A few split ends here and there it otherwise weathered the season much better than her own.

Beth could feel its feathery lightness, the tingle from her sister's fingers as she worked raising goosebumps on her arms and neck. It was a soothing massage, almost dreamy in its effect. She found her eyes closing, her head gently swaying to the movement of her hands as they caressed each strand from its base to the end. She drifted, her thoughts and her mood becoming airy, insubstantial and exquisitely inconsequential.

"Okay, all done."

With the comforting numbness reaching the tips of her toes she barely took notice. Slowly opening her eyes she found Audrey standing in front of her looking from side to side, admiring her work. She didn't like it, the tired thought of being her sister's canvas haunting her again.

"Do you like what you created?" she asked contemptuously.

Audrey frowned, hoping a better reception was on offer this time. "Just look."

Turning to face the mirror she felt suddenly ill catching sight of herself. It wasn't the person she expected to see, the Beth with whom she'd shared a lifetime in reserve, the girl with unremarkable hair, indifferent lips and familiar eyes. She expected a few minor enhancements but this was an altogether different person staring ostentatiously back, her precious accoutrements and garish luminosity on heartbreaking display. It was Audrey.

Disconsolate, she sat mute for a long time gazing at the reflection. For all her sister's trying, and all her own resistance, she in the end was becoming, had become, just like her. It was a realization she greeted with loathing, ashamed of the echo, dismayed of the certainty. But she shouldn't have been surprised, she was her mother's daughter, she was Audrey's sister, and the curse of that physical, undeniable, inevitable truth was perhaps the hardest of all to swallow.

"Take it off," she demanded evenly, repeating it again when Audrey didn't respond.

"Why?"

"Because that's not me," she replied glaring at her sister.

"Yes it is, a beautiful you."

"No, it's you."

Audrey tried to console and reason with her but it fell on deaf ears. So fixated was she on the reflection no words could dissuade her from the belief she was someone else and she'd somehow been fundamentally changed and damaged. It was an irrational discussion, the more so because Audrey thought it a simple cosmetic display, the trick of a woman's delight. And that was just the problem, Beth lived for unvarnished truth and she knew it. The eyes who stared back made a mockery of the ideal she cherished so dearly.

"Look Beth," she said dolefully sitting on the edge of her bed, "I hardly put anything on you so who you see is you. Besides, the way you look is not who you are."

"Said the girl who's every bit as she looks," she replied spitefully.

"How would you know? Can you say you know me or do you just presume?"

Slumped over picking at her nails Beth refused to acknowledge her sister's questions. She retreated into herself, a comfort she found ever difficult to leave behind as much as she'd been trying over the last few days and weeks. Looking at her Audrey was moved to the same pity she felt the day she watched her sitting cross-legged in front of her locker. It was the same hopeless girl mired in her own self knowing little how she got there and even less how to escape.

"Okay, you asked what I meant when I said I wanted to be anywhere but here," she confided, "I meant that I wanted to be away from here and this house, this life."

Beth looked at her with the revelation, confirmation of her own considered opinion more startling now it was spoken aloud.

"What?" Audrey asked, "Do you think you're the only one who wants out?"

"But why?"

"What do you mean why? Look around you. Do you think I want to be like this all my life, trying to make do with pennies, hungry half the time and cold the other half?"

"I know that but you seem to enjoy your life."

"And I do, and so should you."

"Well it doesn't come so easily for me," she mourned.

Audrey got up and walked to the window staring at her likeness in the lighted glass. It was pleasing to her, the hair, the eyes, the lips. She was every bit what she wanted to be and, unlike her sister, was as comfortable with the picture she presented herself as anyone could be. The difference, she reasoned, was she knew who she was and who the reflection was and the difference between the two. Absorbed with these thoughts she began to pace the room stopping only when she realized she was chewing her nails. Forcing her hand away in frustration she went back and sat on the bed.

"It's because you make it so damn hard."

"Like it's really that simple."

"But it is," she contradicted, "you just get so bogged down in the little things that you're losing focus of the bigger picture. Look at me."

She picked her eyes up, briefly scanning her sister's features.

"No, really look at me."

She took in her sister's soft, pale skin, a hint of redness on the cheek, her vital lips and delicate nose framed by the long hair, a tinge of strawberry paying compliment to her features. She wore little makeup, eyebrows lively and natural, forehead a beautiful and broad expanse, unmarked by emotion or thought. But it was looking in her eyes, the browns so deep they almost washed out the black of her pupils, that she stopped. It was where everyone stopped, basking in the confusing weight and lightness of her gaze.

"Envious, aren't you?" she asked seductively.

Beth turned away angrily. "Why are you doing this?"

"Isn't it obvious? Because I can use this to get what I want, even from you."

Thinking she'd been taken in once more Beth was crestfallen, torn between the need to flee and the desire to reach around and pull her sister's hair out by the roots. The duplicitous nature of the girl was so detestable she wondered what more could she do to thwart her every effort at a quiet, happy and unassuming existence? Was she trying to slowly reduce her to nothing or was she after a more rapid and violent end, a life cut short by her own hand? Either way it was masterful the way she worked, far more clever than she had even imagined.

Audrey saw the changing formations in Beth's mind, the storm brewing and passing in the confusion. "Now look at yourself again."

"Why?"

"Just do it."

Beth faced the mirror, quickly turning away again when she couldn't consider the reflection.

"Now I'm envious," Audrey said.

"Why?"

"Because you're a very beautiful girl, another beautiful Kane girl. The difference is there's an honesty to your beauty. Look," she said more softly, "I'm not trying to be cruel, I'm just trying to show you something. I learned a long time ago that if I look and act a certain way I can get pretty much what I want. It's terrible to say but it works, it always works. You know, people can deny it all they want but a beautiful face can get just about anything they want. I just reflect back their assumptions and they give it all to me. And for some reason they're confused by that."

"We all are."

"Maybe, maybe not. I think you're smart enough to understand, at least I want to believe you are. Now, you presume to know me, and have pretty much always hated me for it, but you only know some of me because you never took the time to know much else beyond your own expectations just like the rest of them. So I used that to get what I wanted."

"And you don't see a problem with that?"

"Of course I do, that's why we're having this talk."

Beth got off the chair and began to walk the room stopping to watch through the window. "So what did you get from me?" she asked without turning.

"It wasn't so much what I got from as I got in spite of." She took a deep breath, "Look, you told me you thought mom doesn't love you. But you're wrong. She doesn't love me more than you, if she even does at all, she's just confused by me. And you know why? Because even though I look just like her I act in a way that is so alien to her she doesn't quite know what to do around me. She doesn't look at you that way because she

191

understands you. And as much as you don't want to see it, she does because you're very much like her. Not just like, just very much like. But with me, she doesn't know what to do because she's looking for a reflection I won't provide. It keeps her off balance."

"And so you get what you want."

"Yes, you don't have to like it but it works. And you know what, contrary to what you believe, I honestly think she loves you more than me."

Beth gave her last argument little credence. It was inconsequential anyhow, vying for her mother's love no longer something she felt compelled to do having lost the battle long ago. And perhaps there was some truth in her sister's questioning whether her mother could love at all, indeed if it was something that could ultimately be gained by anyone. Misery was about the only company she kept and the closeness of that bond was as near to love as she deemed her mother capable.

"So why are you saying all this?"

Audrey thought for a moment, "There's a lot of reasons. Guilt is one. But I also don't want you to end up like her."

"What is that supposed to mean?"

"You ever notice that she just seems to be waiting, like something grand is going to happen to make her life so much better. And she's forever disappointed, with everything. Her marriage, the place she lives, the things she does, or doesn't do, even in us. She's tired of being poor and I think she blames dad for all of that."

"Be careful," Beth admonished.

"I don't blame him, she does. I know he works hard and does the best he can, he just doesn't have much to work with and she doesn't help. And I also know she blames me so don't think I'm putting it all on his shoulders. I just don't want you to end up that way, yet all I see is you sitting in here alone all the time and can't help but think that maybe you will."

"I won't."

"I'd like to believe that." She stared at the back of her sister. "Look, the reason I'm envious of you is because your beauty is so honest. Mine isn't. And I feel guilty about it because I know I haven't acted well, especially toward you, and for that I'm sorry. But in a way, you're teaching me to be a little more truthful."

"Glad you can still get something from me," she replied cynically.

Audrey ignored the sarcasm, "You know, we're after the same thing Beth and I just want to be sure we get it."

"And what might that be?" she asked turning to face her.

"Escape."

"You're sure of that?"

"Other than me I don't think I've ever known anyone with the desire to flee more than you so yeah, I'm sure. I"m just trying to get you to work with the tools you have and maybe use them a little better than I have."

Beth wondered if it was all that simple. The argument her sister presented was so tightly bound together she'd be lying to herself if she didn't admit to its intriguing logic. Audrey's life did appear simple and happy enough, especially when held in compare with her own dour existence. There was little doubt the girl would escape, it was only now too clear how hard she'd been working to be certain of that. But escape to what and to where? And what would she have to give in return? Her self-respect, her solace, her family? The price seemed too steep, the ends hardly worth the means.

"I don't think our ideas of escape are quite the same."

"Maybe not, but in that I'm a little more circumspect."

"Big word for you. How so?"

"Save the insults," Audrey glared at her, "I'm every bit as smart as you just a little more wise. You can think brains are going to get you somewhere but I'll be willing to bet you they won't, at least not as quickly and easily as I and clearly not to where you want to go."

"Some happiness you'll have," she replied haughtily.

"Oh, you don't think so? Let me tell you something honey," Audrey responded in a small fury, "you can't eat happiness. You can think what you want but you know as well as I that poor and happy are incompatible. That doesn't mean to be rich is to be happy, but to be poor is a guarantee you won't."

Beth returned to gazing through the window looking for something on which to settle her thoughts. She was reminded how little the two shared in common other than the bond of family and maybe that wasn't enough. Their worldview was so radically different from one another that if they'd met as strangers they would have remained so and in the end her sister was only providing further confirmation she was exactly who Beth thought she was.

Yet, as much as she tried to dissuade herself, her sister's sardonic outlook varied little from her own, it really came down to the means. She was under no illusion as to how crushing poverty was to the spirit. The incongruity of it with happiness wasn't a novel revelation to her own mind. She'd thought much of it over the years, most often when her stomach was knotted with hunger. But if she gave her life to a pursuit of one end, the escape from poverty, hoping the presumptuous benefits, namely her own happiness, would necessarily follow then wouldn't it be a dishonest pursuit? And what if it failed, if happiness never followed? In that Audrey's argument had some strength if only to herself because if she were to be miserable anyway she might as well be so with a full belly.

"You know what I wish," Audrey offered having come back down a bit, "is that there was a little of me in you and a little of you in me."

"Yes, then it would be a perfect world."

"Perhaps, but our paths would probably be easier and more fulfilling."

"Wait just a minute," the realization striking her, "you succeeded in getting only one thing right, we both want to escape. But it's from different things."

"Yeah, I know, though it doesn't make me wrong."

"Oh?" she asked smugly.

"Yeah, the destination's still the same. Look, Beth," she admitted, "you can find fault with what I do, and God knows I do, you've shown me that and I love you for it. But I know you and I'm just trying to show you a way to escape from what you're so desperate to."

"And what might that be?"

"Yourself."

Beth turned and walked from her, the certainty of the pronouncement inflaming, made more so by knowing she was right. It had little to do with her surroundings, her mother or her family anymore. Probably hadn't for a long time, maybe ever. It was her own self she wished to escape, the other excuses little more than convenience. She was tired of her awkward life, her graceless body, the artless floundering she couldn't avoid when in the company of others, the embarrassment she met when closeness appeared near, even with her own father. She'd spent a lifetime trying to conceal herself from others when in the end she only succeeded in hiding from her own self.

Looking through the window she noticed snow falling, large puffy flakes already covering the ground, sparkling in the distant streetlight. She watched it scatter like great schools of fish each time a small breeze blustered by and then resume its slow meander when it was again still. It calmed her, the quiet of the night passing to a more beautiful and transcendent peace, a virgin love affair between land and sky.

18.

Barely were the first rays of light showing in the east Christmas morning than the boys were downstairs in front of the tree poring over the small store of gifts. Picking each one up they shook, hazarded a guess and then put it neatly in the appropriate stack segregated by recipient. With that done they took an eye to determine who had the most, their sign of the best behaved through the year and of who in turn was most deserving of their parent's love. The logic of it all lost, and Andy coming out on the short end, it was deemed appropriate to instead count the gifts certain of the truth in numbers. Again coming up short by one Andy was insisting there had to be more when they heard someone waking and stirring, little doubt from the noise of their haggling. Quickly mixing and piling them back up under the tree they escaped to the kitchen where they put the kettle on and busied themselves preparing mugs of coffee.

It was Carl who first came loping down the stairs, giddy despite his exhaustion. For him the snow that fell over the prior couple of days came with a heavy and most unwelcome burden. Since late that night when Beth was peering through her window watching the first flakes touch the ground he'd been at his job plowing the streets. Though the lightness of the snow made the job easier, the tedium of the hours did not and only through the virtue of an occasional nap was he able to keep going. It was a rare thing to have a storm fall so close to Christmas, in spite of everyone's collective wishing, and for that he was glad, their hopes were his despair. Ordinarily he wouldn't mind quite as much, the overtime pay a boon and more than fair compensation for the misery behind the wheel, but this year, feeling his gift to the family a pure stroke of genius, he anticipated the day as much as anyone.

He wasn't the only one in need of consolation as the snow fell that night. Light and fluffy in the cold, it was quick to stick, freezing and turning to ice with the first few cars that spun their way up the streets. As travel became increasingly treacherous the last minute shoppers were kept home, some presents nothing more than an explanation or promise of post-holiday giving, the question of whether they really deserved or needed it burning longer. Travelers were equally frustrated, their destinations and families left to carry on without them, their cheer found alone in a mug of coffee in an empty house or apartment, the mirth buried with every inch of new snow. It was a poorly timed start to a late winter.

It was a sentiment Audrey could share. She was unused to spending so much time in the house and was surprised when she began to miss the pull of others and the effort of being on constant display. Her restlessness grew the longer she was trapped and the more coffee she consumed so as the day wore on and she wandered from room to room she took little pleasure in the company she found. Yet it was relatively shortlived so by evening she was again swept up in the tide of good feeling, the excitement of tomorrow no more evident than in the boys begging and she obliging to chase them around the house only further agitating their mother.

In one sense Lily was glad of it, hoping their energy burn may finally allow her a decent night's sleep knowing what was to come the next day may forever put an end to a good night's rest. And if it was to be the last it would be the first in years, the boys early risers like the girls never had been. She knew some day it would have to stop it just seemed to be carrying on longer than it should. At times her only holiday wish was they would grow up, and fast. But in the end it was an empty hope, the boys up at the crack of dawn digging away at her already fragile spirit. With Carl stirring first, she was left with the one last hope she could roll over and sleep for a little while longer, the rays of the sun and Christmas morning unwelcome in her room.

Feeling lively Beth followed him down the stairs practically leaping the last few as her thoughts were wholly consumed by the puppy. She'd slept little at first deliberating what they should name it realizing she didn't know whether it was a boy or girl simply picking the most vulnerable. She found herself also wondering how her mother's reaction would be to its presence with the noise and mess it would surely bring. It must have been a tough sell for her father knowing just how she felt about being in the company of small furry creatures. Then the magnanimous idea struck her that maybe they should allow her to name it thereby giving her a vested interest in the dog she would have to tolerate for years to come. With that and the knowledge the boys would be as happy as she come morning she found the distraction she needed and eventually a contented night's rest.

"So when's it getting here?" she whispered before they reached the kitchen.

"Around nine."

Feeling anxious at the mention of it, she tried hiding her excitement when they entered together and found the boys innocently preparing them all coffee. Seeing only the two of them Andy was quick to lift the kettle from the burner when it started to whistle knowing some people in the house would remain grumpy through the whole of the day if forced from her bed earlier than wanted.

"Merry Christmas," Carl said softly.

The boys returned the greeting, Cary jumping in his arms and Andy giving him a hug. Pulling themselves free they ran over and gave Beth the same treatment almost knocking her over and causing a small ruckus until with a wink and smile she quietly shushed and scolded them to behave. Just as quickly forgetting they noisily readied the mugs of coffee and sat marveling over the snow and all they could do with the day. Beth and Carl merely looked at one another knowing whatever they planned it would soon change.

They sat like this until eight thirty, the boys becoming ever more difficult to silence, their anticipation busting at the seams. Eventually Audrey's loud entrance and the failed attempts to quiet her were enough for Carl to rouse Lily whether she was ready or not. There was plenty of time later to enjoy the coziness of her bed, for now they needed to get the smaller gifts open before the big family one arrived.

Handing them out with barely time for a sip of coffee she watched with disgust as the boys greedily snatched and tore into their presents. Showing no restraint they showed less in their disappointment when socks, underwear or a new hat were unwrapped. It was a bruising and thankless affair she endured every year, the pleasant uncovering of a new sled for Andy, the gift missing from his pile, or an electric blanket for Beth doing little to alter her mood. When a knock came at the door she could do nothing but huffily withdraw to the kitchen where she prepared a warm mug of coffee in the hopes it would calm her nerves and still her voice.

With the boys looking around curious as to who might come knocking so early on Christmas morning Carl laughingly feigned his own ignorance telling them to go to the door and find out. Sensing a ruse was at hand, Cary just beat Andy to the door and threw it open. Shrinking back inside he retreated leaving it wide.

"Well, invite him in," Carl ordered.

He nodded and over the threshold stepped Jeremy Watson followed by his father. Beth recognized him immediately and could do nothing but stand in awe watching he and the boys stare at one another with neither daring to say a word. Carl got up warmly embracing Earl and kneeling to wish his young son a merry Christmas. He merely echoed the greeting never losing focus of Andy and Cary. With only an inkling of what was going on Audrey went and stood by the boys resting her hand on Cary's shoulder. Coming from the kitchen Lily stopped in disbelief, her greeting stuck dry in her throat.

"Come on in, come on in, and don't worry about wiping your feet," Carl beckoned. "Lily, get Earl a cup of coffee. You got time for that, right?"

Lily moved her gaze from the young boy to Earl noticing how beaten he looked since last she'd seen him. Skin pallid and rough, scant hair poking from beneath his hat, he was gaunt, even the little paunch he carried the last few years gone. With his exhausted features worn, the genial and alert eyes were all she could remember.

"Sure I do. Got a little something of yours in the car too."

He motioned for Jeremy to go out and retrieve it. The boy lingered, gaze now fixed squarely on Cary, finally moving once he was ordered a second time.

Only when he was out the door were the boys able to exhale. Looking at one another Cary reached up and clung to Audrey hoping she would remain by his side. She squeezed his hand whispering reassurances in his ear. Andy, bypassing his father who was anyway oblivious helping Earl off with his coat, went to Beth asking what they should do. She couldn't think, the whole situation queer knowing why the boy had gone to the car.

Telling him to calm down, she promised if nothing else she would have a few words with him before he left. Hardly a comfort, he knew there was nothing more he could achieve under the circumstance.

Jeremy returned with the puppy in a carrier placing it down in the middle of the room where he stood again keeping a wary eye on the two boys. Poking her head from the kitchen Lily scrutinized him while waiting with regret the moment he opened the door for the animal to scamper through the house. Already its whining was a nuisance her morning could have done without.

"So," Earl clapped his hands together, "I think this belongs to you," he said looking at Cary as he flipped the latch of the small cage.

The puppy dashed out wagging its tail, circling in fits, yapping, chirping and greeting everyone in turn before finding Earl who was again seated. Running over the top of him it made it to the back of the couch where bounding across it surveyed the surroundings and then launched itself to the floor below. Coming around the other side it found the tree and a ball of discarded wrapping paper tearing it into dozens of smaller pieces before making a jump at some low hanging tinsel. Nipping at Jeremy's fingers when he tried shooing it away it then spied Lily and made a mad dash for her. Startled, she remained still allowing it to sniff her feet and run back and forth between her legs, the soft fur tickling as it brushed her shins. She looked over to the boys expecting a bigger reaction but they just stood incredulous by all that was happening.

"Come here girl," Jeremy called bending down and coaxing the puppy. Running to him he picked her up holding her forepaws to discourage squirming. "Cary, come take her."

Looking to his father who was motioning him over he tried communicating a refusal but it went unnoticed. Loosening her hold on his shoulder Audrey gave him a gentle nudge telling him it would be okay. Approaching nervously, he found himself watching Jeremy more than the puppy.

"Okay, hold her just like this and hold those paws tight so she doesn't jump," he instructed handing her over.

With the puppy licking his face and nibbling his chin he couldn't help but giggle. Watching his struggles Beth burst into laughter. Even if it was in part a measure of the situation's absurdity it didn't matter, her reaction put him more at ease and for the moment his guard dropped, the acknowledgment of the puppy's existence in his arms a revelation to his nervous spirit.

"So what's her name?"

"Anything you want it to be."

Jeremy started teasing her by running his fingers through her open mouth before she could clamp down, her frustrating cries growing louder with each failure. Andy joined them rubbing her bright pink belly and begging Cary to give him a chance to hold her.

With Beth and Audrey playing along the men retired to the kitchen to enjoy their coffee. Lily sat with them disturbed over the collapse in Earl's health. Politely taking part in the conversation she couldn't help but stare searching out his warm eyes rather than allow herself to study the rest of him. She was thankful he kept his hat on, the loss of hair more than she would want to see. Feeling he was a mere corpse, she found herself inexplicably torn between pity and disgust only averting her eyes with the shame of this new thought poisoning her mind. Excusing herself she went to the living room just in time to witness the puppy urinate on the hardwood floor. She saw it as the beginning of her personal Hell, as though the years leading up to it weren't enough.

It was late in the week and they still hadn't found a name for the newest member of their family. Finding Beth's suggestion a good one Carl tried to get Lily more involved yet she refused, naming the beast the last thing she wished to do. She'd grown tired of it far sooner than she imagined, the urine, feces, chewing and crying worse than she remembered from any of the children. She even sought to indulge it from a different perspective, that shared by the rest of the household who'd grown instantly enamored of the black and white ball of energy, but it was of no use, their joy a reminder of her own sadness at having agreed to such a foolhardy idea. Worse still was the reality she'd be left alone to care for and entertain the creature when the kids returned to school. The only consolation on that point was Earl left behind the carrier so it could be crated when no one was about. In that way she could stuff it in its little cage and ignore it when the others were gone or she herself was off to work.

Not surprisingly promises were already broken. Before leaving Earl advised the kids the dog was very clever and required a lot of exercise so she would need to be out frequently even suggesting they start training her off leash early so she could run free without straying and thereby release her energy in appropriate ways. No one heeded his warnings. Instead they played with it inside realizing only after it had already gone on the floor they were perhaps late in getting it out to stretch. Broaching the subject of a chain to leave it outdoors and meeting with an instant refusal from all, including Carl, she used it as a threat if things didn't change. They didn't, and the chain never materialized.

"So what about Puff?" Cary asked, the kids all gathering in the girl's room to brainstorm the possibilities.

"Puff? Where in the world did you get that?" Audrey questioned.

"My head. She's just a little puffball so I thought..."

"Not likely, squirt," Beth chuckled.

"Well what about Squirt?" Andy laughingly suggested. "Mom could agree with that one."

"Please," Audrey gibed, "serious names only."

"Well you think of something then."

"Okay, it's got to be simple though, no more than two syllables. So how about Kate or Eva, maybe just Eve?"

"Why just two syllables?"

"So it's easy to call her. What do you want to do, yell out something like Geraldine or Penelope?"

"Those are just stupid names," Cary complained.

"Oh, I don't know, I like those actually, especially Penelope."

"No, Beth, they're too long."

"Not really. You know it'll just end up being shortened like my name or Andy's. So it would be Geri or Pen. I really like Pen."

"Yeah, so do I," Andy agreed.

As they continued to debate the still nameless puppy started scratching at the door trying to pry her way out. Resigned to the fact it was her turn Beth got up joking she was going to take Puff out for her walk, an unnecessary jab at Cary she regretted the instant his face turned sour. Audrey consoled him on her behalf promising his next suggestion would be taken under thoughtful consideration.

Opening the door the puppy rushed the stairs with Beth shuffling behind gathering her hat and gloves as she went. Reaching the front door she could hear her running through the kitchen, her mother cursing all the while. In an instant she came bounding out hiding behind her legs with Lily chasing after, a newspaper in hand. Raising it to strike at the dog Beth stayed her arm squeezing her wrist so tightly she let out a small gasp of pain.

"What the Hell do you think you're doing?" she seethed at her mother. "Let go of me."

She refused, holding and squeezing her arm even tighter causing the skin to break, a small trickle of blood seeping from the wound. With her other hand Lily sought to loosen the grip but when that failed she slapped a glancing blow across her daughter's face. Enraged, Beth let go and with the full force of her dominant hand now free she returned the violence striking her mother square, the blow staggering her more with the shock it was done than with the power it could deliver.

"If I ever see you try to hit that dog again I will lay you right here in a pool of your own blood," she threatened, the ice in her stare enough that Lily was left with no question as to the sincerity.

Confused and angry, a flustered Lily ran the stairs retreating to her room slamming the door behind where she paced trying to control her rage and mourning the loss of her dignity. She was wracked with indecision, wondering if she should call Carl or risk another confrontation with the girl.

Downstairs a composed Beth picked the puppy up hugging her close. Clasping the leash she took her out for a long walk feeling as good as she could ever remember.

Hearing a knock on the door she knew it was her father coming to dole out his punishment for her behavior. She cared little, the necessity of protecting their puppy and the satisfaction of finally delivering to her mother what she deserved well worth the price. It had been a long time coming and though she was flying solo, the boys and Audrey expressing deep reservations at her reaction, she felt the justness of her actions were above reproach. Besides, if he felt it right to scold or ground her then it just served to show he was still blind to her mother's true nature. Her righteousness assured, she bid him enter.

"Well, I'm outta here," Audrey said taking the puppy with her when she saw both parents coming through the door.

Beth sat upright, skewering her mother the moment she entered, almost gloating in her stare. Lily did likewise, the two never moving eyes from one another. Carl came in just behind, moving out of the way enough for Audrey to rush past. She didn't go far, the boy's door open she joined them in a concerned and excited vigil. It was uncommon for tumult of this magnitude to occur under their roof so the mixed emotions were new and exhilarating even if it meant one of their own was about to be torn down. The three sat listening, struggling to keep the puppy quiet so they wouldn't miss a word behind their sister's closed door.

"What's she doing here?"

"She," Lily answered, "is here because you're going to apologize."

"You can hope."

"I'm not finished. And when you're done, if I accept it, you will then take your punishment."

Beth continued glaring at her, "Then I'll ask again, what is she doing here?"

"Now listen," Carl intervened, "you're going to apologize to your mother."

She looked at him for the first time. Despite the seriousness with which he directed her she could tell he was nervous. She wasn't sure if it was a result of her mother, the situation, perhaps even of herself. Regardless, she stiffened and released him from her icy stare returning it to her mother.

"No chance in Hell."

"Listen you little -" Lily took a step toward her just catching herself.

Beth jumped from the bed and stood facing her. "Bitch. I think that's the word you were looking for."

Andy started giggling though Cary failed to find the humor. Audrey shushed him and, tiring of the fight and need to entertain her, let the puppy wander. She found a sock to occupy her attention where gnawing on it she quickly found the elastic and pulled delighting in the resistance.

"That's enough," Carl yelled, "sit back down. Lily, back off."

Beth noticed her wrist, a deep crimson clot of blood surrounded by a growing purple bruise, and couldn't help but smile. Worth the price even more, she thought.

"I tell you what young lady, if I may be so bold as to call you that...

"Go on, keep up the insults," Beth replied smugly.

"I will have Carl take that damn dog back."

She looked to her father. He betrayed no judgment, his accord neither evident nor absent.

Across the hall Andy failed any longer to find humor in the exchange. Looking at Cary and seeing the tears well up Audrey soothed and assured him the puppy was going nowhere. Beseeching her he only prayed she was right. Andy joined the benediction.

"You wouldn't dare."

"Oh no?"

"No. For one, this was dad's big family gift. For two, all you'd be doing is punishing everyone else and, though I wouldn't put it past you, I don't think it will happen."

"You seem pretty well self-assured."

"I am. Because three, what I said downstairs wasn't a threat, it was a promise."

Lily turned and stomped from the room slamming the door behind. Glancing into the boys room and seeing her three other children sitting on the floor apprehensively watching her she looked past to see the puppy chewing on and tearing out the elastic of a sock.

"Is that one of your new socks? Give me that damn dog," she shouted stepping over the boys.

Audrey ran and scooped her up before her mother could get near. Cradling her in her arms she turned her back protecting the puppy from her mother's grasping hands. Cary started crying as Andy pushed him out the door where following he took him by the hand and led him downstairs. Lily kept repeating the demand, Audrey spinning away each time she reached out to snatch the dog from her.

"No," she yelled back stopping finally, "stay the Hell away from her."

Giving up the fight Lily sought the refuge of her own room where Audrey could hear her hurling things about, the adjacent wall absorbing the indignity of each object thrown and taking the brunt of her punishment.

Rushing downstairs she found the boys hiding in the kitchen. Producing the puppy she coaxed them out with guarantees it was safe and she was unharmed. Giving her over to Andy she knelt down and brushed away Cary's tears pulling him close and promising she would never let anything happen to their new friend.

Upstairs Carl held his head in his hands despairing at all he could hear going on around him. Beth approached trying to pry his hands away but he wouldn't let her. Returning to her bed she sat and watched him.

"Why did you have to do that to your mother?"

"Dad, I warned you and I told you I didn't want her near me."

Looking up, face reddened, the stress being told through the blotchy rims of his eyes, the wrinkle of his forehead, the handprints that were still visible on his cheek, he fell back on Audrey's bed groaning.

"I'm sorry dad."

"Arggh," he sat back up, "why couldn't you have said that to your mother?"

"Because she didn't deserve it."

"But you can't do what you did, can't you see that?" he begged.

"No, I can't. Look dad, it's a helpless creature that needed protection and so I gave it."

"I know, I know, but you can't hit your mother."

"Well, then keep her away from me."

"Oh boy, this is gonna be a long night," he muttered. "Look, you're going to be punished. Just what it is I don't know but you will and you can be sure of that."

"Fine. And if you're done you can leave now."

Carl left the room looking in both directions when he got into the hall. He could hear Lily melting down and taking her anger out on the few possessions they had. He only hoped it was her own things she was damaging and breaking. Either way, she was a problem that could wait. Creeping downstairs he found Audrey hugging Cary on the couch, Andy sitting on the other side stroking the puppy he held in his arms. She was still as he soothed her, the stress of the last few minutes sapping her energy. Thank goodness they're resilient, Carl thought.

"So, have you decided on a name yet?" he asked sitting on the edge of the chair opposite.

Andy shook his head.

"Well, we need to do that soon."

He went over and tousled Andy's hair taking a moment to rub the puppy's belly. Looking over at Audrey she met his gaze and mouthed everything was okay as she stroked Cary's hair. He could see his young son's glistening eyes watching him in the half light. He smiled and winked at the boy before climbing the stairs.

Later that night and long after everyone had their chance to find peace Audrey came back to the room. She'd spent most of it talking with the boys and playing with the puppy across the hall where Cary took great care to clean everything up and move any little thing she could get her teeth around well out of the way. It took some time but eventually she had them smiling and again feeling less sorry for themselves. When she got up to leave they were insistent she take the dog with her.

"I heard what you did," Beth commended.

"Well, I saw what you saw."

She kicked her shoes off and walked over to the bed handing Beth the puppy and sitting next to her. She started in biting right away, Beth playing the same game with her that she watched Jeremy play a few days before. The more she did the more aggressive she became to where the bites with her little teeth and jaws began to smart. Putting her hand under the blanket for protection she moved it all around with the puppy scampering to keep up and pouncing every time she stopped.

"You know, the boys and I took a vote and we want you to name the puppy."

"Yeah? What happened to Puff?"

"Well, it took some convincing but he gave it up."

She thought for a minute letting the puppy bite her hand and try to pull the blanket away.

"Okay. Penelope it is, Pen for short."

19.

The night passing like a whisper, New Year's Day dawned cold. Toasting the old each in their own way, they were glad to be through and praying it shut the door behind. It had been a hard year, another of many, and yet they still held on and were still together. With reminders of the past haunting their dreams they looked forward with promise, a better and warmer tomorrow just over the next horizon. And perhaps that's what made the year feel so hard. There was a better tomorrow to come, they could see it and they longed for it and that very impatience for change, any change, tarnished the old more than any other. When one day passes into the next with hardly a difference one has no use for a calendar nor any use for counting the days, their essence nothing more than a marker in the sand. For the Kanes that's just what each day came to represent, another day closer to their own oblivion, for some its coming the only welcome release the universe had to offer.

But the old didn't go quietly, claiming Earl just before the stroke of midnight. Putting the receiver down Carl abruptly departed the evening with word his old friend may not last the night. Keeping vigil with the Watson family it was one of his last wishes, friends and family there to comfort and ease his transition to the great empty beyond. It was the last spasm, a year passing with the excruciating fear and sorrow of a man who wasn't ready to let go, a man for whom the promise of nothingness was too much to overcome. It wasn't his life flashing before his eyes that night it was what his life wasn't to be, the future erased as sure as one wished to erase the past.

Carl carried that weight back home with him near dawn, the mind-numbing cold an afterthought as he walked the path to his stoop. Lily was waiting for him there wrapped only in her robe and slippers, a warm coffee and cigarette at the ready. Lighting it she handed him both and sat with him wordlessly watching over the land, the trees cracking as the suns weak rays warmed the branches, a clutch of crows heralding the dawn, stretching their wings to catch what little warmth they could. He wondered about the life of a crow, so often seeing a pair walk either side of the road, a wary eye on the traffic and always one step ahead. It was a hard life they led, the ease of a southern winter somehow a missing part of their DNA, instead eking out a miserable existence in the cold and the snow, picking at whatever providence cared to provide. Yet they were undoubtedly the smartest birds he'd ever known, their every move an efficient and calculated response to ensure their own survival and there they were, preparing for a new day high in their tree, a watchful eye below for gifts the night may have left.

"I never want to see that again." He looked away, a solitary tear rolling off his cheek.

It was the first Lily could ever remember him shed. For all his faults in her mind it was a reminder of why she loved him, of why she stayed and above all of why she felt the loss of his love and esteem was more than she could bear. His warmth even in her coldest moments was enough to pick her head up, to wake her in the morning and help her plod through another day, allow her time alone wishing for more and spend time together thankful there wasn't less. She could never leave him, she knew that now, her life neither singular nor alone.

Putting him to bed, tucking the blankets and rubbing his back, she left him to stare at the wall, the sorrow he carried his own as he drifted off to sleep. She returned to the kitchen where she stared from the window watching blue jays jump from branch to branch, their noisy chat welcome company to spoil the uncomfortable stillness of the morning. A solitary cardinal settled in a bush on the other side of the road, its scarlet coat standing stark against the white, knowing no equal for beauty in a winter garden. Listening close she could hear a woodpecker in the distance, its staccato drumbeat echoing through the crisp air. She imagined it, the black and white feathers, the long beak, chunks of bark falling to the forest floor below. She could just see it climbing higher in the tree, leaping to another branch, calling to its mate and sharing the find. What a wonderful thing to be a bird.

Pulling herself away it was time to make breakfast. She started in on the french toast before filling bowls with fresh fruit and nuts, powdered sugar, whipped cream and a jug with plenty of maple syrup. She even took time the day before to visit Brett's Cafe and without much convincing get little French flags to decorate their plates which she lay out next to the stove ready to top off whatever the children wished. As she was putting on these finishing touches Pen came running into the kitchen making a dash for her water and then for Lily. Giving her a quick pat she put a scrambled egg in her bowl. She greedily lapped it up. Coming in behind, jacket thrown hastily on, leash in hand, Beth glanced at her mother and then at her bandaged wrist. Hanging her head she called to Pen and took her outside. Lily watched her go before picking up and rinsing Pen's bowl.

Within a few minutes the boys came clamoring down the stairs stopping just short of the kitchen door, enough to peer in and confirm what their noses were already telling them. Putting her finger to her lips and explaining their father was asleep she helped them into their chairs at the table and took their order effecting the best Leslie Caron accent she could. Cary got a hearty laugh out of that, she sounding more like Marlene Dietrich but he none the wiser. Audrey joined just in time to hear and in her best tongue tried to mimic her mother. It was no better, the laughter greeting Beth as she came back in with Pen and sat at the table. Done trying, she prepared Beth's plate with none of the fanfare delivering it with a weak smile and a flag that toppled over when she placed it down.

Later that day there was a knock at the door. Alone downstairs Lily opened it to a boy she didn't recognize but who was clearly cold as he stood asking for Elizabeth. Bringing him inside she looked him over before calling for her. He was unremarkable, longish hair poking from beneath his hat, an olive drab military coat, black scarf he'd been using to cover his mouth judging by the frost that still clung despite the warmth of the house. Pleasant enough, exceedingly polite, he seemed almost familiar in his bearing even if a bit clownish in his canvas sneakers, wool socks pouring over the top. She puzzled at the inappropriateness of his footwear in such weather and more so over the idea of a visitor for her young daughter, one who used her proper name.

Coming down the stairs Beth stopped halfway, perplexed over who she saw standing just inside the door. With the boys filling in the top, sitting down and watching, she calmly descended the rest stopping again at the bottom.

"Hey Chris."

She could hear the boys giggling behind her, Andy putting two and two together and coming up with a million in his own mind before explaining the new math to his brother. She glared back up at them where they pretended to be still, a smirk playing across their faces.

"What are you doing here?"

"I was just out and thought I'd stop by to see you."

"Well here I am," she replied smartly regretting it the moment the words popped out, old habits so frustratingly difficult to kill.

Audrey joined the boys at the top of the stairs as surprised as Beth to see him standing by the door. Backing off before he could notice she listened from just inside the door to their bedroom.

"Well, do you maybe want to go for a walk?"

"In that cold?"

"Yeah, I know..."

"No, no, it's fine, just let me get my coat."

She ran back up to her room glowering at the boys as she passed. Audrey jumped on her bed pretending not to know who had come calling. Rummaging through the clutter clogging the dresser and causing bottles, paper and all manner of things to fall Beth searched frantically for the hairbrush.

"It's under the magazine."

"Thanks."

Audrey chuckled watching her brush through in a desperate rush, the friction causing her hair to stray, the knots getting worse the harder she worked.

"Slow down, you've got plenty of time."

Getting off her bed Audrey took the hairbrush from her and worked the knots out slowly, spritzing it lightly with water as she went. Finished, she took her makeup bag and held it up for Beth to see in the mirror and waited for her to nod before emptying its contents on the bed.

"Just a little."

"Of course. Like I said, you're too refined to have more than a little."

Gathering her hat and gloves Beth made a dignified descent of the stairs, head held high, back straight. It was her practiced entrance, the one she imagined making a thousand times. Her only regret was the staircase wasn't more grand, the house more elegant. In a way she was sorry he'd come, the squalidness of how she lived pricking her still fragile ego. Yet she knew there was nothing she could do to change it, or the way he saw her as she gained the bottom.

"So, anywhere in particular you had in mind?" she asked as they stepped to the stoop closing the door behind.

"No, I just thought we'd walk, talk a bit, whatever."

They started off toward town, the only direction with a destination at its end. It was a quiet walk, more purposeful than she imagined it should be for two people with nowhere in particular to go and, despite the chance for time with him, somehow bothersome when she couldn't for the life of her fathom why he wanted to go in the first place. It was just too damn cold, especially so if he had nothing to say.

"So, we've got the walking part of the plan down, what about the talking?"

"Yeah, yeah, sorry about that. I was just thinking," he replied without offering his thought.

"Okay?"

"You look different."

"Is that good?"

"No, yeah, I mean yeah, it is, you just, you kind of look like Audrey."

"Well, she is my sister."

She thought about it and how a few days ago she probably would have ended their walk then and there. The connection to her sister was something she could never escape, nor that to her mother. And though it would take a while longer before she could fully understand what that meant, it didn't seem to bother her now as she walked quietly in the cold receiving what she believed a compliment.

"But thanks."

As they continued their march to nowhere she wondered about the kiss he shared with Audrey. There was no getting around the fact he would have enjoyed it and he was surely the envy of so many who dreamed of a moment such as that even if it was devoid of any romantic notion. But if ever he kissed her would it feel the same, would he imagine her instead of she, would he care or perhaps enjoy hers more? In the end she reasoned it didn't much matter, he wouldn't be walking with her if it wasn't for the carelessness of that kiss.

Stopping at her favorite neighborhood haunts along the way she had him look over the gardens they offered. Though mostly covered in snow she felt he could still get the sense of what they represented if he just used his imagination. Failing in that she sought to show him what they looked like in the full splendor of spring by describing every detail she could recall from her many visits to the front of their homes. He seemed not to understand, the old man's house a wreck, the car unimpressive, another piece of junk added to the disaster. The same opinion came out when they got to Mrs. Jensen's, his quip he should offer to mow her lawn, at double the price, his most meaningful contribution.

With no understanding why he couldn't see what she did she marked it down as a fault in his personality, his mind, or both. Even less could she understand why she turned him around and brought him to her refuge on the hill in back. Clearing off the bench they sat shivering, he making comments about other houses in the neighborhood never realizing he was holding hers in compare. Yet she listened, quietly picking details of buildings around town, the church spires, the library and the field on the hill opposite where in the early morning of summer she could see the dots of deer moving through on their way to daytime cover. When he went back to the houses in the neighborhood she couldn't help but wonder if indeed he was a gift better left unwrapped. Yet he was attentive, and for the moment that was enough.

Sitting on the stoop sharing a cigarette Carl and Lily were talking about the year just past, the year to come and the hope they had for a better tomorrow sure this time it would come true. She was pleased, able to get him to laugh at times, the edge of the night dulled by the rest he was able to gain during the day. She knew it was brief, the hurdle of a funeral and a changing workplace still to come. They would get through, they always did, so she didn't worry, a resolution she was desperate to keep.

"So what's yours?"

He thought for a moment. "Cigarettes. I'll give up my cigarettes."

"Yeah right, cowboy, that'll never happen."

She nuzzled into him trying to steal his warmth. Beth and Chris came walking around the corner, he introducing himself to her father and bidding his goodbyes to them both. She walked him to the road and said her own goodbyes brushing his arm with her hand before turning and going inside.

"Who the Hell was that?"

"Oh yes, I didn't tell you, he came calling for Beth today."

"Huh. Imagine that?"

They watched him disappear around the corner walking gingerly, every step rushed with discomfort. Carl smiled in the thought the boy was smitten enough with his daughter that he stood in the cold with her despite the fact his toes were near to falling off with frostbite.

"You know," Lily observed, "I know why that boy seemed so familiar, he reminds me of you when you were that young."

She nuzzled in further, smiling at the thought.

ABOUT THE AUTHOR

A graduate of the University of Vermont, Stephen Jennings holds degrees in Sociology and History. Despite extensive travel he continues to make his home in New England splitting most of his latter years between Vermont and Maine. An avid hiker, photographer and dog owner he still finds a little time to play ice hockey whenever he gets the chance.

Made in the USA
Lexington, KY
23 March 2012